Resist them if you can!

Styr Hardrata has travelled to Ireland with his wife Elena to save their marriage. They have grown apart and, when he is captured and she kidnapped, both find themselves faced with irresistible temptations...

Handsome warrior Styr is captured by beautiful Irish maiden Caragh in

TO SIN WITH A VIKING
August 2013

Lonely Elena is stranded with husband's best friend, Viking warrior Ragnar Olafsson, in

TO TEMPT A VIKING
Coming soon

Read both stories in this powerful new duet of forbidden passion
by Michelle Willingham

AUTHOR NOTE

Sometimes arranged marriages in historical romance end in happily-ever-after. And sometimes two good people are never meant to be together. I wanted to explore the idea of a marriage between a husband and a wife who want to make it work but are unable to connect. And what will happen to them when they meet their true soul mates?

This duet of books, beginning with TO SIN WITH A VIKING, explores that theme without trespassing into the realm of adultery. Both Styr and Elena Hardrata deserve a happy ending...but it will not be with each other. Styr is taken captive by Irishwoman Caragh Ó Brannon, and the forbidden attraction between them is searing. He must decide whether to maintain his loyalty to a wife who is heartbroken in their marriage or whether to reach out to the woman who has taught him how to love. Elena's story will follow, when she is rescued by fellow Viking Ragnar Olafsson.

I hope you'll enjoy these Irish-Viking stories. If you want to read more about my Hardrata heroes, Styr is the ancestor of Tharand Hardrata, the hero of THE VIKING'S FORBIDDEN LOVE-SLAVE, and later of Kaall Hardrata, hero of *The Holly and the Viking* in WARRIORS IN WINTER.

You're welcome to visit my website at www.michellewillingham.com for excerpts and behind-the-scenes details about my books. I love to hear from readers, and you may e-mail me at michelle@michellewillingham.com or via mail at PO Box 2242 Poquoson, VA 23662, USA. I can be found on Facebook at: www.facebook.com/michellewillinghamfans and Twitter at www.twitter.com/michellewilling.

TO SIN
WITH A VIKING

Michelle Willingham

First published in Great Britain 2013
by Mills & Boon, an imprint of Harlequin (UK) Limited.
Harlequin (UK) Limited, Eton House, 18-24 Paradise Road,
Richmond, Surrey TW9 1SR

© Michelle Willingham 2013

ISBN: 978 0 263 89844 6

Harlequin (UK) policy is to use papers that are natural, renewable and recyclable products and made from wood grown in sustainable forests. The logging and manufacturing process conform to the legal environmental regulations of the country of origin.

Printed and bound in Spain
by Blackprint CPI, Barcelona

RITA® Award Finalist **Michelle Willingham** has written over twenty historical romances, novellas and short stories. Currently she lives in south-eastern Virginia with her husband and children. When she's not writing Michelle enjoys reading, baking and avoiding exercise at all costs. Visit her website at: www.michellewillingham.com

Previous novels by this author:

HER IRISH WARRIOR*
THE WARRIOR'S TOUCH*
HER WARRIOR KING*
HER WARRIOR SLAVE†
THE ACCIDENTAL COUNTESS††
THE ACCIDENTAL PRINCESS††
TAMING HER IRISH WARRIOR*
SURRENDER TO AN IRISH WARRIOR*
CLAIMED BY THE HIGHLAND WARRIOR**
SEDUCED BY HER HIGHLAND WARRIOR**
TEMPTED BY THE HIGHLAND WARRIOR**
WARRIORS IN WINTER*
THE ACCIDENTAL PRINCE††

Also available in Mills & Boon® Historical *Undone!* eBooks:

THE VIKING'S FORBIDDEN LOVE-SLAVE
THE WARRIOR'S FORBIDDEN VIRGIN
AN ACCIDENTAL SEDUCTION††
INNOCENT IN THE HAREM
PLEASURED BY THE VIKING
CRAVING THE HIGHLANDER'S TOUCH

And in M&B:

LIONHEART'S BRIDE
  (part of *Royal Weddings Through the Ages*)

The MacEgan Brothers
†prequel to *The MacEgan Brothers* mini-series
**The MacKinloch Clan*
††linked by character

**Did you know that some of these novels
are also available as eBooks?
Visit www.millsandboon.co.uk**

Chapter One

Ireland—ad 875.

The tribe was slowly starving to death.

Caragh Ó Brannon stared at the grain sack, which was nearly empty. One handful of oats remained, hardly enough for anyone. She closed her eyes, wondering what to do. Her older brothers, Terence and Ronan, had left a fortnight ago to trade for more food. She'd given them a golden brooch that had belonged to their mother, hoping someone would trade sheep or cows for it. But this famine was widespread, making anyone reluctant to give up their animals.

'Is there anything to eat, Caragh?' her younger brother Brendan asked. At seventeen, his appetite was three times her own, and she'd done her best to keep him from growing hungry. But it was now evident that they would run out of food sooner than she'd thought.

Instead of answering, she showed him what was left. He sobered, his thin face hollow from lack of food. 'We haven't caught any fish, either. I'll try again this morning.'

'I can make a pottage,' she offered. 'I'll go and look for wild onions or carrots.' Though she tried to interject a note of hope, both of them knew that the forests and fields had been stripped long ago. There was nothing left, except the dry summer grasses.

Brendan reached out and touched her shoulder. 'Our brothers will come back. And when they do, we'll have plenty to eat.'

In his face, she saw the need to believe it, and she braved a smile she didn't feel. 'I hope so.'

After he went outside with his fishing net, Caragh stared back at the empty hut. Both of their parents had died last winter. Her father had gone out to try to catch fish, and he'd drowned. Her mother had grieved deeply for him and had never recovered from the loss. She'd given her own portion of food to Brendan numerous times, lying that she'd already eaten. When they'd discovered the truth, it had been too late to prevent her death.

So many had succumbed to starvation, and it bled Caragh's conscience to know that both of her parents had died, trying to feed their children.

Hot tears rose up as she stared at her father's forge. He'd been a blacksmith, and she was accustomed to hearing the ring of his hammer, watching the bright glow of hot metal as he shaped it into tools. Her heart was as heavy as the anvil, knowing she would never hear his broad laugh again.

Though his boat remained, she didn't have the courage to face the larger waves. Her brothers knew how to sail, but none of them had ventured out again after his death. It was as if evil spirits lingered, cursing the broken vessel that had returned without their father.

She wished they could leave Gall Tír. This desolate land had nothing left. But they lacked the supplies to travel very far on foot. They should have gone last summer, after the crops had failed to flourish. At least then, they would have had enough to survive the journey. Even if they now travelled by sea, they had not enough food to sustain them beyond a day.

The hand of Death was stretched out over everyone, and Caragh had felt her own weakness changing her. She could hardly walk for long distances without growing faint, and the smallest tasks were overwhelming. Her body had grown so thin, her *léine* hung upon her, and she could see the thin bones of her knees and wrists.

But she wasn't ready to give up. Like all of them, she was fighting to live.

She picked up her gathering basket and stepped outside in the sunlight. The ringfort was quiet, few people exerting the energy to talk, when there was the greater task of finding food. Her older brothers weren't the only ones who had left to seek supplies. Most of the able-bodied men had gone, especially those with children. None were expected to return.

A few of the elderly women nodded to her in greeting, with baskets of their own. Caragh thought of her earlier promise, to find vegetables, but she knew there was nothing out there. Even if there was, the others would likely find it first. Instead, she made her way towards the coast, hoping to find shellfish or seaweed.

She stopped to rest several times when her vision clouded and dizziness came over her. The water was nearly black this morn, the waves still and silent. Her brother was standing along the shoreline with his net, casting it out into the waves. He waved his hand in greeting.

But it was the sight of the longship on the horizon that evoked fear within both of them. The vessel was large, a curved boat that could hold over a dozen men. A massive striped sail billowed from the mast, and a single row of white and red shields hung over the side. In the morning sun, a bronze weathervane gleamed upon the masthead and a carved dragon head rested at the prow. As soon as she spied it, her heartbeat quickened.

'Is it the *Lochlannach*?' she cried out to her brother. So many tales she'd heard, of the barbaric Vikings of the Norse lands who ravaged the homes of innocent people. If their ship was here, they had less than an hour before the nightmare began. Gooseflesh prickled upon her skin at the thought of being taken by one of them. Or worse, being burned alive if they attempted to seize her home by force.

'Go back to our house,' Brendan commanded. 'Stay inside, Caragh, and for God's sake, don't let anyone in.' He pulled in his fishing net and hurried back towards the ringfort.

'What are you going to do?' She caught up

to him, afraid he was about to do something foolish.

Her brother's grey eyes turned cold. 'They have supplies, don't they? And food.'

She was horrified at his sudden thoughts. 'No. You can't try to steal from them.' The Norsemen were ruthless warriors who would murder her brother without a second thought.

'They'll try to raid the fort. They'll be gone while I take what's on board their ship.'

'And what about the rest of us?' she demanded. 'If we're fighting for our lives, we might all be dead by the time you return. *If* you return,' she added. 'No, you can't do this.'

Her brother entered their father's hut, searching for a sword among the blacksmith tools. 'If you'd rather, go and hide in the forest. Climb one of the trees as high as you can and wait until it's over.'

'I can't abandon the tribe.' There were elderly folk remaining, who were too weak to fight. Though her own strength was waning, she couldn't turn her back on their kinsmen.

Her hands were trembling, the fear rising up from inside. Brendan took her hand and squeezed it. 'If we don't take their supplies, we'll die anyway. Either today or a fortnight from now. We both know it.'

She did. But she didn't like stealing. Though she'd lost nearly every possession they'd owned, she still had honour. And that meant something.

'We could ask,' she said. 'If they see how little we have, they may share with us.'

Her brother's expression darkened. 'Since when do the *Lochlannach* possess mercy?' He belted the sword at his waist. 'Gather the others and take them from here, if you wish. Leave the ringfort unprotected, and perhaps they'll take what they want without hurting anyone.'

She stared at him, her thoughts caught in a tangled web of fear. 'Don't go, Brendan. The risk is too great.'

'Don't be afraid, *a deirfiúr*.' He bent down and kissed her forehead. 'I'd rather die in battle than die the way our parents did.'

She could see that no argument would influence him. But perhaps she could speak to his friends. He might listen to them, though he paid no heed to her warnings.

All she could do was try.

No man ever wanted to admit his marriage was dying.

Styr Hardrata stared out at the grey waters cloaked with mist, watching over his wife Elena. She stood with her hands upon the bow of the ship, her long red-gold hair streaming behind her in the wind. She was beautiful and strong, and he'd always been fascinated by her.

But that strength had now become a coldness between them, an invisible wall that kept them apart. She blamed herself for their childlessness, and he didn't know what to say. He'd tried everything until now, she grew sad every time he tried to touch her. Lovemaking had become a duty, not an act of passion.

Though he'd tried to ignore her growing reluctance, he was tired of her flinching whenever he tried to pull her near. Or worse, feigning pleasure when he knew she no longer wanted his touch.

The slow burn of frustration coiled inside him. This was a war he didn't know how to fight, a battle he couldn't win. Styr approached the front of the boat and stood behind her. He said nothing, staring out at the grey waves that sloshed against the boat.

'I know you're there,' she said after a time. But she didn't turn around to look at him. There was no smile of welcome, nothing except the quiet acceptance she wore like armour.

He didn't know how to respond to her cool-ness but said the only thing he could think of. 'It won't be long now before we arrive.' And thank the gods for it. Their ship had been plagued by storms, and he hadn't slept in three days. None of them had, after the strong winds had threatened to sink the vessel. His mind was blurred with the need to find a pallet and sink into oblivion.

In fact, the moment his feet touched ground, he was tempted to lie there and sleep for the next two days.

'I'll be glad to reach land,' she admitted. 'I'm tired of travelling.'

He reached out to touch her shoulder, but she didn't turn to embrace him. She held her-self motionless, staring out at the water. In time, he lowered his hand, suppressing the disappointment.

In truth, Elena had startled him when she'd agreed to leave Hordafylke and jour-ney with him to Éire, for a new beginning. Though their marital troubles had worsened over the past year, he wanted to believe that she wasn't ready to give up yet. He held on to the hope that somehow they could rekindle what they'd lost.

Styr waited for her to speak, to share with

him the thoughts inside, but she offered nothing. He considered a thousand different things to say to her, questions about what sort of house she wanted to build. Whether she would want a new weaving loom or perhaps a dog to keep her company when he was fishing at sea. She loved animals.

'Do you—?'

'I'd rather not talk just now,' she said quietly. 'I've not been feeling well.'

The words severed any further conversation attempts, and he stiffened. 'So be it.' He went to the opposite end of the boat, needing to be away from her before he said something he would later regret.

Disappointment shifted into anger. What in the name of Thor did she want from him? He wasn't going to lower himself and beg for her affections. He'd done everything in his power to make her happy, and it was never enough.

Frustration surged inside him, though he knew it was unwarranted. She was tired from the journey, that was all. Once they built a new home and started over, things might change.

The shores of Éire emerged on the horizon, and he stared at the desolate, sun-darkened grasses. Though he'd heard tales of how green the land was, from this distance, it appeared that they were suffering from a drought.

His friend Ragnar stepped past the men rowing and stood beside him. 'I still don't know why you wanted to settle here, instead of in Dubh Linn,' he remarked, pointing towards the east. 'The settlements there are a hundred years old. You'd find more of our kin.'

'I don't want Elena surrounded by so many people,' Styr admitted. 'We'd rather begin anew, somewhere less crowded.' As they drew nearer, he thought he glimpsed a small settlement further inland.

Ragnar sat across from him and picked up an oar. Styr joined him, for the familiar rowing motion gave him a means of releasing physical frustration. He was glad his friend had decided to journey with them, along with a dozen of their friends and kin from Hordafylke. It made it easier to leave behind his home, when his closest friends were here. He'd known Ragnar since he was a boy, and he considered the man like a brother.

'Has she said anything to you about this journey?' Styr asked, nodding towards Elena. She, too, had known Ragnar since childhood.

It was possible that she might confide her thoughts in someone else.

Ragnar sobered. 'Elena hasn't spoken much at all. But she's afraid—that, I can tell you.'

Styr pulled hard on the oar, his arms straining as the wooden blades cut through the waves. Afraid of what? He would protect her from any harm, and he was more than able to provide for her.

'What else do you know?' he demanded.

'The men are tired. They need rest and food,' Ragnar said. His friend's face mirrored his own exhaustion, after they'd been awake for so long.

'I wasn't talking about the men.'

Ragnar rested the oars for a moment, sympathy on his face. 'Just talk to Elena, my friend. She's hurting.'

He knew that was the obvious answer. But Elena rarely spoke to him any more, never telling him what she was thinking. He couldn't guess what was going on inside her head, and when he demanded answers, she only closed up more.

He didn't understand women. One moment, he would be talking to her, and the next, she'd be silently weeping and he had no idea why. It made him feel utterly helpless.

As their boat drifted closer, he eyed Ragnar. 'I've been saving a gift for her. Something to make her smile.' He'd bought the ivory comb in Hordafylke, and the image of Freya was carved upon it. When he showed it to his friend, Ragnar shrugged.

'It's a nice gift, but it's not what she wants.'

Though his friend was only being honest, it wasn't what Styr wanted to hear. 'Do you think I don't know that? Do you think we wanted to be childless all these years?' His temper broke out, and his words lashed out louder than he'd intended. Elena was holding on to her waist, and she didn't glance back at either of them. He didn't doubt his wife had overheard their argument. But as cool-headed as she was, she'd never confront him.

'I've made offerings to the gods,' he admitted, dropping his voice lower. 'I've been a good husband to her. But this curse is wearing on both of us. It has to end.'

Ragnar stood, preparing to lower the sail. 'And if it doesn't?'

Styr stared at his hands, not knowing the answer to that. But he strongly suspected that there was nothing he could do to make his wife happy again. He stole a last look at her, and at that moment she turned back. Her pale face was shadowed, her eyes holding such pain, he didn't know how to heal it.

In the end, he busied himself with the ship, unable to bridge the growing distance between them.

The *Lochlannach* were here. Caragh's heart beat so rapidly, she could hardly breathe. There were a dozen men walking through the shallow water, and their size alone dwarfed her kinsmen. Battleaxes and swords hung from their waists, while they carried round wooden shields. Several of the men wore chainmail corselets and helms with narrow nose guards. One man was taller than all the others, possibly their leader. His eyes narrowed upon the ringfort, and Caragh remained hidden behind a pile of peat bricks.

She'd managed to evacuate most of the people, aside from Brendan and his friends. The young men worried her, for they seemed intent upon attacking the *Lochlannach*. If they did, doubtless they would be slaughtered in the attempt.

She didn't know what to do. Should she approach them and find out what they wanted? Their leader drew closer, and he was so tall, he stood a full head above her brother Brendan.

He had fair hair bound back, and his shoulders were broad, like a man accustomed to hacking his way through a battlefield. His cloak was black, and a golden brooch fastened it on one side. Beneath it, she caught the glint of chainmail, though he wore no helm. There was no trace of mercy in his visage, as if he'd come to plunder and take everything of value.

She tried to calm the wild beating of her heart, but in the distance, she spied her brother moving behind the men. Four others were approaching from opposite corners, intending a surprise attack.

Why wasn't Brendan moving towards the boat? With horror, she realised that he'd changed his intent. No longer was he planning to raid their supplies.

It seemed her younger brother and his friends were planning an attack of their own. Caragh swallowed hard, praying for a miracle. If only her older brothers were here to stop him. Or any of the other men. She had to do something to protect Brendan, but what?

She started to rise from her hiding place, when suddenly, she spied a female standing back from the men. Her skirts were sodden from walking through the water, and she stared at the ringfort as if she were nervous.

If these men had come to raid, they would never have brought a woman along. Who was she?

Caragh had no time to consider further, for her brother and his friends made their move. Within seconds, they surrounded the woman, dragging her away from the other men.

Her scream cut through the air, and the Viking leader charged after the young men. The other *Lochlannach* followed, but their movement lacked energy, as if they had not fought in some time. The leader showed no weakness at all, and a roar erupted from him as he ran, his battleaxe unsheathed.

He was going to kill them.

Caragh bit her lip so hard, she tasted blood, when the Viking was surrounded by her kinsmen. He swung his battleaxe, his chainmail shirt outlining immense muscles and a honed body well accustomed to fighting. The blade sank into one of the young men trying to hold him back.

She closed her eyes tightly, her blood pulsing so hard, she felt faint. Although the Norseman was outnumbered, the young men's efforts would come to naught. They would die for this—Brendan among them.

She couldn't stand aside and let it happen.

Caragh slipped back into the blacksmith's hut, searching for a weapon she was strong enough to wield. Precious time slid away and she tried to lift her father's hammer, without success.

Something. Anything. She whirled around, and this time, she saw a wooden staff in the corner. Although it was heavy and thick, at least she could lift it.

She rushed out of the hut, only to find that several more of her kinsmen had returned from their hiding places, and had surrounded the *Lochlannach*. Older men charged forwards with their own weapons, and several lay dead. Others had managed to subdue several of the enemy men, tying them up as hostages.

But it was the Viking leader who held her attention now. He'd torn his way free of the people and was running after the woman, blood lust in his eyes.

Straight towards her brother.

Caragh didn't think, but raced after him, her lungs burning as she ran. She didn't know what she could possibly do to stop the warrior, but she gripped the wooden staff in her hands, praying for strength she didn't have. Her terror seemed to slow, magnified by the need to save Brendan. Her brother had seized the woman with both hands, leaving him powerless to defend himself.

'Brendan, let her go!' she shouted, but he didn't. The Viking raised the battleaxe above his head, prepared to strike.

Without knowing where her strength came from, Caragh swung the staff at his head. The man turned at the last second and the staff caught him across the ear. He dropped hard, the axe falling from his hand. The woman screamed, reaching towards him as she cried out words in an unfamiliar language.

Caragh felt the woman's pain, and she met the woman's eyes with her own, wishing she could make her understand. She'd had no choice in this.

Chapter Two

Styr awakened, feeling as if someone had crushed his head. When he tried to sit up, a rush of pain poured through him.

It was eerily quiet, and it took him a moment to reassemble what had happened. He smelled a peat fire, and when he tried to sit up, he realised that his wrists were chained behind his back, around a thick post. He was now a prisoner.

Where was Elena? Had they taken her, too? His eyes adjusted to the darkness and he struggled to stand. There was only a woman standing on the far end of the room, watching him with wariness. He listened hard for the sound of his language, for any evidence that his kinsmen were alive. But there was nothing.

He knew the Irish language, after his father had taught him many foreign tongues. As a voyager, Styr knew how valuable it was, and he'd mastered several languages as a boy. But he asked the woman no questions, not revealing his ability to understand her words. He might learn more about Elena and Ragnar, if he pretended he knew nothing.

'Where have you taken the others?' he barked out, using a Norse dialect he knew she wouldn't understand.

She flinched at his tone and remained far away. Good. In the shadowed light, he couldn't quite make out her features, but it surprised him that her family had left her here alone with him. Where were the other men? Why was there no one else to guard him?

He began examining his bonds more closely. They had chained his arms behind his back, around a thick beam on the opposite wall. He guessed the circumference of the beam was the width of his thigh, for when he leaned his weight against it, it did not budge.

'Let me go,' he demanded, still using the Norse language. To emphasise his words, he strained against the chains.

When the woman stepped into the light, he was shocked by what he saw. Her face was terribly thin, her eyes sunken from lack of food. The bones of her wrists were narrow, and though he recognised her as the one who had struck him down, he couldn't imagine how she'd done it.

There was no possible way she'd had the strength to move him here and put him in chains. She looked as if a strong wind would knock her over.

Her eyes were a strange blue, so dark, they were almost violet. Her brown hair hung to her waist, unbound except for a small braided section at her temples.

She might have been beautiful, if she'd had enough to eat.

He found himself comparing her to Elena. His wife was nearly as tall as he was, with long reddish-blonde hair and eyes the colour of seawater. Their families had arranged the marriage in order to ally their two tribes together. Although she was a quiet woman, the first few years had been good between them.

A chill took hold within him as he wondered what they'd done with her. Was she alive?

But demanding questions of this waif would accomplish nothing. Better to bide his time and gain her trust. Perhaps then he could get her to unlock his chains, and he'd slip away into the night.

'I can't understand your language,' she admitted, drawing nearer. She was far shorter than Elena, and the top of her head only reached his shoulders. 'But I'm sorry for all of this. I just...wanted to protect my brother.'

He said nothing, staring at her. The young woman's voice revealed her fear, but there was also a sweetness to it, as if she were trying to soothe a wounded beast.

'My name is Caragh Ó Brannon,' she informed him. Touching her chest, she repeated, 'Caragh.'

Styr said nothing at all. If she wanted his name, then she'd have to set him free first. He sent her a hard look, willing her to release him.

'If you'll allow it, I can tend your wound,' she offered. 'I truly am sorry for hitting you. I was afraid I'd killed you for a moment.' She lowered her gaze, wringing her hands together. 'That's not the sort of woman I am.' Her mouth tightened, and she sighed. 'I don't know why I'm even speaking to you, for you can't understand a single word.'

It didn't seem to stop her, though. Caragh began talking in a stream of conversation, and Styr was so taken aback by her ceaseless speech, he had trouble following some of her words. She kept apologising while she found a basin of water and a bowl of soup. Then he came to understand that it was her way of hiding her fear. By talking her enemy to death.

When she stood an arm's length from him, Caragh stopped mid-word. Her eyes stared at him with regret, and she set down the bowl of soup at his feet, along with another basin, presumably for his personal needs.

'I'm sorry to keep you like this,' she said quietly. 'But if I let you go, you'll kill my family.' Her eyes drifted downward again. 'Possibly me, as well.' She dipped the linen cloth into the water and hesitated. Water dripped down into the bowl, and she admitted, 'I probably shouldn't have taken you prisoner. But if I hadn't, you'd have gone after my brother again.'

It disconcerted him that he'd been captured at all. If he and his men had been at their full strength, it never would have happened. The lack of sleep had slowed their reflexes, making it difficult for them to respond to the surprise attack.

Caragh reached out and touched the cloth to his temple, washing away the dried blood.

The gentle gesture was so unexpected, he gaped at her. She was intent upon her work, though from the slight tremor in her fingers, he sensed her fear of him. The cool water soothed the swelling, but he spoke no words.

Why would she bother tending his wound? He was her enemy, not her friend. No one had ever touched him in this manner, and he couldn't understand why this waif would attempt it. Either she had a greater courage than he'd guessed, or she was too foolish to understand that a man like him didn't deserve mercy.

'I wish you could understand me,' she murmured, while a water droplet slid down his cheek. She was staring at him intently, her blue eyes so dark, he found himself spellbound. When her fingers touched the drop of water, an unbidden response flared inside him. Styr moved forwards, stretching the chains taut.

Forcing her to be afraid.

She jerked back, stammering, 'I—I'm sorry. I must have hurt you again.' She pointed towards the bowl of soup on the ground. 'I haven't much I can feed you, but it's all there is.' She shrugged and retreated again, nodding for him to eat.

Styr eyed the bowl of watery soup and then sent her a questioning look. Exactly how did she expect him to eat with his hands bound behind his back?

She waited for a moment, ladling a bowl for herself. With a spoon, she began to eat slowly, as if savouring the broth. 'Don't you want—?' Her words broke off as it dawned on her that she would have to feed him if he was going to eat at all.

A slow breath released from her. 'I should have thought about this.' She stood and reached for another wooden spoon. For a moment, she studied him. Her mouth twisted with worry, but she picked up the bowl again.

Styr could hardly believe any of this. Not only had she treated his wounds, she'd offered food and was about to feed it to him.

For a captor, she was entirely too merciful. And it enraged him that he was trapped here with a soft-hearted woman attempting to make the best of the situation while Elena was out there somewhere. He had to escape these chains and find his wife.

Regret stung his conscience, for he'd failed to protect Elena. He didn't know if she was alive or dead, and guilt weighed upon him.

What if another man had violated her? What if she was suffering, her body ravaged with pain?

Styr ignored the soup and called out in a hoarse voice, 'Elena!' There was no reply. Again and again, he shouted her name, hoping she would hear him if she was within the ringfort. Then he called out to Ragnar and each of his kinsmen as he tried to determine if he was the only hostage. Or the only one left alive.

'They're gone,' Caragh interrupted when he took another breath. 'I don't know where, but the ship isn't there any more.' Her face flushed and she admitted, 'Brendan took the woman hostage. I saw your men lay down their weapons, but I don't know what happened after that.'

Her gaze dropped to the ground, and he suspected she was withholding more information. He turned his gaze from her, so she would not know that he'd understood her words.

Turbulent thoughts roiled within him, igniting another surge of rage. Where was his wife? Was she still alive? And what of his men?

When Caragh dared to touch a spoonful of broth to his lips, he used his head like a battering ram, sending the bowl flying. She paled and retrieved the bowl, wiping up the spilled soup.

In fury, he kicked at the wall, smashing the wattle and daub frame until he'd created a hole in the wicker frame. He roared out his frustration, straining against the manacles in a desperate need to escape. Over and over, he pulled at the chains, trying to break them.

And when he'd failed to free himself, he cast another look at Caragh. She'd picked up the remains of his soup and added it to her own bowl. When he stared at her, she showed no fear at all. Only a defiant look of her own, as if he ought to be ashamed of himself.

Caragh slept fitfully, awakening several times during the night. Dear God in Heaven, what had she done? Imprisoning the Viking had seemed like a good idea at the time, but now, she regretted it. She shouldn't have saved his life. He was planning to kill Brendan and had already killed two others. He didn't deserve to live.

It was several hours before dawn, but she rose from her pallet and tiptoed over to the fire, adding another peat brick. A flicker of sparks rose up, and she stoked the flames to heat the cool interior. In the faint amber light, she studied the *Lochlannach* man who lay upon the earth.

She had removed his cloak and brooch, not wanting him to use the pin as a weapon. He wore a rough linen tunic beneath the mail corselet protecting his chest, while his fair hair was tied back in a cord. His face was strangely compelling, even in sleep. She sat upon a foot-stool and studied him.

Though he was harsh, his body strong from years of battle, she couldn't deny that he was handsome, like a fallen angel. None of the men she'd met over the years even compared to this man's features.

He was the sort of man to carry a woman off and claim her. Without warning, her mind conjured the image of kissing a man like this. He would not be gentle but would capture her mouth, consuming her. A hard shiver passed over her, for she'd never before imagined such a thing. It was madness to even consider it.

But she'd glimpsed the fury on his face when the woman was taken. He'd fought hard for her, striking down any man who threatened her.

Caragh studied his profile in the firelight, wondering what sort of man he was. Was he a fierce barbarian who would kill her as soon as she freed him? Or did he possess any honour at all?

In his sleep, he moved restlessly, and she realised he was exposed to cool air from the wall segment he'd broken. Though it was summer, the nights were often cold, and no doubt he was feeling the chill. The practical side of her decided that he ought to be uncomfortable for smashing the wall.

Wouldn't you have done the same thing, if you were a captive? her conscience argued. *Wouldn't you have done anything to escape?*

She might have. But he'd killed her kinsmen. He deserved to suffer for it.

They took his woman. He was trying to protect her.

He'd called out the woman's name, Elena, for a long time. Likely she was his wife or possibly his sister.

That was what plagued her most. If their situations were reversed, and she had been captured, her brothers would have slaughtered anyone who dared to harm her. She couldn't fault this man from trying to guard a family member.

But if she hadn't intervened, he would have killed Brendan. And if she released this man now, he would hunt her brother down and exact his revenge.

Worry knotted her stomach, for she didn't know where Brendan was. Her last fleeting vision of him was when he'd kept his blade at the woman's throat, dragging her backwards towards the ship. Caragh had been so busy securing her own prisoner, she'd only caught glimpses of what was happening around her.

One of the older men had helped her to drag the prisoner away from the others, for she'd been too weak to do it herself. After she'd chained the Viking, she'd returned outside, only to find the man's body cut down by a sword. Her stomach wrenched to think that he'd died because he'd tried to help her.

In her mind, she reconstructed bits and pieces of what she remembered. Brendan with his hostage…and the *Lochlannach* had dropped their weapons on the sand before they'd waded into the water.

Though a few of Brendan's friends had joined him, they were outnumbered. Even weaponless, Caragh didn't doubt that their enemy intended to ambush her brother, re-claiming the ship and the woman. They needed no blades to kill Brendan.

It had been impossible to help him, without drawing the *Lochlannach* back on herself and the others.

Why had he lured them away from Gall Tír? It was reckless and dangerous.

Unless Brendan was trying to lead the enemy away in a desperate act of bravery.

She closed her eyes, steeling herself against the possibility that her brother was already dead. Hours had passed, but he hadn't returned at all. She could only pray that he was still alive.

Disbelief and fear welled up inside her. All of her brothers had abandoned her. She hadn't argued when Terence and Ronan had gone, confident that they would return with the promised supplies. But now, it had been nearly a fortnight, and there was no sign of them.

What if none of her brothers returned? What if all of them were dead?

The idea of being alone, with no one to protect her, was terrifying.

With a heavy heart, she searched inside for the right decision about what to do now. She couldn't release her prisoner. If she did, she had no doubt he would strike her down. His dark, callous eyes bespoke a ruthless nature. There was nothing tame about him, and she saw no alternative except to keep him chained until her older brothers returned.

If they returned.

She closed her eyes, forcing away the thoughts of doubt. No, Terence and Ronan would come back. They had to.

Caragh picked up a woollen *brat* that she used as a winter wrap and tiptoed over to the section of the wall that the man had destroyed. She reached up to secure it over the hole, using it to block the wind.

When she turned around, she saw him staring at her. She pressed her back against the broken wall, just as he rose to his feet. His eyes were a dark brown, and she couldn't read the expression on his face. But she wouldn't make the mistake of trusting him. She inched further away until he spoke a word she didn't understand.

'What do you want?' she asked.

His gaze followed her, and he paused a moment. 'Water.'

It startled her to hear her language spoken by this man. 'You know Irish?'

But he only repeated, 'Water.'

Caragh went to fill a wooden cup with water, and she felt his eyes watching every move. When she drew close, she hesitated, not wanting to be so close to him after he'd already spurned the bowl of soup. But with his hands chained behind his back, there was no other alternative.

She swallowed back her apprehension and raised the cup to his lips, tilting it slightly. He drank, and in the shadowed light, she saw the rough stubble of facial hair. It was the same light blond colour as his hair, and when she lowered the cup, her eyes were drawn to his mouth. His lips were firm, a slash of a mouth that she doubted had ever smiled. In his dark eyes, she saw a worry that mirrored her own.

'Where is she?' he demanded in her language.

Caragh stepped back from him. 'So you do know Irish.' It meant he'd understood every word she'd spoken.

'Where?' he repeated. The ice in his voice held the promise of vengeance, and she retreated further. Though he could not harm her while he was in chains, she didn't doubt that he'd kill anyone who threatened the woman called Elena.

Her face paled, but she repeated what she'd said before, 'I told you already. I don't know.' She tried to calm the roiling fear in her stomach, admitting, 'Brendan took her as a hostage and set sail.'

Frustration drew his face taut with silent rage. 'I have to find her. Let me go.' His command was spoken in a steel voice, one meant to be obeyed.

Though she understood his need, she couldn't possibly free him from the chains. 'I can't release you,' she protested. 'You'll kill me if I do.' In her mind, she envisioned him taking his chains and wrapping them around her throat.

'I don't usually kill women. Even the ones who try to crack my skull.' He tested the post, straining against his bonds.

'I'm sorry for your wound, but I had to protect Brendan,' she argued.

'And I had to protect my *wife*.' He half-snarled the word, his rage erupting. 'She's an innocent. She did nothing to you.'

'The men were wrong to attack,' she admitted, crossing her arms. 'I tried to stop my brother, but he wouldn't listen.' Though it wouldn't make any difference, she offered, 'We were starving and needed supplies.'

'And you thought you'd take them.' Bitterness clung to his tone, and he let out a cynical breath of air. 'We would have shared what we had, if you'd asked.'

'Attacking you was never my idea,' she insisted. It shamed her that this man thought of her as nothing but a thief, when she wasn't.

'Let me go, Caragh.'

'Not yet, *Lochlannach*,' she countered. Frowning, she added, 'I don't even know your name.'

'I am Styr Hardrata. My wife is Elena.'

'I saw her with the others. She's beautiful.' Caragh returned to the cold pot of soup and moved it closer to the hearth to warm. 'Be assured, my brother doesn't plan to hurt her. He's only seventeen…and thoughtless, I'm afraid.'

'He plans to ransom them or sell them as slaves, doesn't he?'

She hadn't thought of that, but it was doubtful. 'I don't know what he plans to do.' Truthfully, she doubted if he'd considered any of his actions, it had all happened so fast. 'All I know is that I can't free you until my older brothers are here. Once they are, then you can go as it pleases you.'

'And I'm supposed to stay here and ignore what's happening to the rest of my family? You expect me to wait and do nothing?'

She lifted her shoulders in a shrug. 'I won't let you hurt my brother.'

His dark eyes gleamed in the stillness. 'If she's harmed because of what he did, I'll kill him. Be assured of it.'

She believed him. There was a darkness in this man, a soulless being who wouldn't falter when it came to retribution. It didn't matter that Brendan was young and foolish. In the Viking's eyes, she saw the promise of vengeance.

Her hands were trembling as she ladled more soup into a bowl. 'Do you want anything to eat?'

'What I want is to be released.' He glared at her, and she tightened the hold upon her fear.

Ignoring his demand, she said, 'I have very little food. If you want to eat, I will share what there is. But if you're going to push it away, tell me now, and I'll keep it for myself.'

He said nothing for a time, staring towards the fire. 'I suppose I'll have to keep up my strength for the day when you set me free.'

'I regret hurting you. But I had no choice.' She picked up the bowl with both hands, steam rising from the soup. It felt as if she were nearing a dragon as she approached the warrior.

He waited, and when she stood before him,

he said, 'You look as if you haven't eaten well in weeks.'

She hadn't but didn't say so. 'There was a drought, and we lost a good deal of our harvest last summer. Many died during the winter, and it's too early to harvest this year's crops.'

Caragh raised the bowl to his lips, and this time, he drank. The soup wasn't good, watery with only a bit of seaweed. But there was nothing else.

'What of your animals?' he asked. 'Sheep or cattle?'

She shook her head. 'They're gone. My brothers went to trade for more food.' To him, it might seem that they'd done little, but she knew the truth. They'd given up most of their possessions for food. 'Believe me when I say there is nothing to eat,' she continued. 'I've looked everywhere.'

'You live near the sea,' he pointed out. 'There's no reason for you to starve.'

But it wasn't that easy. 'The fishermen left, months ago, and took their boats with them,' she explained. 'We can only get the smaller fish near the shore. It's not enough.' She didn't mention her father's boat, for they had not touched it in months. The others, too, had left it alone.

Styr's hard gaze fastened upon her. 'There is no reason to starve if you know the ways of the sea.'

When she took the bowl away, she noticed that the side of his face was swollen red and would likely be bruised black and blue by morning. Seeing his wound bothered her, for it was her fault he'd been hurt.

Caragh went to fetch a linen cloth, soaking it in more cool water. Without asking his leave, she went and touched the sore spot, bathing it to prevent the swelling from growing worse.

He stared at her in disbelief. 'Do you always strike your enemy and then tend his wounds?' His eyes held suspicion, as if he weren't accustomed to anyone taking care of him. It made her feel foolish, and she pulled the cloth away.

'I've never taken a man prisoner before.' Her cheeks burned, and she retreated, wishing she'd never dared to touch him. Everything about this man threatened her, from his fiercely handsome face, to his raw strength. It was like chaining a predator, and she needed to remember that he was not to be trusted.

'How long before your brothers return?' he asked.

She shrugged. 'They've been gone a fortnight. I have no way of knowing when they'll be back.'

'And if they don't return?'

Caragh shook her head, not wanting to imagine it. Inwardly, she tightened the invisible bands around her fear and frustration. Ronan and Terence had sworn to return, and she believed they would.

But it was Brendan who gave her the greatest cause to fear. Her younger brother hadn't considered the consequences of his actions, and he might pay the price with his life.

Returning to the far side of the hut, she washed out the bowl and set it to dry. Her voice was quiet, but she admitted, 'If they don't return, I'll let you go. It would be more merciful for you to kill me than to starve to death.'

He sat down, leaning back against the post. And though she was desperately tired, Caragh sat beside the fire. Absently, she picked up a comb and began to run it through the long dark strands, hoping to calm herself. She was aware of him watching her, but she tried to ignore his gaze.

'Why did they leave you here?' he asked. 'Don't your brothers believe in protecting their women?'

She pulled at the comb, not looking at him. Aye, she did feel uncertainty at her future and a sense of hurt that they'd gone off without her. But she wouldn't reveal it to him. 'I can care for myself.'

'Can you?' He eyed her, and beneath his gaze, she felt embarrassment at her thinness.

'I haven't given up hope. My brothers will return, and—'

'—and you'll starve in the meantime.' His scorn irritated her, for he behaved as if she weren't lifting a finger. 'The women of my country would be out hunting for food, scouring the land instead of waiting at home.' He gave a shrug, and his diffidence infuriated her. 'But then, you're Irish.'

How did he dare to mock her, when she'd given up her own share of food on his behalf?

'What is that supposed to mean?' she demanded.

He only sent her a sardonic look, as if she could guess which insult he'd implied. Aye, she might not be a sword-wielding warrior, but she wasn't weak. Not by half.

She glared hard at his unsympathetic face,

wondering how he dared to criticise her. 'What would you have me do, were you in my place?'

'Leave. Find a man to protect you and care for you if your brothers won't take the responsibility.'

'Sell myself, you mean.' Though he might be right, she hated the thought of giving her body in exchange for survival. She'd rather die.

'You wouldn't have to sell yourself,' he said. His dark eyes fastened upon hers, his voice deepening. 'Most men are weak when it comes to women in need. And you've a fair enough face.'

Though his words were spoken with no innuendo, she felt herself blushing. It wasn't at all true. The men in her tribe wanted a demure, modest woman who rarely talked. Not one who spoke her mind and questioned everything.

'I'd rather survive using my wits,' she admitted. She stepped backwards, adding, 'And if I'm to find any more food for us in the morning, we should both get some sleep.'

'If you set me free tonight, you won't have to feed me at all,' he pointed out.

She ignored the suggestion. 'I can't do that.'

'Because you're too afraid?'

'I captured you, didn't I?' she shot back. 'I doubt if any of your women could say the same.'

'Only because I was unconscious,' he admitted. 'In my homeland, many wanted to capture me, but only one other succeeded.'

His wife, he meant. Caragh crossed her arms and stared at him. 'She must have the patience of a saint, then.' Putting up with a man of such arrogance would be a true test of any woman.

'She likes me well enough,' was his answer. But she caught a sense of brooding in his tone. Almost a reluctance to speak of Elena.

'I hope you find her,' Caragh said quietly, 'and that she's unharmed when you do.' It was the truth. She'd seen the agony on the woman's face when Caragh had struck down her husband. She didn't want to be the cause of any suffering between them.

Styr stood up again and stepped forwards, testing the length of his chains. 'Oh, I *will* find her,' he warned.

His brown eyes turned foreboding with a violent edge. 'But I'm not going to wait around to be murdered by your brothers. One morning, you'll awaken, and I'll be gone.'

Chapter Three

The hours spent alone were gruelling. Not only was Styr's stomach snarling from lack of food, but Caragh had been gone from sunrise until evening. It was as if she were seeking revenge for his earlier remark about the women of his country. This time, she had indeed left him alone all day. He'd used the time to study his chains, trying to determine how the manacles were fastened. It seemed they were attached with iron pins, ones that could only be removed with a hammer and an awl.

He'd tried to kick at the support beam to loosen it, but to no avail. His wrists were bloody after trying to squeeze his hands through the manacles, and again, it was no use.

Never in his life had he been any man's

captive, let alone a woman's. Though Caragh might eventually free him, it wouldn't be soon enough to suit him. Elena was at the mercy of those men, and although they'd had their marital troubles, she was still his wife. He was bound to protect her, and he couldn't stop until he'd freed her.

The image of Elena's face haunted him with the fear that she'd been dishonoured or hurt. *A man protects his woman*, his father had said, time and again. *He is merciless to those who threaten her.*

Styr turned to face the top of his post. There was a way to free himself, if he was willing to destroy Caragh's dwelling. He studied the structure, at the way the beam supported the house. It was possible…

Where was Caragh now? Was she even planning to return? His mouth was parched with thirst, and the water in the bucket on the far side of the room seemed to taunt him.

The door swung open, and a younger man entered the hut. His mouth curved in a sneer. 'So, this is Caragh's new pet. I heard she captured a *Lochlannach*.'

Styr said nothing at all, pretending he didn't understand a single word. Even so, he adjusted his stance, in case he needed to fight.

'Why is she keeping you here? Does she need a man that badly?' His enemy circled him, as if taking his measure. From his stance and the possessive tone, Styr suspected the man desired Caragh, but she'd spurned him.

'She shouldn't have kept you alive, *Lochlannach*.' Rage coloured the man's voice as he unsheathed a blade. 'You killed our kinsmen.'

Styr never took his eyes off his enemy, for he had only one opportunity to save himself. He gathered up the chains until there was no slack and they were locked tight against the wooden beam.

The man raised his knife, the blade slashing downwards towards his heart. Styr gripped the post and swung his legs out, tripping the man. The edge of the blade caught his leg, but the cut was shallow.

He locked his legs around the man's neck, squeezing until the man began to choke. A coldness settled within him, with the bitter resignation that he had no alternative—it was this man's life or his own. Seconds ticked by and his enemy's muscles grew limp.

A moment later, the door flew open. Caragh ran forwards. 'No! Release him!'

Styr held on until the man lost consciousness. 'Would you have rather he killed me?'

He struggled to his feet, ignoring the blood that ran down his leg.

She paled at the sight. Her gaze shifted to the other man, and her emotions held a trace of regret.

Taking the fallen knife, she hid it among her possessions, leaving both of them weaponless. When the man started to revive, Caragh helped him to his feet. Quietly, she ordered, 'Leave my home, Kelan.'

The look in the man's eyes was murderous. His voice was hoarse as he gritted out, 'Why did you save him? He doesn't deserve to live, Caragh.'

'Go,' she repeated. 'He is my prisoner, not yours.' Though she kept her voice calm, Styr sensed her unease with the man.

Kelan's gaze swept over her, lingering over her body. 'You're not safe with him.'

She shielded her thoughts, her violet eyes growing cold. 'It's no longer your concern.'

A dark flush came over Kelan's face. 'He slaughtered our kin, or did you forget?'

'Our brothers attacked them first,' she reminded him.

'You're defending a murderer?' The disbelief in his voice held venom. 'He's worth nothing at all, Caragh.'

She gave no reply but opened the door in a silent command to leave. Although the man obeyed, Styr knew it was only a matter of time before Kelan attacked again. And next time, he might not be able to save himself. His earlier resolve to free himself was now critical.

Caragh closed the door and lowered her head for a moment, not facing him. Her shoulders slumped, and he realised she was trying not to cry. The weight of the world seemed to bear down on her, and he saw her swipe her hands across her eyes before she turned to face him.

Her gaze drifted to his wounded leg. 'He hurt you.'

Styr shrugged. 'It's nothing. Just a slight cut.' But despite his insistence, she was already reaching for water and a cloth to tend it.

She was entirely too soft-hearted. Too trusting and naïve, especially with a man like him who knew nothing of forgiveness.

'Who was he to you?'

Her mouth tightened, but she shrugged. 'He's a member of our clan, that's all.'

'No. He was more than that.' Styr hadn't missed the underlying tension between them.

Caragh let out a sigh. 'He wanted to wed me once. But I refused him.' Before he could voice another question, she met his gaze squarely. 'And I don't want to talk about it any more.'

As soon as she touched his thigh with the damp cloth, he reflexively jerked.

'I'm sorry. I'll try to be gentle,' she assured him. But it wasn't the touch of her hands against the knife wound. It was the sudden softness of female fingers, perilously close to his groin. Though he told himself that the sudden response would have happened to any man, he felt himself tightening with an unwanted arousal.

Styr gritted his teeth, pressing his temple against the post to evoke the harsh pain of his head wound. He needed something to distract himself from Caragh's hands. He could imagine her palm sliding up his inner thigh, cupping his arousal. Elena had never done such a thing but usually lay beneath him while he'd joined with her.

Sometimes…he wished she would have

touched him in return. To know that she desired his attentions instead of accepted them.

He let out a hiss of air as Caragh finished cleansing the wound. 'It doesn't need to be stitched,' she agreed. 'You were right.'

Thank God for that. She stepped away, but as she did, he spied the redness around her dark blue eyes and remembered that she'd been crying.

'You were gone a long time,' he said. 'Did something happen to upset you?'

She shrugged. 'I walked for miles, but there was still no food.' Her eyes gleamed again and she admitted, 'I was angry with myself. There was a rabbit, but my stone missed him. I couldn't catch him while running because I lost my breath.' Her features tightened with anger. 'We're going to run out of food tonight.'

The desperation in her voice affected him more than he wanted it to. He should ignore it for, once she was out of food, she'd have to free him.

But he heard himself saying, 'You live by the sea. You won't run out of food.'

'Our nets have been empty for some time now.'

'Go out further,' he said. 'The large fish are in the deeper waters.'

'I can't.' She trembled a little, as if too afraid of the sea. There was danger in the deepest waves, true, but Styr revelled in the adventure of sailing. Harnessing the wind was like trying to steal the power of the gods. Even during the wild storm on the journey here, he'd welcomed the reckless force of the waves. It was freedom in its purest form.

'You also need bait,' he continued. 'Go out to the beach with a torch. Look for crab along the shoreline. Search near the seaweed.'

'I haven't seen crab in weeks. There aren't—'

'Trust me,' he insisted. 'More of them come out at night. You'll need them for the fishing lines.'

'I shouldn't leave you here alone. Kelan might return.'

He sent her a disbelieving look. 'I can defend myself, Caragh. Or did you forget that I defeated him even while I was chained?'

She ignored him and let out a rough sigh. Opening her basket, she revealed a bunch of clover and changed the subject. 'I'm afraid this is all I could find. I have enough grain for us tonight, but that's all.'

'So you'll run out of food and starve to death, without a fight. You won't even try.'

He stood up, hoping to provoke her anger. In her eyes, he could see the hopelessness, the physical weakness dragging her lower.

'It's not about trying.' She dropped the basket and confronted him. 'Do you think I haven't scoured the shores, looking for food? Don't you think all of us have tried?'

'I think you'd rather wait on your brothers to save you than try to save yourself.' He deliberately spurred her temper, knowing it would overcome the fear. Rage was the best weapon against the suffocating doubts.

'Perhaps I should have let Kelan kill you,' she muttered. 'Then there'd be one less person to feed.'

'You haven't fed me today,' he reminded her. 'And from the look of it, you haven't eaten, either.'

And at last, her fury got the best of her. Tears of frustration streamed down her face. 'I haven't eaten for nearly a fortnight, save a few greens and a soup that's mostly water. I can't remember the last time I had meat, and I'm so hungry, I can hardly walk anywhere without getting tired.' She tore down the woollen cloth from where it covered the hole in the wall.

'Then *you* had to come and destroy the only

home I have.' She wrapped the *brat* around her head and shoulders, holding on to herself as if she could hold back the emotions. 'I don't know what to do any more. It's frustrating to have nothing to show for my efforts.'

He said nothing at first, for this woman wasn't his responsibility. She'd taken him prisoner, and there was no reason to offer his advice.

But when he saw her shadowed face, he could think only of his wife. Was Elena hungry, as well? Was anyone watching over her? Or had they turned their backs on her?

If Caragh died, none of the others would free him. She was his only hope of escaping. And the only way to do that was to gain her trust.

'Set me free, and I'll help you get food,' he said at last. 'Then you can guide me to find my wife and kinsmen.'

She shook her head slowly, a rueful smile on her face. 'You'd only abandon me here, as soon as I let you go.'

Of course she would believe that. But he wasn't about to spend any longer, waiting until her brothers arrived. He would keep trying to free himself, no matter what he had to do.

Caragh took a branch from her supply of kindling and made it into a torch, lighting it in the fire. 'I suppose I could try to look for crab for a little while. Wait here, and I'll return within the hour.'

As if he had a choice.

He leaned back against the post, determined to do anything necessary to make his escape.

Styr tested the chains behind his back, lifting the manacles as far up as he could, to his shoulders. He leaned against them with his full body weight, stepping against the post. Though his wrists burned from the effort, he walked backwards up the post, lifting the chains with every step. After falling back down several times, he realised he had to keep the chains taut. Inch by inch, he guided himself up, gritting his teeth against the ache. It was the thought of freedom that pushed him past the edge of pain, while he twisted the chains and continued higher.

The support beam reached up to the ceiling. Slowly, he pulled himself up, until his shoulders touched the thatch. Sweat beaded against his forehead as he fought to keep his balance. If he could just lift his arms a little higher, he could raise the chains over the top of the post. It was attached to the roof, but the other beam was thinner, perhaps the width of his wrist.

Every muscle in his body cried out with agony, but he pushed past the pain. He would endure this for Elena's sake.

His shoulder nearly dislocated when he shoved the chain over the top of the beam. He hung, suspended, from the smaller piece of wood, and his body weight strained against the beam.

Come on, he pleaded. *Break.*

He gulped for air, swinging against the wood while he feared it was his wrists that would break. In his mind, he pictured the face of Elena and her haunted sadness.

She needs you.

With a Herculean effort, at last the smaller beam cracked and he fell to the ground against his knees.

He couldn't move, and for a long moment, he rested his cheek against the earthen floor. His wrists were slick with blood, and they throbbed with pain.

But he'd done it. He was free to move, free to leave this place. Though his hands were still bound in chains, no longer was he confined to Caragh's hut.

Styr rose up to his knees, letting out a shuddering breath. It was better to wait until morning to go after Elena. This land was unknown to him, and he needed to plan his journey.

That meant gathering supplies and food—if there were any to be had. He sobered, for he'd travelled enough to know that he couldn't go off blindly trying to track down Elena and Ragnar. Since they'd gone by boat, they could be anywhere along the coast.

He needed a ship of his own, to travel the same path. And he needed to break free of these chains.

Slowly, he stood, eager to escape the confines of this place. He struggled to open the door, but when he stepped outside, he breathed in the scent of freedom. All was quiet, the night cloaking the sky with darkened clouds. In the distance, he spied the flare of a single torch.

Caragh.

He gripped the chains to hold his silence as he tiptoed into the night. Soundlessly, he made his way towards the beach where he saw her staring intently at the sand. Alone, with no one to help her.

In her face, he saw the dogged determination to survive. It was breaking her down, but she kept searching. He'd known men who were quicker to give up than her.

She walked alongside the water, the torch casting shadows upon the sand. In the faint light, her face held a steady patience. Her skin was golden in the light, her brown hair falling over her shoulders in untamed waves.

She was far too gentle for her own good. What kind of a woman would capture a Norseman and then give up her own food? Why would she bother treating his wounds, when he'd threatened her?

And why was there no man to take care of her? No husband or lover...unless Kelan intended to offer his protection. From her coolness towards the man, she wouldn't want him near.

Styr remained in the shadows, even knowing that he shouldn't be here. He ought to be studying the perimeter of the ringfort, searching for hidden supplies or information about these people.

Instead, he couldn't take his eyes off

Caragh, as if she were the vision of Freya, sent to tempt him. Like the women of his homeland, she possessed an inner strength he admired. Though Fate had cast her a bitter lot, she'd faced the grimness of her future.

Taking him prisoner had been the action of a desperate woman, not a cruel one. He knew within his blood, that if he left her now, she would starve to death.

He shouldn't care. Because of her, he'd been helpless to look after his wife and his men. He owed her nothing.

And yet, he couldn't bring himself to walk away. Perhaps it was the way she'd tended his wounds…or the way she'd wanted to protect her brother. He understood loyalty to family.

He cursed her for weakening his resolve, but he couldn't leave until she had enough food to survive a little longer. Turning his back, he returned to her shelter, his mind filling up with plans of how to gain a boat.

Once he'd found fish for Caragh, he'd have his own supplies, too. Then, he could go out in search of his wife.

Caragh sat upon a large stone, watching the sand for any sign of movement. Styr had claimed that she might find crabs at this time of night, but she doubted there would be anything.

His accusation stung, that she would rather wait on her brothers than try to save herself. Of course she'd tried to survive. She'd done everything she could to find food.

Every breath was a fight to live, and she'd grown accustomed to hunger. The emptiness inside her was a constant reminder of how capricious Fate could be. But the *Lochlannach*'s words had bruised her feelings.

The familiar dizziness blurred her vision, and she took slow, deep breaths to keep from fainting. In time, the ringing in her ears stopped, and she concentrated on the water once more.

A flicker of movement caught her eye, and she raised the torch. She was startled to realise that Styr's prediction was right. There were crabs underwater at night. Quickly she reached for one and placed it in her basket. Though it was too tiny for meat, if she caught enough of them, they could make a good soup.

One by one, she saw more crabs and added them to her basket, feeling her spirits lift.

* * *

After another hour passed, she decided she'd caught enough. Though there were only a dozen, they would provide sustenance. She smiled with relief, covering the basket to protect her catch.

It was late, but she was so hungry, she hardly cared. Right now, she wanted to boil some of the crabs for food. Hurrying back, she opened the door and saw the Viking exactly where she'd left him. When he spied her, his eyes seemed to say: *I told you so.*

'You were right,' she admitted, revealing the crabs she'd caught. But she hardly cared what he thought. She couldn't stop herself from smiling. 'I'll boil these and make a soup.'

The *Lochlannach* shook his head. 'Don't. You'll catch fish if you bait lines with the crab tonight. Put them where the tide comes in and you'll have bass or flounder in the morning.' He gave her further instructions about the kind of fishing lines she needed and the hooks.

Caragh put up her hands, not listening. 'No. We should eat now. I know you must be as hungry as I am.'

'We'll eat the grain tonight,' he corrected. 'Fish in the morning.'

'If there *are* any fish.'

'There will be,' he promised. 'I was right about the crabs, wasn't I?'

She eyed her basket in dismay, wanting so badly to eat them. But they were no bigger than the palm of her hand…and the promise of large fish made her mouth water.

'I'm afraid of losing the crabs,' she confessed. 'What if I bait the lines and get nothing for my trouble?'

'It's possible,' he told her. 'But I've spent my life living off the sea. I know how to catch fish.'

Caragh regarded him. If so, then it might be their salvation. She'd never been able to catch anything but small fish in the shallow water.

She pulled out some of the fishing lines belonging to her brother and Styr repeated his instructions, explaining how she should pierce the shell with the hook.

'Set out the lines,' he said. 'And in the morning, you'll see.'

He appeared confident that it would work, but Caragh wasn't so certain. The sea was unpredictable, and more often than not, she'd caught nothing.

She placed the bait and the fishing lines in her basket, walking slowly past Styr. His demeanour was stoic, almost arrogant in his belief that she could not fail in this. But when he turned to look at her, there was a slight shift in his expression, almost as if he held empathy towards her.

His dark eyes held a steadiness, willing her to believe in this. A tightness seized up in her chest, for she desperately wanted to hope. Her gaze passed over his wounds. The cut upon his leg didn't seem to be bleeding any more, but his head wound was still swollen.

'Thank you for helping me,' she said. 'I pray that this will work.'

In the dim light of her house, she noticed a difference in his posture. There was something unusual about the way he was sitting.

Frowning, she started to approach, but he said, 'Go and set the lines before your torch dies out.'

'All right.' She reached for her basket and the torch, adding, 'If I do catch any fish, I promise I'll free you in the morning.'

He sobered, giving a single nod. Though

she didn't know if it was safe to make such a vow, she was a woman of her word. And their lives depended on catching these fish.

Styr crept outside, shadowing Caragh. Immediately, he noticed that she was choosing the wrong location for her lines. No fish of any size would swim near the pools where she'd set the bait. He remained hidden, watching as she moved from one line to the other. In all, she set out a dozen, in various locations along the shallow waters. He waited until she was further away and then knelt down, using his shackled hands to pick up the first line, moving it out into deeper water.

Thor's blood, he shouldn't be interfering like this. But there was no choice. He needed supplies and food before he could go after Elena.

The tide was going out, and Styr crouched down, searching for a place where the line would lure larger fish. Though his hose grew soaked, he waded towards a sandbar. He gripped the baited line behind him, searching until he found the right place. Luck was with him, and his foot pressed against a stone, one large enough to hold the line. Kneeling down in the water, he manoeuvred his hands until he was able to secure the line with the stone.

When he turned back, he was startled to glimpse the outline of a boat, anchored near the shore. Caragh had said nothing about it, claiming that the fishermen had taken their boats with them. This one was set apart from the settlement, almost as if someone had tried to hide it.

But now, he had a means of leaving this place. A way of retracing the path of his wife and kinsmen. Thank the gods.

With a quick glance, he saw that Caragh was starting to return. Styr rose from the water and hurried towards the shore. He melted back into the shadows, running towards her hut. Though a close glance would reveal that he was no longer bound to the post, he hoped he could feign sleep. His clothing might dry by morning, though it was doubtful. He leaned against the post, curling his body to hide his chains.

Within minutes, the door creaked open. 'Styr?' Caragh whispered.

He didn't answer, hoping she would go to sleep and leave him alone. The wind blew against his back, making his wet clothing more uncomfortable.

With his eyes shut tightly, he ignored the footsteps approaching, willing her to leave him alone. Before he realised what was happening, she had laid his cloak over him. The wool was warm from where she'd set it by the fire.

Her scent clung to the cloak, and it rendered him motionless. No one had ever done anything like this for him. He doubted if she'd even realised the significance. Kindness came to Caragh as naturally as breathing.

He closed his eyes, damning himself for a fool. There was no way he could leave her behind now, even if they did catch fish. It would haunt him for the rest of his life if she starved to death.

Whether or not she wanted it, he was going to take Caragh with him when he went in search of his wife.

Someone had to look after her.

Chapter Four

There were no fish. Caragh cursed and stared at the empty hook on the seventh line she'd checked. Seven crabs…all gone. Her mind bordered on hysteria, for if she hadn't listened to the *Lochlannach*, she could have had crab meat last night, instead of cooked grain. Furious tears rose up, but she refused to weep. It would do no good at all.

The eighth and ninth lines were empty, as well. When she reached the tenth, she sat down upon the rock, almost trembling with the knowledge of what she would find. Or wouldn't find, in this case.

'Did you catch anything, *a chara*?' An elderly female voice broke the stillness and she spied frail Iona, standing on the beach.

'No.' She picked up the tenth line, and saw a crab still dangling from the hook. 'But take this.' She unhooked the crab and held it out to the old woman. 'It's not much, but perhaps it will help a little.'

Iona smiled and shook her head. 'You're a dear one, Caragh, but no. I see what's before me, and my days are numbered. Why waste it upon an old crone like me, when it's a young woman like you who needs it more?'

Caragh ignored her and moved forwards, pressing the crab into her hand. 'Boil it and you'll have meat and broth. Please.' She folded the old woman's fingers over the crab, and a softness entered Iona's eyes.

She raised her hand to Caragh's forehead. 'You're a good child. How I wish you and Kelan had wed.'

The smile froze upon her face. Once, the handsome man had made her laugh, spinning stories that had made it easy to be with him. She'd believed that the rest of their days would be filled with happiness. But he'd tossed it aside for someone else.

Iona wanted to believe that her son was a good man, but Caragh wasn't about to disillusion the older woman. Too late, she'd learned that Kelan had a wandering eye. On the day they were meant to wed, he'd left her standing alone, humiliated before her friends and family. And when she'd sought him out, she'd caught him with another woman. The bitterness of that day hadn't diminished, even after a year.

'He still wants you,' Iona said. 'You should forgive him for his mistakes.'

Caragh said nothing. She'd loved Kelan, only to have it thrown back in her face.

Iona's gaze grew distant, staring suddenly at the waves. 'You've a rough journey ahead of you. And your heart will break.'

The eerie tone in the woman's voice curled into her spine. Iona spoke like a soothsayer, her voice faraway as she continued. 'But you'll be stronger for it.' Her clouded eyes narrowed. 'The path before you will only end in disappointment.'

'You're not making me feel better,' she told Iona with a dark smile, 'if that was what you were trying to do.'

'I say what I see,' Iona countered. 'And you will find your happiness, when you learn to walk away from what was never meant to be.' With that enigmatic message, the old woman returned to her home.

Caragh rubbed her arms as the sea wind

swept across the sand. She was cold and hungry, and her stomach wrenched with the pain of emptiness. Ignoring the last two fishing lines, she strode back to her home, planning to tell Styr exactly what she thought of his advice. Baiting the lines with the crabs had given her nothing at all.

She pushed the door open and her heart nearly stopped when she saw him standing a short distance away from the post where she'd chained him. 'How—how did you get free of the post?' His hands were still chained behind his back, but no longer was he confined to the place where he'd been.

'I told you I would free myself,' was his nonchalant answer. 'Did you find any fish?'

She stared up at the post and saw the broken beam near the top. How he'd ever managed to climb that high, sliding his chains over the top, was beyond her ken. 'No. There was nothing.'

'You didn't put the lines in the right place.'

'I did!' she insisted. 'I spread them all over the shoreline.'

'You put them in places where the water was too shallow.'

'And how would you know?' She had a suspicion that he had been free, long before this morning.

'Because I followed you last night.' He moved in, and when he stood before her, she felt intimidated by his immense height. Simply to look into his eyes meant craning her neck back.

'I changed one of your lines,' he said. 'Did you check that one?'

She shook her head. 'But all the others—'

'The others would have been washed away by the tide. Or the smaller fish would take the crab.' He used his shoulders to push the door open, waiting for her to lead.

But she didn't move. 'If you freed yourself already, then why are you still here?'

'I'm not free.' His voice grew harsh, his expression filled with frustration. 'You still have to remove the manacles.'

She said nothing, unable to trust him. He led the way outside, changing the direction to walk along a rocky ledge that extended out beyond the shore. 'There.' He nodded towards the sea, but she could not see what he was referring to. 'Wade into the water and you'll come upon a sandbar. I secured the line under the water.'

'I'm not going out there,' she insisted. 'The tide has come in.'

'Do you want fish or not?'

She stared at him, not knowing whether or not he was serious. The idea of wading into the water didn't appeal to her, though the early summer air was warm. 'How do I know you're not lying to me?'

'I'll walk with you,' he said and stepped into the water up to his knees. Wading through the waves, he continued towards the sandbar, his arms still bound back by the chains.

He turned back, but Caragh still didn't move. 'Do you see anything?'

'Come and find out for yourself.' His expression was unreadable, and though she didn't at all want to get wet, she stepped into the frigid water, wincing at the cold.

When she reached his side, he said, 'Reach into the water near my foot. I'm standing on the stone and you can lift it to grasp the line.'

His muscular thigh was close to her, and she brushed against his calf as she reached for the stone. Beneath it, she felt for the fishing line, and was startled to realise that there was something at the other end of the hook. Something was fighting hard, and in her excitement, she pulled against the line. Moving backwards, she gripped it steadily as she approached the shallows.

'Styr, we have a fish!' She couldn't tell how large it was, but joy brimmed up inside her. When at last she pulled the fish from the water, she found that it was not large, only the length from her wrist to her elbow. But it was food.

She laughed, holding the fish and imagining how good it would taste. Thank God.

The Viking emerged from the water, and she hugged the fish to her, not even caring how foolish it was. For now, she had hope of surviving a few more days. But a moment later, her elation dimmed.

'What is it?' he asked, walking alongside her towards the hut.

'I—I should share this with the others,' she admitted.

He sent her a hard look. 'Did they ever share anything with you?'

'It isn't right to have so much and not offer it to anyone else.' She thought of Iona and some of the other elderly folk who remained.

'We aren't going to eat all of it,' he told her. 'Half, maybe, but we're using the rest for more bait.'

She stared at him, incredulous. 'We lost

most of the bait last night. I'm not using this fish, only to lose half of it.'

He waited beside the door, and his expression was unyielding. 'I allowed you to try it your way, last night. But it's clear to me now that you need my guidance.'

His guidance? He spoke as if he were a sea god, able to control the elements. 'And what do you suggest?' She swung the door open, not even certain if he would follow. Caragh reached for a knife, preparing to clean the fish.

'I saw a boat anchored off the shore last night,' he said. 'We'll use it to catch enough fish to store over the next few months. And then we'll take the boat when we search for my wife and kinsmen.'

We? Her skin went cold at the thought. She wasn't about to go with this man on a boat. He would take her as his hostage, sailing far away from here.

'I'm not going with you.'

'Oh, yes, you are.' His voice turned commanding, and he stood above her, using his physical presence to intimidate her. 'I'm going to exchange your life for my wife and companions.'

She stared back at him. 'Not if you're my prisoner.'

His face tightened, and his dark eyes flared. 'I freed myself already, *søtnos*. And I can find a way out of these chains. With your help—' he leaned in, his warm breath against her cheek '—or without it.'

Styr broke his fast with the meagre portion of baked fish that Caragh had shared with him. The other half of the fish lay upon the board where she'd cleaned it. As he'd ordered, she'd kept the scraps.

Though she didn't want to go out on the boat with him, he knew she would. He'd whetted her appetite with the small fish, and she'd surprised him when she'd cooked a delicious meal, seasoning the fish with herbs and salt. Yet, neither of them was satisfied by the small amount of food, and he pressed her further.

'Miles off the coast, you'll find the larger fish,' he promised. 'We'll get more bait and then catch enough that you won't be able to eat any more.'

She stared down at her empty plate, her mood melancholy. He'd thought she would be eager to go out, but instead, she appeared to dread it.

'We will return by nightfall,' he swore. 'I give you my word.'

She still wasn't answering, and he moved to sit across from her. Waiting for her to speak. To say something.

But just like Elena, she was closing off her thoughts. She didn't want to go, and she didn't trust him at all. He couldn't fault her for that, but already he'd spent two nights here. The fierce need to find his wife and kinsmen went beyond longing. He had to save them and bring them back.

'Bring the fish and all of your family's fishing supplies,' he ordered. 'We'll go out now.'

She stood, taking a moment to wash the wooden platter they'd shared for the fish. Then she went by the fire and he saw how the damp gown hung against her knees.

'I'm afraid,' she admitted. 'It's been months since I went on a boat.'

He sensed there was more to it, but he didn't press her. 'Change your gown, and bring a warm wrap,' he ordered. 'I'll stand outside and wait for you.'

Caragh lifted her dark blue eyes to his, nodding. 'I will go. But only because I believe you can help me get the fish I need. And because the others need your help, as well.' She reached out to touch his arm, and the coolness of her fingers sent a shock of sensation through him. 'If we do catch fish, then I will go with you to help find your wife.'

'First, remove my chains,' he ordered quietly. 'You gave your promise.'

Her violet eyes met his, uncertainty lining her face. 'Not yet,' she whispered. 'Perhaps tonight.'

His rage magnified, that she would not keep the vow. 'You said you would free me, if we caught fish. And so we did.'

She gripped her arms, her gaze lowering to the ground. 'Only one.'

He moved in so close, she was trapped against the back of the wall. Her hands moved up to press him back, but he didn't move. 'You try my patience, woman.'

'I'm not your woman.'

'No, you're not,' he agreed. But her hands moved over the chainmail hauberk, and though it was only her effort to break free, a sudden vision flashed into his mind...of her hands continuing to move lower.

Damn her for conjuring such images.

'Your brother took Elena. And he will suffer for it.'

She took a breath, her expression turning serious. 'Promise me, you won't kill Brendan. He's just a boy.'

Styr stepped back, releasing her. 'If she is unharmed, then I might let him go. But if she has endured any pain at his hands, I will make no such vow.' When he reached the door, he turned back. 'Nor will I spare him, if you don't remove these chains.'

He stepped outside, not waiting for her answer. The day was a clouded grey, and rain was likely. Still, he would not delay any longer. If he could have left now, he would have. He hated being at the mercy of someone else, locked up in chains that prevented him from going after Elena.

And worse, having no supplies to take along. Without his ship, he had none of his wealth, nothing save the clothes on his back and the battleaxe that had been taken from him.

After several minutes, the door opened. He turned and saw Caragh approaching with two baskets in each hand. She wore a gown dyed a rich blue. Though it was a simple long-sleeved garment, the colour contrasted against her dark hair, bringing out the violet-blue of her eyes.

An uneasiness slipped over him, for she appeared beautiful. Styr gave her a nod, revealing nothing of the wayward thoughts inside him.

'That gown is too fine for fishing,' he said. 'You should choose another.'

She shrugged. 'It's the only other gown I have.' A hint of sadness passed over her face as she added, 'I should have given it to my brothers to be sold.'

Without explaining herself, she led him further down the beach until he saw the small boat anchored a short distance out. The mainsail was tied up, but the vessel appeared to be intact.

'If you don't free me from the manacles, you'll have to do all the work,' he pointed out. 'I won't be able to help you.'

She sent him a sidelong glance as if she hadn't thought of that. But in the end, she shook her head. 'I'll manage.'

Styr stepped into the water and turned his back to her. 'Climb on my back, and you won't have to get wet again.'

A look of startled surprise crossed her face. 'That's kind of you.'

She ducked beneath his chained arms, wrapping her arms around his neck with her legs around his waist as he walked from the shore to the boat. Though it was awkward with his chained manacles, he was aware of how light her body was. She was too thin.

He would take her out to find more fish today, no matter how long it took. No woman should ever face starvation, and he was determined to see her enjoy a true meal this night.

Styr climbed back to the stern, taking command of the rudder while she drew up the anchor. They sat beside one another, each with an oar, as they rowed out to sea. Though he had enough slack in the chains to move his arms, it was difficult for him to row with his hands behind him. He changed his position on the bench to face backwards, half-crouching as he pulled the oars behind him. Though it was awkward, Caragh lacked the energy and knowledge to manage it alone.

Silence descended between them, and as the land grew more distant, Styr ordered her to unbind the mainsail. He directed her how to tie it down, gathering the wind, and her hair streamed past her face as she obeyed.

His thoughts turned dangerous as he saw the curve of her body and her slender hips. She was so unlike Elena. While his wife had a muscular, toned body, Caragh's was delicate.

But she did possess curves where he shouldn't

be looking at all, curves that seemed impossible, from her thinness.

He drew his thoughts back to Elena, hoping she was all right. The urge to find his wife was strong, along with the frustration at being unable to pursue them. The wind blew against his face, the familiar freedom easing his dark mood. The vessel had picked up speed, and he directed Caragh on how to adjust the sail. But even after she'd obeyed him, he could see the fear in her eyes.

'You don't like the water?' he questioned.

She shook her head. 'My father drowned last winter. This boat came back to the shore, but he was gone.' She rubbed her arms as if to ward off a chill. 'My brothers believe it's cursed.'

'I've been on boats all my life,' he said. 'You've nothing to fear.'

Though Caragh nodded, he could see that she didn't believe it. She moved closer to him, sitting a few feet away while the boat continued south. 'Why did you come to Éireann?'

The reasons were too many to name. To save his marriage. To escape the conflict surrounding his brother's leadership as *jarl*. And the truest reason of them all—to journey across the sea to foreign lands, experiencing a way of life different from his own.

He met her gaze and shrugged, unwilling to say the reasons. As a distraction, he ordered her to cast the weighted net over the side of the boat, letting it drag along the bottom while the boat continued to sail.

'You don't like to share anything about yourself, do you?'

Her pointed question tightened his frustration. 'Why should I? This isn't a journey among friends. I'm helping you get food because I'll need it when I search for my wife and kinsmen.'

Caragh studied him. 'You're right. This is a trip of necessity. And I don't suppose a *Lochlannach* like yourself would ever be a friend to someone like me.'

Her posture had stiffened, and he knew he'd offended her. But he had to draw a clear line between them, to ensure that she saw him for what he was—an enemy.

'Pull up the net,' he commanded. She reached for it, but her thin arms had difficulty pulling the heavy net. She strained against it, using her body weight, but it did little good at all.

'I'm beginning to think I should have un-chained you,' she mused.

Styr balanced himself and came close. With his back to hers, he said, 'Hook your arms around mine, and then grasp the net.'

She hesitated. 'What are you planning to do? Cast me overboard?'

'If I'd wanted to kill you, I could have done it long before now,' he reminded her. 'I'm going to help you bring in the net.'

With his legs spread out for balance, he waited until she drew her arms within his. Then as she grasped the net again, he leaned back, pulling her body off her feet as she held on. Despite herself, she began to laugh. 'Well, that's one way to catch fish, I suppose.'

As he'd hoped, she was then able to pull the net back into the boat. There were only small fish within the net, but he found a few oysters as well, which Caragh saved.

Over the next hour, he instructed her on baiting the hooks and setting the fishing lines. The activity seemed to take her mind off her fear, especially when they caught a few small fish. But the longer he watched her, the more his chains irritated him. He wanted to control the sails, to command the sea and catch the fish. Standing around in chains only simmered his resentment more.

After she let down the fishing line, Caragh tucked a strand of hair over one ear, suddenly appearing nervous around him. 'Will we catch any more, do you think?'

He shrugged and stared at the horizon.

She sent him a look and then deepened her voice, as if mimicking him. 'You couldn't catch a minnow, Caragh, as weak as you are.'

In her own voice, she continued the singular conversation. 'I know that, but I am trying.'

'Not enough,' she countered, pretending to be him. 'And if you don't catch a fish, I'll toss your useless body overboard and sail away.'

He stared at her in disbelief of what she was doing. 'You're mad,' he muttered.

'And you're in a foul mood,' she shot back.

'Because you've chained me. Do you think I should be happy about this? Do you think I should be talking with you about fishing and the weather? I'm still your prisoner because you won't trust me.'

'I have no reason at all to trust a man who wants to kill my brother,' she countered.

'I might not kill him.'

'Might not? If anything at all happened to Elena, he'll take the blame for it.'

'And it would be well deserved.' He knew Caragh wanted to protect the boy, but seven and ten was old enough to understand the consequences. 'He can't hide behind your skirts for what he did.'

She glared at him. 'And now you understand why I'm reluctant to release your chains. The moment I do, you'll go after Brendan.'

'He will answer for what he did, Caragh.'

She stared out at the calm waters of the sea, dismay lined upon her face. 'Then I have no choice but to come with you. For nothing I say will change your mind.'

'I am a man of actions, not words.'

'I'm aware of that.' Imitating his voice again, she added, 'Warriors don't talk, Caragh. They kill people. And I'm quite good at killing things.'

'Good at killing things who talk too much.' But there was a glint of humour in his eyes. The line was starting to pull, and he went to stand against her. His back pressed against her own, to lend his strength.

Caragh linked her arms with his and gripped the fishing line, leaning back. 'Something is biting.'

Styr pulled hard, helping her with the fish.

The line moved violently and Caragh gasped as it cut into her palm.

'Don't let the line go,' he commanded. 'Keep a steady pressure upon it.'

He continued pulling, and Caragh began talking again, encouraging him to help her. At last, she guided the line into his hands and used a hand net to bring the fish into the boat. It was a large flounder, the length of her arm.

At the sight of the fish, she let out a cry of exultation. 'We did it! Styr, we have food!' She was laughing and crying at the same time. Her joy was so great that she threw her arms around his shoulders, embracing him hard.

He stood motionless, startled by her. The reckless gesture was something Elena never would have done, and he didn't know how to respond.

But his body knew. Though the embrace was brief, he'd felt the touch of her breasts against him, her hips pressing close. The spontaneous affection meant nothing, but it was as if she'd awakened a part of his spirit that had been shielded for a long time. It was rare that anyone had touched him in such a way, and he was so taken aback, he returned to his seat at the rudder.

'I'm sorry,' she said. 'It's just that I've never

caught a fish this large before.' Her face was flushed with excitement as she stored the fish in a corner of the boat.

Styr grunted a response, and ordered her to set out another line. She did, and while she worked, her joy spread over her face. The sunlight gleamed upon her brown hair, and when she looked back at him, her smile slid beneath his defences, diminishing his dark mood.

He turned his gaze back to the sea, a sense of guilt permeating his conscience. It had been a long time since any woman had smiled at him. Especially when he'd done so little to deserve it.

'Are you still afraid of the sea?' he asked.

Caragh shook her head, her smile remaining serene. 'I suppose it's not so terrible. The weather was bad that day, and my father never should have gone out.' Her gaze drifted towards the water, and she let out a sigh. 'I miss him terribly, and it hurts to think of losing him.'

She glanced back at him and sent him an apologetic smile. 'I shouldn't have touched you, I know. It was too impulsive of me.'

He said nothing, half-afraid she would see how it had affected him. If he weren't bound to Elena, he might have enjoyed the embrace, pulling her closer. But honour demanded that he leave this woman alone, that he lock away any attraction he might feel.

She knelt down on the boat, the blue dress damp from the sea. 'This fish means life,' she admitted. 'It may seem like nothing to you… but it's everything to me.'

'It's enough to last us the journey, if we preserve it.' He needed the reminder of his purpose, and she nodded.

'We'll find them, Styr. And perhaps, when you return, we can make peace between our people, even after all that's happened.'

'No,' he responded. He couldn't remain here, not so close to Caragh. The contrast between this woman and his wife was dangerous, for although he'd done nothing wrong, he sensed that staying near her would be unwise. 'We'll settle elsewhere.'

Her expression dimmed, and she turned her attention back to the fishing lines.

They caught five more fish before returning to shore. Caragh was exhausted, but her spirits had never been more joyous. There was food, such as she'd never seen in months. Not only enough for herself, but also enough to share with the others. The sun had drifted lower in the sky, and Styr shadowed her as she brought the largest flounder back to her home. Though she doubted if anyone would try to steal the fish, she also knew that many had become desperate—particularly Kelan. She hoped to ease their hunger by gifting them with some of the extra fish they had caught.

One by one, she visited the other families, and seeing their elation at the food lifted her mood even higher. Iona's husband Gearoid gave her a small keg of mead in thanks. Though she protested, he refused to take no as an answer, and balanced it on his shoulder as he struggled to bring it to her home. Styr was waiting by the fire, and when the old man saw him there, he blinked.

'Are ye well enough, Caragh?' Though he kept his tone calm, she didn't miss the worry in his eyes. None of them had agreed with her decision to chain Styr; they'd wanted him dead.

'I am fine. And were it not for this *Lochlannach*, we'd still be hungry this night.'

Gearoid didn't seem comfortable leaving her, but Caragh opened the door and walked out with him.

'He hasn't done anything to harm me,' she reassured him. 'I promise you, I am safe.'

It was stretching the truth, but she didn't want the others to be afraid. 'Go back to Iona and enjoy the fish,' she urged.

'If you have need of us, you have only to ask,' he said. With a squeeze of her hand, he hobbled back to his wife.

After he'd gone, Caragh returned and set to work cleaning the fish as best she could. It was work she didn't mind at all, and she carefully saved the scraps, which could be used for stews or soups. Her joy was so great, that when she set several chunks of fish over the hearth to bake, she returned to her father's work space.

She stood in the darkened space, breathing in the ashen scent of the forge. If she closed her eyes, she could almost imagine her father's presence and his hearty laugh.

Am I making a mistake, Father? she wondered. *Do I dare take the risk?* She reached for an awl and her father's hammer, wondering what to do. Styr had proven himself this day, taking her out to find fish. They'd caught enough to survive a little longer…or to travel in the search for Brendan.

In her heart, she knew the Viking had saved her life. And for that, he deserved his freedom.

Don't let him hurt Brendan, she prayed inwardly. Taking a deep breath, she lifted the hammer and awl, returning to her hut.

Styr was seated near the fire when she returned, and as soon as he spied the hammer and awl, his eyes lit up.

'I owe you my thanks,' Caragh said, 'for helping me to find fish today. And in return, I will keep my promise to remove the chains.' She watched him, meeting his eyes with her own. 'I ask only that you grant me my brother's life in return. Show him mercy.'

Styr gave her no answer, but she could only pray that he would spare Brendan. Crossing behind him, she reached for his wrists. Upon his skin, she saw dried blood and heavy bruises. Clearly he'd tried to free himself and had suffered in the process.

She hammered at the pin that bound the manacles closed until his first hand was free. Then the second.

Styr drew his hands in front of him, flexing his wrists, as he breathed with relief. 'Thank you.'

Having him unchained made her suddenly more aware of his presence. Though she didn't believe he would harm her, she couldn't stop the prickle of uneasiness. She busied herself with cooking the fish, remarking, 'I'm surprised you haven't left yet.'

'As I told you, I'm taking your father's boat in the morning,' he said. 'And you're coming with me.'

She made no refusal, for she wanted to protect Brendan. 'I won't go as your hostage.'

His gaze turned harsh, but his eyes seemed to warn her that he would use her in any manner necessary.

Caragh's hands trembled as she gave him his portion of fish. *Fool*, she cursed herself. This man wasn't safe. He might have helped her to get food, but he could not be trusted.

But she forgot about her uncertainties, the moment she tasted the delicate white fish. 'Oh heaven,' she breathed, eating the first piece so fast, she nearly choked on it. The second piece disappeared nearly as fast, and she cooked more portions, knowing that Styr was as hungry as she was. To pace herself, she poured each of them a cup of mead, and the sweet, honeyed taste was delicious. Even though she knew it was unwise to drink it quickly, she couldn't stop herself.

'Slow down,' Styr ordered. 'Or you'll make yourself sick.'

She did, concentrating on the drink instead.

It made her head feel lighter, and a pleasant airiness seemed to surround her. 'Did you get enough to eat?'

He nodded, leaning back beside the fire. 'If you salt the remaining fish, we can preserve it for a few days.'

She nodded her agreement and went to cut the remaining fish into pieces the size of her hand, salting them heavily and covering them. As she worked, a dizziness made her unsteady on her feet. The room seemed to be a faraway place, but she took another sip of mead.

When she had finished preserving the fish, she washed her hands and walked unsteadily towards the fire.

'How many cups of mead have you had?' Styr asked, frowning.

'Two. Perhaps three,' she answered.

'You shouldn't have anything else to drink,' he said, taking the cup from her. 'You've already had too much.'

A lazy smile curved over her. 'It tasted so good.' When he drank the rest of her mead, her gaze settled upon his mouth. My, but he did have a wonderful mouth. So firm and fierce. It was a shame that a man like this was already wed. It would be interesting to kiss him.

'Are you as wicked as the other *Lochlannach*?' she asked, warming her hands before the fire. 'Do you pillage the homes of people, taking their women?'

His gaze turned enigmatic. 'What do you think?'

'I think you could...if you wanted to.' Her head was still buzzing, but she found herself saying whatever words came to her mind. A startled laugh broke free. 'But this time, I took you.'

He looked irritated at her reminder, but she added, 'You weren't nearly as bad a man as I thought you were.'

'Don't.' He cut her off, reaching out to grasp her chin. Though his gesture was meant to be threatening, it didn't hurt. 'Don't try to pretend I'm harmless.' His hand moved back to grasp her nape, and a thousand tremors poured through her skin. There was power in his touch, a ruthlessness that held her spellbound.

Her traitorous mind suddenly imagined more than a kiss. She envisioned his bare skin and what it would be like to run her fingers over him. With his hand still tangled in her hair, she reached out and rested her hands against his chest.

Chapter Five

Styr didn't move. He knew Caragh wasn't thinking clearly, that her actions were dictated by the mead. But when she rested her head against his chest, a part of him wanted to hold her. He wanted to feel a woman's arms around him, to inhale the delicate scent of her skin.

His heartbeat pounded beneath her fingertips, his treacherous body responding to her nearness.

Gently, he extricated her and stepped back. 'Did you get enough to eat?'

A soft smile transformed her face. 'For the first time in months. Yes, I did.' She busied herself with clearing away their wooden dishes. But although Caragh washed and put them away, she did not clean every part of the dwelling or straighten the furnishings. Instead, she sat by the fire, smiling at him. It occurred to him that never had Elena stopped to relax after a meal. She spent her time cleaning, straightening, and scouring their home.

Caragh drew up her knees by the fire, her face golden in the light. All the while, his mind replayed the image of her hands touching him, her face pressed against his heart. The hunger for affection roared through him, and he cursed the instincts he couldn't control.

It had been so very long since Elena had reached out to him. Time and again, he'd tried to tempt her, even to hold her, only to be pushed away. Her resentment at being childless festered like an open wound, one that wouldn't heal.

Sometimes, he wished they could start over. That there was a way to be friends again, with no tension between them. The last time that had happened, they had been hardly more than adolescents. Once they'd been betrothed, Elena had grown more serious, putting all her concentration on becoming a good wife. And she'd refused to accept their failure to have children.

When she'd finished putting away the

food, Caragh asked, 'What would you like to do now?'

Her voice held energy, a restlessness that conjured up memories of bare skin, and what it was to touch a willing woman, burying himself deep inside her yielding flesh. He felt himself harden, and he cursed himself for drinking too much mead.

Odin's blood, but he needed to stay away from this woman. He had no doubt that the goddess Freya had set him upon this path, to test his willpower. But no matter how this woman tempted him, he refused to betray Elena.

'We should get some sleep before our journey on the morrow,' Styr told her, tossing another peat brick on the fire. He moved to the furthest side of the room, intending to block her from his mind.

'I can't sleep,' Caragh protested. 'It's still so early.' Without asking his consent, she went to a trunk on the far side of the room and returned with a board. 'Don't go to bed so soon,' she pleaded. 'We could play a game.'

'I don't play.' He'd gambled before with dice, but it wasn't a pastime he'd engaged in very often.

Caragh moved towards his pallet, giving

him no means of escape. She set the wooden board on the ground between them, and he recognised it as a variant of *duodecim scripta*, a game he'd known from his homeland. 'Where did you get that?'

'My brother won it off a traveller from Burgundy.'

The board consisted of two opposing rows of black triangles with game pieces made of bone. The dice were carved from antlers, and she gave him his pieces, explaining the rules which were similar to those he already knew.

'You must move the pieces to your home ground and afterwards, you can begin removing them. Whichever of us removes all the pieces first will win.'

He took a sip of his mead, watching as she set out her own pieces. A long lock of dark hair hung over one shoulder, and her cheeks were flushed from the drink. Her blue eyes held merriment and a trace of wickedness as she said, 'Are you prepared to lose, *Lochlannach*?'

His sense of competition sharpened, and he took the dice from her, his hands brushing against her warm fingers. 'And what if you lose?'

'Then I'll have to pay a forfeit. Just as you

will.' When she leaned on one arm, the neck-line of her gown slipped down one shoulder, revealing bare skin. Styr dropped the dice rapidly, wrenching his gaze away as he moved the first game piece.

'And what could you possibly offer me?' His instincts heightened, wondering what she would say.

'Your weapons and your cloak,' she offered. 'They are mine now, since I took you prisoner.'

'And what would my forfeit be, if by some miracle of the gods, *you* were to win?'

She smiled. 'More food for me and my people.'

Her honesty diffused his tension, as he realised that she was respecting the boundaries between them. Earlier, when her hands had touched his chest, she'd looked like a woman waiting to be kissed.

By the gods, if he were unwed, he'd have taken her. He'd have captured her mouth, pulling her slender body to his and exploring those curves with his hands.

Tasting and touching her until she broke forth a throaty moan.

Odin's blood, but the sexual abstinence was taking command of his senses. When he found

Elena again, he intended to coax her back into desiring him. His blood was hot, his needs making it impossible to think clearly.

With effort, he wrenched his mind back into reality. 'Where do you think your brother took Elena and the others?'

'Possibly Áth Cliath. Or Dubh Linn,' she admitted, moving her own piece. 'He's been there before with my father, when he was a boy. But even if he did, I'm not certain what he planned to do with his prisoners. He might have released them along the shore.'

Styr didn't believe it. If his kinsmen had let themselves be taken captive, it was for Elena's sake. More likely they had killed Brendan and the other Irishmen. He moved his pieces again, taking one of Caragh's. 'We'll sail at dawn to find them. Enough time has been wasted.'

He made his next move, but she captured his piece, taking it for her own. 'Your wife is unharmed,' she promised. 'I believe that.'

Releasing a slow breath, she contemplated her next move, while he rolled the dice. As they played, she kept his goblet full of mead, and he used it to drown out the voices of betrayal in his mind.

Caragh was winning the game, and her smile was triumphant as she moved the piece again. In the golden firelight, her face was haloed, her blue eyes filled with excitement. Her gown mirrored the intense colour, and it made him frown when he made his next move.

'You said you kept this gown, when you should have sold it. Was there a reason?'

'I was to be married in it.' She rolled the dice, considering where to move the next piece.

'What happened?'

She captured another piece of his and shrugged. 'I found Kelan sharing another woman's bed.' Though she spoke in a calm tone, he caught the note of anger in her voice.

'You're well rid of him,' Styr said. He couldn't imagine Caragh betrothed to a man like that. It explained Kelan's jealous behaviour, but he didn't know why she would have agreed to wed him in the first place.

'Perhaps.' She shook her head, her lips drawn in a line as she studied the board.

There was no perhaps about it. Why would Caragh lower herself to a man like that?

She removed one of her pieces from the board. 'My brothers were angry and wanted to kill Kelan for me. I refused to allow it.'

His estimation of her brothers rose a notch.

'He hasn't given up on you, has he?' He took one of his own pieces off the board.

'No. He wants my forgiveness, but I can't bring myself to forget what he did. He said he loves me, and it was a moment of weakness.'

Styr snorted. 'Loves you?' He moved another piece across the board and shook his head. 'You don't believe that, do you?'

'Once, I did.' Her face furrowed, and she slid a game piece to a darker triangle. 'Don't you love your wife?'

'Love has nothing to do with marriage. I owe her my protection, and I intend to find her.' The idea of love had been beaten out of him as a boy. His parents had trained his brother and him to be a future *jarl*, as was their duty, but there was no love involved in his upbringing.

Absently, he reached a hand up to his chin, fingering the scar where his father had struck him. He'd learned not to weep or show any sign of emotion. Emotions were for the weak-minded, and they never served a man well in battle.

Styr moved another game piece, not wanting to reveal more. The truth was, he did care about Elena. He'd wanted her to be happy in their marriage, although when her barrenness was evident, she'd begun refusing him. She didn't love him, if she ever had—that was clear enough. But now, it was rare to see her smile.

Divorcing her was possible, but he didn't want to admit his own failure. And she'd agreed to come here, which meant she wasn't entirely ready to give up on their marriage. What kind of man would he be if he'd taken her from her homeland, only to leave her?

No, somehow, they would solve the problems between them.

'Elena has been a good wife to me,' he admitted. 'I respect her.'

But Caragh's expression held confusion, as if she didn't understand. 'Was your marriage arranged?'

He nodded. 'I agreed with my father, that the match was a strong one. Her family approved of it, as well.' It was only Elena who had seemed intimidated by the marriage. She'd hardly spoken to him after their betrothal.

Now, he wondered if she had objected to it. No one had said anything to him in the past…but had they forced her to wed him? He frowned at the thought.

Caragh removed another piece, leaving

only two remaining. 'It hurt, when Kelan turned to another,' she continued. 'I caught him embracing her and—' she closed her eyes '—touching her.'

'It's good that you didn't wed him.'

'I can't help but think that I should have done something differently.' She gave him a rueful smile. 'I might have a husband and children now, if I had. Maybe if I hadn't talked so much, or maybe if I tried to be more careful with the way I looked.'

'There's nothing wrong with you, Caragh.'

She shook her head, not listening. 'Then why am I still alone?' Heartbreak resonated in the words.

Styr rolled the dice again, taking a sip from his mead. It was clear that love *did* matter to a woman like Caragh. He was tempted to speak words of reassurance. To tell her that those men were fools not to want her. But he kept silent, not wanting her to suspect his own thoughts.

Her blue eyes watched him, as if trying to discern an answer. To avoid it, Styr took his final piece from the board.

'You win,' Caragh conceded, drawing her knees up beneath her gown. 'I suppose I'll have to return your cloak now.'

'No, the battleaxe,' he corrected. 'Put my cloak over the wall I damaged.' If they were staying, he might consider repairing it. But it wouldn't matter, once they were gone.

Caragh yawned and began to put away the pieces. Styr helped her, and when the game was put away, she turned abruptly and nearly stumbled. He caught her, to prevent a fall, but her hands rested upon his forearms a moment too long.

'Your wife is a fortunate woman,' she murmured, her gaze upon his. Her violet eyes were studying him in a wistful way that was far too dangerous. The warmth of her hands upon him was more welcome than it should have been. Styr felt the touch sinking into him, like a balm. He shut down the thought immediately.

'Caragh, don't. You've had too much to drink.'

She nodded, pursing her lips. 'I have, yes. But, for a moment…you looked as lonely as I feel.' She closed her eyes a moment, as if gathering courage. 'And I wondered if everything was all right between you and your wife. You looked sad, for a moment.'

Styr put her hands aside and walked away. 'What's between Elena and myself is no concern of yours.' He didn't care how hard his words sounded. The reason for their estrangement had everything to do with her inability to conceive a child, nothing more. Once she became pregnant, all would be well again. He believed that.

He didn't like the direction of his thoughts. The more time he spent around Caragh, the more he found himself wanting to ensure that she was protected, that she had enough to eat. If his thoughts towards her were of a sisterly nature, it wouldn't bother him so much. But they weren't. He admitted to himself that he was attracted to her, much as he hated himself for it.

'I'm sorry,' she said quietly. 'You're right. It has nothing to do with me.' With that, she retreated to her pallet and pulled a coverlet over her body.

Styr stoked up the fire, watching the sparks float into the air. The mead had discoloured his judgement, and he didn't like the direction of his thoughts.

He *was* lonely.

And he would be a liar if he didn't admit he'd considered ending his marriage. For all he knew, the fault could be his, and perhaps he had been the one cursed with the inability to have children. What right did he have to bind Elena into a marriage where she would never have a child, when he knew how desperately she wanted one?

The thoughts plagued him as he returned to his own bed, wondering what would happen when he found her once more.

The sound of the door opening awoke him from sleep. Styr stared into the shadows, the faint glow of the peat fire offering the only light.

The intruder didn't speak, but crept towards the food Caragh had preserved in baskets. Styr had a strong suspicion of who the thief was. He watched the man as he took the basket, sneaking outside again.

Without a warning to Caragh, Styr reached for the battleaxe that she'd returned to him last night. Following the intruder, he caught up to the man and saw that it was Kelan, as he'd suspected.

'Drop the basket,' he commanded.

Kelan spun, and the flash of his blade gleamed against the morning fog. He dropped the basket, advancing upon him.

'Are you that dishonourable, that you would steal food from a starving woman?'

Styr demanded. 'When she shared what she had with you?'

'She shared with you as well,' the man accused. 'And you're nothing but a murderer. That makes her a traitor to us.' He sliced his knife through the clouded air, circling him.

Styr dodged the blow, swinging with his own weapon. He heard the sound of a door striking against the frame, Caragh calling out to him.

'Please don't fight,' she begged, as Kelan moved in with his blade.

'He's a thief, Caragh,' Styr countered. 'I should have killed him when I had the chance.'

She darted forwards and seized the basket. Styr blocked another blow with the axe and struck out at the man, his fist connecting with Kelan's jaw. In his enemy's eyes, he saw desperation and the mark of a coward.

Caragh came closer again, pleading, 'Stop this. I don't want either of you to be hurt.'

'I suppose you're sharing his bed, aren't you, Caragh? Whoring yourself to the enemy.'

She stumbled back, her face flushed. 'I've done no such thing. He was my prisoner, until last night.'

'I suppose he was glad to be chained up, for your use,' Kelan taunted. When she covered her mouth with her hands, appalled, he back-handed her, sending her to the ground. Reaching for the basket of fish, he started to flee, but Styr dived upon him. He ignored the knife and rolled with his enemy on the ground, determined to protect her.

Fury raged through Styr. Kelan was a dishonourable thief, one who ought to be punished for his deeds.

He raised his battleaxe, prepared to slice the man's throat, when suddenly, strong arms dragged him backwards. Two men, with strength to equal his own, hauled him away from Kelan. Though Styr tried to break free, they held him back.

'Kelan was trying to steal food from me,' Caragh explained to the men. She stood before them, and from their physical resemblance, Styr guessed who they were.

'Take your belongings and leave the ringfort,' the taller man commanded Kelan. 'If you set foot upon Gall Tír again, your life will be the forfeit.'

The man's face was murderous as he stood. But he moved towards his own home within the ringfort. Caragh's shoulders lowered with relief when he'd gone.

'Let the *Lochlannach* go, Ronan,' she ordered, reaching past Styr to hug the taller man. 'Terence, you, too. He was only defending me.'

Her brothers, he guessed. And from the dark look in their eyes, they were wondering whether or not to kill him. Behind the men, he spied two horses burdened with large bundles that likely contained food and supplies.

Caragh came to stand beside him. 'This is Styr Hardrata.' Though her words were steady, Styr caught the warning flash in her eyes. He couldn't quite tell what she wanted, but held his tongue.

'And why would my sister be harbouring a *Lochlannach*?' Ronan demanded. 'Were you attacked?'

Styr gave no answer, but nodded to Caragh, letting her give what explanation she would.

'Brendan attacked them when they arrived a few days ago,' she explained. 'He and his friends were planning to steal their supplies.'

Styr eyed the two brothers, and the taller man stared back, his face set in a grim line. 'Where is he now?'

Caragh shook her head. 'I don't know. We were going to search for him today, in Father's boat.'

Ronan expelled a curse, and then his gaze

tightened upon his sister. 'We?' From the dark look in his eyes, Styr knew what the man was thinking.

'Yes.' Caragh lifted her chin as if to defy her brother. 'At first, Styr was my prisoner,' she confessed. 'But...now, he is...' She faltered as if searching for a reason.

Desperate, she caught his gaze and abruptly moved her arm around his waist. She managed a smile for her brothers, as if her action were explanation enough.

The touch of her arm around him sent up a flare of warning. Styr didn't know what her intentions were, but the unexpected touch was far too familiar. She was trying to make her brothers believe that there was more than friendship between them, and the gesture bothered him.

Worse, he was acutely aware of the soft heat from her skin, the scent of her hair. He tensed, as if that could stop him from feeling anything at all. Frustration coiled inside him, but he didn't push her away. Not until he understood what she was trying to do.

'But now?' Terence repeated, eyeing his sister with distrust. The man rested his hand upon the sword hanging from his scabbard. Though he kept his tone calm, his grey eyes held a warning. 'Give me a reason why I should spare the life of a *Lochlannach.*'

Caragh took a deep breath, choosing her words carefully. She didn't look at Styr, but neither did she release him. 'Now, he has come to mean far more to me.' She tightened her grip around Styr's waist, as if pleading with him not to speak. 'Don't harm him, Terence. You saw for yourself, how he defended me.' Her hand moved up to rest upon Styr's heart, her fingers grazing the skin beneath his throat.

That was all it took for his body to respond to her. His heartbeat quickened, and he loathed himself for the involuntary reaction. Gently, he removed her hands and remarked, 'I don't need your protection, Caragh.'

There was a glint of approval in Ronan's eyes. Styr suspected he might be the leader of the tribe, from the way he stood back, assessing both of them. He was taller than his brother, with dark hair like his sister. His beard was sheared close to his skin, and there was a leanness to him, as if he, too, had suffered from the famine. Even so, from the protective nature of the man, Ronan wouldn't take kindly to anyone speaking against Caragh.

'Why did you come here?' Terence demanded. The shorter man was thin, like his brother, but still heavily muscled. There was a hint of darkness to his tone, as if he were trying to provoke a fight.

'We came to trade, and to settle here before your brother attacked us.'

Terence smirked. 'Then you were defeated by adolescent boys. I'd have liked to see that.'

Styr's hand shot out and gripped the man's throat. He squeezed just hard enough to make his point. 'My men hadn't slept in days, after the storms at sea. They were not at their full strength.'

'Let him go, *Lochlannach*,' Ronan ordered. The point of his blade rested at Styr's throat. 'We have more questions that need answering.'

Styr loosened his grip, though he stared hard into Terence's eyes with a silent threat of his own. When he released the man, Terence stepped back, rubbing the skin of his throat.

'You said you were going to search for Brendan,' Ronan interrupted. 'Where do you think he sailed?'

'Caragh thinks he may have gone to Áth Cliath.' He made no mention of Elena's capture, for he was still uncertain of Caragh's intent. He doubted if her brothers believed her suggestion that they were more than friends, because the men were staring at him with distrust. Yet, despite the fact that he'd nearly strangled Terence, they viewed him with a wary respect. Like him, they were warriors. And they now knew that he could defend himself.

'Is this true?' Ronan asked of his sister. 'How long has Brendan been gone?'

'It's true,' she admitted. 'He's been gone a few days now. We were going to begin our search today.'

'And who else was going to accompany you?' Terence asked. 'You weren't planning to go off with this *Lochlannach* on your own, were you?'

A flash of anger darkened Caragh's face. 'And what choice did I have? You and Ronan left me here alone. I didn't know when—or even if—you were coming back.'

'Brendan was supposed to defend you,' Terence countered.

'And a fine job he did,' she shot back. 'He and his friends stole a ship and disappeared.'

Ronan came forwards, his expression sombre. 'We never intended to be gone longer than a sennight. I'm sorry if Brendan failed in his duty to you.' His gaze shifted to Styr. 'How many were killed in the attack?'

'Two of yours,' Styr said. He crossed his arms and warned, 'If your brother was foolish enough to take only a few men with him, it wouldn't surprise me if my men feigned capture and took back the ship. There were more of my men than yours.'

Caragh paled. 'Do you think Brendan is still alive?' There was a stricken note in her voice, as if she hadn't wanted to believe otherwise. Styr gave no answer. If he'd been among his men, he wouldn't have hesitated to lash back at those who had dared to threaten Elena. It was possible that his men had already killed her brother.

'We'll know when we find my ship,' was all he could say.

'We will accompany you,' Ronan said. He took a step forwards, resting his hand back on his dagger. 'We've brought back more grain and other supplies that will serve us well for the journey. I've also arranged for more sheep and cattle to arrive later.' He sent a pointed look towards his sister. 'Caragh, you will remain here.'

'No, I won't.' She moved between them, her face flushed. 'The last time you left, I nearly starved to death. If it weren't for Styr, I'd have run out of food.' She continued talking, jabbing her finger at her older brother. 'I'm weary of staying behind, and I won't do it. I trust him, more than I do either of you, to find food. He helped me find crab, and fish, and—'

'I thought you took him captive?' Terence interrupted.

'I did. It took almost an hour to get him chained up. Seon helped me, but they killed—' Her words broke off, and she took a deep breath to hold back the emotion.

Terence sobered at the mention of the old man, and Caragh composed herself. 'Enough of this. What matters now is finding Brendan.'

'There's also the problem of you spending several nights alone with this man,' Ronan pointed out.

Caragh's face turned scarlet, and Styr stiffened, waiting for her to confess that he was married and nothing had happened between them. Instead, she reached up to touch his face. 'Don't harm him, Ronan. He's a good man. One who has defended me, given me food, and one who…I have come to care for.'

Styr froze in place as Caragh came up before him, standing on tiptoe. Before he could protest, she pulled his face down to hers, kissing him lightly. What was she doing? He couldn't—

Every thought deserted him when she deepened the kiss, daring more. He understood that this was a false kiss, one meant to reassure her brothers that he wasn't going to harm her. It was a ruse, and that was all.

The softness of her lips upon his were innocent, unknowing of the ways between a man and a woman. It startled him, and instinct warned him to break it off. But the gentle kiss reached inside his stony heart and breathed life into him.

He couldn't remember the last time a kiss had affected him in this way. His body and mind were at war, his honour caught up in the softness of a woman's mouth.

Caragh was trying to deceive her brothers. He understood that this kiss was only her effort to spare his life, though he didn't need her protection.

She continued kissing him, but a dark rage blistered inside him, that she would try to use him in this way. Did she honestly believe that he would betray Elena for a woman he hardly knew?

She wanted him to kiss her back, to continue the deception. But if he kissed her back, he intended it to be on *his* terms—not hers.

Caragh wasn't about to let her brothers slaughter the *Lochlannach*. The kiss was a reckless act, one meant to fool them into believing she and Styr had come to love each other.

But Styr was standing there in shock, not at all returning the kiss. Her brothers were going to see right through it, to know that she was making this up. His life blood would be upon her hands, and he wouldn't be able to save Elena.

This means nothing, she willed to him silently. *Kiss me back and help me deceive them.*

She opened her mouth, wondering if he would ever play along with this. Without warning, his hands seized her face, his mouth conquering hers. Heat poured through her, his tongue sliding within her mouth. She couldn't breathe from the intensity of the desire that poured through her.

It was dark and punishing, a man who refused to be bent to a woman's will. And God help her, she had no choice but to surrender. His lips were hard, his tongue invading her mouth with a forbidden power that weakened her knees.

At this moment, she forgot about her brothers standing there. She forgot about honour and promises, completely captivated by the forbidden kiss.

She clung to Styr, knowing her legs would never support her. The kiss was carnal, as if they had already been illicit lovers. And when he broke free, his eyes held fury.

Her lips were swollen, and Caragh no longer knew what to say. Silently, she apologised, but his eyes were upon her brothers.

'We're leaving now,' he said. 'If you want to bring your supplies and join us in searching for your younger brother, I'll prepare the boat.'

Caragh's heart was pounding, her breathing unsteady as he strode off towards the shore. He was livid with her for daring to kiss him, for forcing him into this position.

She shouldn't have done it. She'd only meant to fool her brothers, to give them a reason to leave Styr alone. Instead, she'd forced the *Lochlannach* into a betrayal he hadn't wanted. Likely he despised her, and she desperately wanted to beg his forgiveness.

'Come with us, if you like,' she said to her brothers, trailing after Styr. She stopped only once to pick up the basket of preserved fish and a container of water, hurrying down to the shoreline.

'She's lying,' Terence predicted. 'If our sister is in love with that *Lochlannach*, then I've grown a pair of wings.'

Ronan studied Caragh and the way she'd run after the Viking. She was wanting to protect the man, but for what reason, he couldn't fathom. It had been almost a year since he'd seen his sister show any interest in a man. Kelan had broken her heart, and she'd shunned any of the others who might have taken the man's place.

Until now. Whether or not there was anything between them, there was no doubt the kiss had affected Caragh.

'I want to watch them together,' Ronan mused. 'She should marry. It's been too long since Kelan.'

'But a *Lochlannach*?' Terence eyed the man warily. 'They're not to be trusted. And did you forget, he nearly killed me just now?'

'If that were his intent, you'd be dead,' he countered. 'You shouldn't have taunted him.' Ronan would have done the same, had he been in the Viking's place. 'When Kelan tried to steal, he fought on her behalf. I saw him go after the man.'

'And you want our *sister* with a man who can't control his temper?'

'He was controlling it,' Ronan said. 'Just as he did when he threatened you.' At his brother's grimace, he continued, 'I want her with a man who can defend her. I don't doubt this *Lochlannach* would protect her from every harm.' He handed the horses to Terence. 'Bring our supplies and leave the animals with Iona. We'll accompany our sister to Áth Cliath, as she suggested.'

His gaze passed over Caragh and Styr, who were standing near the boat. His sister had been unhappy for too long. Although he didn't believe there was anything between them, his sister had defended the man. She did care about his welfare, whatever the reason.

Terence walked at his side along the shore. 'You don't think he'll harm her?'

Ronan shook his head. 'I won't pass judgement over him until I've watched them together. But if he isn't to be trusted, we'll leave him behind in Áth Cliath.'

His brother shot him a sidelong glance. 'You're matchmaking, aren't you?'

Ronan stopped walking, holding his brother

back while he studied Caragh and the *Loch-lannach*. 'Only if he's worthy of her.'

'If he's not, there might be an "accident",' Terence suggested.

Ronan absently rubbed his beard, staring at the two of them. Whether or not his sister realised it, the Viking never took his eyes off her. The man most definitely had feelings towards Caragh, but Ronan couldn't guess whether it was lust or something more.

'We'll know within a day,' he predicted. 'Give them a moment before we join them.'

As he observed the pair of them, he saw the way his sister was looking at Styr. It had been a year since he'd held her while she'd wept upon the evening of her wedding. The day Kelan had ruined by abandoning her, for love of another. He'd watched his sister retreat into herself, spending all of her time with the elderly folk of their tribe. She'd thrown herself into service, as if trying to escape her own life.

And when their parents had died, she'd not allowed herself to grieve, but instead had taken responsibility for Brendan.

Caragh needed a life of her own and a man to give her a home and children. If this *Loch-*

lannach could bring back the sister he loved, so be it.

But if he dared to break her heart, Ronan wouldn't hesitate to tear the man apart.

Chapter Six

'Don't ever try something like that again,' Styr warned. His fury was teetering on the edge, barely contained. While it may have been only a kiss, one meant to fool her brothers, the dishonourable act enraged him. How did she dare to throw herself at him, pretending that they were lovers?

Caragh blanched at his tone, apologising quietly. 'I know my brothers. They drew wrong conclusions from Kelan's words. I was afraid they would harm you.'

'I can defend myself,' he reminded her. Using his full height, he glared down at her. 'I have no need to justify my actions to them. *You* took me prisoner. I was only trying to return to my wife.'

He saw her flinch at the mention of Elena. Good. She needed to remember that he wasn't a man she could use upon a whim.

You didn't have to kiss her back, his conscience reminded him. *You could have pushed her away.*

And that was the splinter that dug into his guilt, blistering his rage. If he hadn't dared to continue the deception, he would never have known what it was to be kissed by Caragh. He had reacted on impulse, only to be stunned by the physical response he'd never anticipated. But there was no one to blame, save himself.

Right now, he wanted to plunge his head into icy seawater, to clear away the confused thoughts. He wasn't a man to be unfaithful. In all his five years of marriage to Elena, never once had he looked at another woman. Honesty and loyalty meant everything to him. He would never forsake his wife, no matter how one woman's kiss had affected him.

'I'm sorry,' she murmured, 'but my brothers aren't forgiving. They won't harm you if they believe that we mean something to one another. That you are a man of honour.'

'I *am* a man of honour,' he shot back. Though it didn't feel like it now. He turned his back on her and waded into the frigid sea, welcoming the wind that tore through his chainmail corselet, soaking his hose against his skin.

But Caragh's kiss haunted him, in the way her soft lips had melted into his, like a taste of sweet honey. She'd lost herself, clinging to him when he'd kissed her back.

While Elena had accepted his embraces, she'd always seemed uncertain—almost unwilling to kiss him. He'd tried to be gentle, but he'd never been able to fully enjoy himself, for fear of hurting her.

Whereas this woman had eagerly opened to him, her tongue touching his. Her breasts had pressed against him as she'd wrapped her arms around his neck, yielding sweetly.

No doubt it was the celibacy coming back to haunt him. He'd left Elena alone for a time, while they'd prepared for the journey. She'd suffered such terrible seasickness, he hadn't bothered her then, either. Over and over, he replayed the image of his wife's face and the sadness in her eyes. And he cursed himself for daring to kiss another.

Styr busied himself with preparing the boat, needing the activity to push away the errant thoughts. No longer would he think of how good it had felt to be in Caragh's arms. He would maintain his distance from her, and lock away the dark cravings she'd evoked.

When she climbed aboard the ship, her skirts were sodden. He should have offered to carry her, but he had been unable to touch her. His willpower was shredded to a weak thread.

She set the basket on the far end, choosing a seat on the opposite side of the boat. When her brothers joined them, he learned that Terence was accustomed to sailing. The man took the side rudder to steer them east while Styr took his place with the oars. He pulled hard, letting the mindless exertion consume him.

Ronan took the place behind him, rowing in rhythm. 'I don't believe that either of you are in love,' he said, beneath his breath.

'You'd be right,' Styr admitted, keeping his voice low. It was a relief to admit the truth to the man. Glancing behind him, he added, 'Caragh took me by surprise with that kiss.'

'Our sister has a soft heart, and she thought we were going to kill you for sharing her hut.' Ronan pulled hard against the oars. 'It's still a consideration.'

Styr said nothing, knowing there was no good reply to that.

'It's a simple matter, *Lochlannach*,' Ronan continued. 'Hurt our sister, and we hurt you.'

'I would expect nothing less.' He understood a man like Ronan, determined to protect his sister. 'But Caragh and I are hardly more than strangers to each other.'

'Yet, she's coerced you into helping her search for our wooden-headed brother Brendan, isn't that right?'

'My intent is to find my kinsmen, who were last seen with your brother,' Styr told the man. 'I hope, for his sake, that they are unharmed.' Once they reached Áth Cliath, he would disassociate from Caragh and her brothers, searching for Elena. They could find Brendan, and that would be the end of it.

'Brendan's lacking in brains,' Ronan said. 'If you have brothers of your own, you'll understand that.'

'I had four sisters. One older brother.'

He stopped rowing and stared back at Styr. Crossing himself, he added in a loud voice, 'My God, it's a wonder you haven't gone mad. Four sisters?' He glanced at Caragh with a shudder.

'Now what is the matter with sisters?' Caragh demanded.

'It would take years to name it all,' Ronan

shot back. 'They cry for no reason. If you make a mistake, they'll hold a grudge for the rest of your life.'

'They talk too much and tell your mother everything you do,' Terence joined in. 'If you tie up the cat's tail or put frogs in the garden.'

Caragh glared at him, and Terence continued. 'But we do love you, Sister.' He winked at her.

'Four,' Ronan repeated. 'I'd have thrown myself into the sea, for certain.'

Styr couldn't help but enjoy the man's humour. There was an easiness about these men, a camaraderie like the friendship he had with Ragnar. 'I often took the boat out to sea, on my own, to get away from them. It's why I'm a fisherman.'

'You don't act like one,' Terence countered. 'I'd have taken you for a tribe leader, with your height and strength.'

Styr shrugged, not truly answering the question. He'd begun his trade as a fisherman, but after his father died, many had wanted him to usurp his older brother's place as *jarl*. To avoid conflict, he'd chosen to leave Hordafylke and those who preferred his leadership had come along.

'Go back and sit with our sister,' Ronan

suggested. 'Terence can take a turn to row until we catch the wind.'

Styr preferred to remain where he was, but he saw Caragh huddled at the stern of the boat. She clutched her woollen *brat* over her hair, and her teeth chattered. When he moved to sit slightly in front of her, she kept her voice low. 'I hope you find Elena.'

'I won't stop until I do.' His purpose was clear, and he added, 'If you see her—'

'I'll say nothing.' She stiffened, trembling. In a whisper, she added, 'What I did was a mistake. It will never happen again.'

The journey to Áth Cliath shouldn't have taken longer than a day, but the winds had picked up intensity, the darker clouds sweeping across the sky. Caragh sat upon the floor of the boat, her hands clenched together. Though her gown had dried, she couldn't stop from trembling. It wasn't merely from the cold— her fears had multiplied as she thought of her father's drowning.

A storm brewed, and she closed her eyes, not wanting to imagine a death at sea. The boat rocked against the waves, and she clung to the bench just in front of the stern, praying for calmer waters. Behind her, Terence held fast to the rudder.

'Should we move in closer to land?' he was shouting above the wind.

Styr made a reply, but she couldn't hear him over the roar. The rain began to pound upon them, a piercing wet shower that made her grimace.

The swells broke over the top of the boat, spraying her with the water. Though it was still daylight, dark mists shadowed their surroundings, making it difficult to see the land. She heard her brothers calling out to Styr as they pulled hard on the sail. Risking a glance at him, she saw his muscles straining, his feet balanced across the boat.

She distracted herself from the fear by remembering those strong arms around her, his hands at her waist. And the shocking heat of his kiss…

Self-hatred and a flushed guilt spread through her. He hadn't wanted to kiss her, and she'd forced it upon him. She'd never meant any harm by it, thinking it would only be a way of redirecting her brothers' suspicions.

Instead, it had become something she'd never expected. Perhaps it was because it was forbidden to kiss a man already claimed by someone else. She'd mistakenly thought it would mean nothing at all to him.

Against his lips, she'd tasted his anger. The kiss had lashed back against her, almost brutal as he'd ravaged her mouth. But somehow, in the midst of it, she'd sensed a change in him. Her surrender had tamed the rising beast inside him, and though her heart had never ceased its pounding, she'd evoked a response from him.

She didn't know what to think of that. Only that there was no sense in dwelling upon it. Soon enough, he would be gone from here, reunited with his wife.

And wasn't that just her ill fortune? Every man that she'd come to care for had been in love with someone else.

Don't think of him any more. He belongs to her and always will.

She wished that one day a man would love her for herself. And that he would never turn from her to choose another. Daring a glance at Styr, she closed off any feelings, knowing they could never be.

Another spray of water hit the boat, and now she was sitting in an icy pool. Gingerly, Caragh got to her knees, planning to sit on one of the benches. But without warning, a hard wave struck the vessel, and she lost her balance.

The world tipped on its rim, sending her flying backwards. She cried out and tried to grasp the edge of the boat, but she struck the waves, her mouth filling up with seawater. Darkness closed over her, the icy current submerging her beneath the depths.

Panic roiled inside her, and Caragh flailed her arms, struggling to break through the surface. Her gown was weighing her down, and she fought to reach the boat.

There was an enormous splash, and she saw Styr swimming towards her. He'd stripped off the chainmail corselet, his chest bare as he cut through the water. When he reached her, he seized hold of her waist. 'Can you swim?' he murmured against her ear.

'I'm t-trying.' Her limbs felt leaden from the cold, and he kept one arm around her, helping her back to the boat. When she gripped the side, he hoisted her up, and her brothers pulled her in. A moment later, he joined her.

Her teeth chattered and she shivered hard, in shock over what had just happened. The boat continued to toss in the wind, but this time, Styr held her steady.

Dimly, she heard something about moving

inland, towards the shore, but her body was so cold, she hardly cared. Styr wrapped a blanket around her, but she couldn't stop shaking.

'Will you…hold me for a moment?' she pleaded. It wasn't merely the cold. It was the terror of slipping beneath the waves, being at the mercy of the sea. She could still taste the salt water, and the frigid water had nearly frozen the blood inside her veins.

Strong arms came around her, and she rested her face against Styr's bare chest. Though he, too, was cold, the longer he held her, the warmer his skin became. She was acutely conscious of sitting in his lap, but he didn't let go of her. He'd taken the blanket for himself, wrapping it around both of them.

'Thank you for saving me,' she said, her voice hoarse. The exhaustion of the day was dragging her down, her body so tired, she could hardly keep her eyes open.

Styr made no reply, but she hadn't expected him to. As she closed her eyes, she couldn't help but wonder why it had been him to jump in after her, instead of her brothers.

He hadn't hesitated, stripping off his armour before plunging into the sea. And now, as her body was starting to warm, he wasn't pushing her aside as she'd expected him to.

Don't, she warned herself. *It's nothing.*

But his heartbeat pulsed rapidly against her cheek. And his hand came up to touch her wet hair, smoothing it behind her ear. Like a caress.

Though she hated the thought of losing his warm embrace, she said, 'I suppose you should help my brothers with the boat.'

It was an offer to release him, a way of letting him go. She'd made him uncomfortable before, when she'd kissed him, and this was just as bad.

'Your brothers are fine.' His voice was brusque, as if he had no intention of letting go of her. He wrapped the blanket around her, and the gesture evoked her own guilt. She'd begged him to hold her, and he'd obeyed.

Shame slid over her when she raised her head to look at Terence and Ronan. They were staring at her with an unreadable expression. They didn't know about Styr's marriage...and she didn't want them to.

The winds had died down, and though the rain continued, she no longer felt as if the waves were going to drag her under again. Gently, she pulled away from Styr, trying to calm the pulsing of her heart.

'Are you all right now?' Terence called out to her.

She nodded. 'I'm just cold.'

'We're bringing the boat in, and we'll build you a fire to get warm,' Ronan informed her. He sent a grateful look towards Styr. 'Thank you for saving our sister.'

The *Lochlannach* only tightened his hold around her and said to Caragh, 'You'll be all right in the morning.'

'But the journey to Áth Cliath—'

'—can wait a few more hours,' he said. 'You need to get warm, after what happened to you.'

She didn't argue, but adjusted the blanket around him. Styr let her remain there a moment longer before he gave it back and went to retrieve his tunic. Her brothers spoke a few words to him before he returned to her. She couldn't hear what they'd said, and the quiet expression on Styr's face revealed nothing at all.

'We'll be at the shore in less than an hour,' he said.

'What did my brothers say to you?' she asked.

But he would give no answer.

It was near midnight, Styr guessed, by the time they had anchored the boat and made camp upon the shoreline. Ronan and Terence built a fire for Caragh, and though it helped, she was still soaking wet. After her eyes kept closing, Styr helped them set up a tent for her. She moved inside and he brought her another dry blanket.

'You should be warm soon enough,' he told her.

'Styr,' she whispered, touching his shoulder. Though she'd only meant to stop him from leaving the tent, the slight gesture made him grasp her hand.

'Sleep,' he bade her.

'I'm sorry,' she murmured.

'It wasn't your fault you were swept overboard,' he argued. She was so light from the hunger she'd experienced, it had been all too easy for her to fall back.

'That's not what I meant,' she said quietly. 'I shouldn't have kissed you. You've been nothing but honourable towards me, and I had no right.'

He stared at her, saying nothing at all. No, she hadn't. And though he understood that she was trying to ease things between them, her brothers had complicated matters even more.

They'd thanked him for saving her life...

and then they'd asked him if he would consider marriage to Caragh.

'*You saved her life,*' Ronan had said. '*And she needs a strong protector.*'

The instinct to blurt out no had risen to his lips, to confess everything about his wife. But he understood that they were speaking of alliances, of blending the Norse and Irish together. They respected his sailing and his fishing, but more, the two men had expressed their concern for Caragh being alone.

'*The only reason you're coming with us,* Lochlannach*, is for her sake,*' Terence had said. '*I'd rather leave you behind.*'

For that reason, he'd kept silent about Elena. He needed this ship to travel east, retracing the path of Brendan, and he didn't for a moment believe that Caragh's brothers would allow it if they knew the truth. He would tell whatever lies were necessary to reach his wife.

In the end, he'd avoided answering Ronan and Terence, saying that he had to speak with Caragh first.

She was eyeing him now, her face flushed with guilt. 'I—I've done nothing but treat you badly since you set foot on Éireann. And you've saved my life twice.' Her hand tightened on his. 'First, by helping me find food, and now, you've kept me from drowning.' She took a deep breath, gathering up her courage. Dark blue eyes held a fragile trust, and she admitted, 'If you weren't already wedded—'

'Don't.' He cut her off, his tone harsh as he released her hand. 'Don't say it.' He wouldn't allow her to speak of thoughts that had no place between them.

Caragh drew up her knees beneath the sodden gown, lowering her forehead.

'I was going to say that I wish we could be friends.'

Styr remained silent, shielding his thoughts from her. Becoming friends with a woman like Caragh was dangerous.

'You look as if such a thing would be impossible,' she offered.

'It is,' he said. 'Men and women cannot be friends.'

She looked taken aback, as if he'd struck her, but she ventured, 'Why?'

Was she truly that naïve? He stared hard at her, willing her to understand the unspoken truth.

Caragh pulled the blanket around her shoulders, trembling as she waited for an answer. Her wet hair was darker, almost black against her pale skin. Her face was damp, her mouth drawing his attention.

'I think you know exactly why we can never be friends,' he said, not caring how harsh he sounded. Without another word, he left the tent, letting it fall closed behind him.

Styr's harsh anger kept coming back, resonating within Caragh's mind. Ever since she'd kissed him, he'd taken her actions the wrong way—as if she were threatening him.

She wasn't trying to steal him away from his wife. Nothing could be further from the truth. Aye, he was handsome enough, but he was far too callous for her. Too demanding.

The longer she was around him, the more he made her heartbeat quicken, setting her nerves on edge. The memory of his raw kiss came rushing back, and her skin prickled with unease. No, she understood now, what he meant. They could never be friends, for she could feel his resentment. It bruised her spirits, for she'd never meant to imply that she wanted him.

The more she thought of it, the angrier she grew.

She peeled away the wet gown, even removing the damp shift until she was naked inside the tent. Carefully, she spread them out, hoping they would dry in the next few hours. Then she rolled up within the blanket, covering her body from neck to ankle.

With each minute that passed, she found it more difficult to sleep. She had never been in a position like this, as if she were a fallen woman trying to lure a man. Styr had saved her life, that was all. And she'd kissed him in an effort to save his. If she'd given the word, her brothers could have slaughtered him where he stood. Didn't he realise that?

'Caragh,' came a male voice. It was Styr.

She bit her lip and tightened her hold around the blanket. 'What is it?'

'Your brothers sent you food.' Without waiting for her to say a word, he entered the tent and set a folded cloth before her. For a moment, his expression tensed when he saw her clothing spread out.

'Why didn't they bring it, instead of you?' she asked, keeping her voice low. He shrugged, but she already knew the answer. It was because her meddling brothers were starting to believe her false story.

Before he could leave, she released the storm of bitterness within her. 'No, don't go. Not until I've had my say.'

He raised an eyebrow at that, but she gripped the coverlet and raised her chin.

'Whether or not we are ever friends, let me be clear that I didn't kiss you because I wanted you. You saved my life, and I tried to save yours with my deception. I didn't want my brothers to kill you. That's all.'

'They couldn't have killed me,' he responded.

'You're wrong. And though I'm glad you saved me from drowning, I'm angry that you think I have no honour at all.' Her heartbeat quickened, and she continued talking, giving him all the reasons why she didn't want him.

By the time she reached the fifth reason, she realised he wasn't listening to her at all. Instead, his eyes were fixed upon the back of the tent, as if he found it fascinating.

He could have left, she supposed. Instead, he'd remained without speaking a single word.

'Well? Have you nothing to say?' she prompted.

'I have never met a woman who talks as much as you do,' he said at last. His impassive expression irritated her even more.

'Don't tease me.' She knew she talked a great deal, but it wasn't her intent. It was simply the desire to fill the empty space, to blot out the discomfort he made her feel.

Styr pushed the food towards her. 'Eat the fish. There's bread, as well, that your brothers brought.'

'Bread?' She couldn't control the delight at the thought of tasting bread again. She didn't care if it was green with mould or the texture of rocks.

When she tasted it, she had to suppress her sigh of delight. She devoured the bread, nearly finishing the last piece, when she suddenly remembered that Styr might not have eaten, either.

'Have you had anything to eat this night?' She offered him the rest of the bread, in case he hadn't.

Styr nodded and sat across from her. He waited for her to finish, and as the uncomfortable silence stretched on, she said, 'Will you tell me about your wife?'

'Why?' His tone sounded disgruntled, as if he wanted to share nothing about Elena.

Because she thought the topic would put him at ease, truthfully. Instead, she said, 'You miss her, don't you?'

'I want her to be safe. It's different.'

Caragh frowned. 'Tell me more about her. I know she's very beautiful.'

Some of his frustration subsided, and he nodded. 'She is.' His expression relented and he admitted, 'I used to tease her about her red hair. I didn't like the colour when I was younger, and she was angry with me for saying so.'

'I can't imagine,' she responded drily.

His mouth twitched. 'She tried to cut off my hair while I was sleeping. I was nine years old at the time.'

She picked at the fish, savouring each bite. As she ate, she was careful not to reveal any of her nakedness. 'What did you do?'

'When I woke up, I caught her with a length of my hair. I tried to hit her, but my father caught me.'

'Did he thrash you for it?'

Styr nodded. 'And he cut off the rest of my hair in punishment. So that everyone would know I tried to strike a girl.'

Her amusement faded at that. 'But you forgave her, didn't you?'

He nodded. 'When I was older.'

When Styr offered nothing else about his wife, Caragh asked another question, though already she suspected the answer. 'Do you have children?'

'No.' The quiet answer held a grim ring to it, and she realised she'd touched upon a delicate subject.

'I'm sorry. I shouldn't have pried.'

'Be ready to leave at first light,' was all he said, taking away the cloth that had contained her food.

Chapter Seven

All night long, Styr had been haunted by the image of Caragh's bare shoulders. Though she'd kept herself covered throughout their conversation, his mood had darkened as his mind turned to other memories.

He thought of Elena and the way she often kept herself covered, even during lovemaking. She'd been shy of her body, never wanting him to see her bare skin...almost as if she were ashamed. Then, too, she'd kept her mind veiled as well, never revealing the thoughts she'd hidden within herself. He'd been married to her for five years, and it still felt as if they were strangers.

He reached towards the pouch at his belt and loosened the ties. The leather was stiff and damp, but he managed to pull out the ivory comb. As he stared at it, a tight fear rose up inside. He should have given it to Elena on board the ship. He should have spoken the words of reassurance that she'd needed to hear.

But then, he'd tried to talk to her, only to be spurned. He wasn't good with words or trying to explain himself.

Caragh was the opposite. Like a small bird, she chattered and revealed everything she was thinking. Sometimes she revealed too much.

A note of danger threaded through his mind, as he thought of her clear violet eyes and her soft mouth. The longer he was around Caragh, the more he compared her to Elena, and it wasn't right.

He told himself it was curiosity, nothing more. They weren't even friends. Thor's blood, she'd captured him and put him in chains. He owed her nothing at all. And because of her brother, he'd lost his wife. A wife he needed to find.

The will strengthened within him as he brushed aside idle thoughts of Caragh. Elena was his focus, and no matter how difficult the past few years had been, he wanted nothing to happen to her.

An insidious voice whispered the possibility that Elena was dead. The thought pierced him with fear. She was his responsibility to protect, and the days of sleeplessness had proved a weakness. It enraged him that he and his men had been brought down by a starving tribe. It never should have happened.

This morning, they had boarded the boat a second time. The sea was calmer now, and it was likely they could finish their journey up the coast without any further problems.

Styr risked a glance at Caragh and saw that her hair was still damp against her face. She wore the blue gown from before, with half of her hair braided back from her face. The rest hung down over her shoulders in dark, curling strands. The morning sun cast a glow over her face, but her expression held worry instead of reassurance. When the wind shuddered past her, he saw the way she gripped her arms, steadying herself.

'She hates the water,' Terence said, beneath his breath, as he joined Styr at the oars. 'Ever since our da died, she's gone nowhere near it.'

'She said he drowned.' He pulled hard, matching the pace of Terence.

'Aye. He went out during a storm and never came back.' The man turned to stare at him.

'She has a gentle heart, our Caragh does. I don't know why she bothered to save one like you.'

Styr made no remark, but increased his pace, forcing Terence to match him. The man did, but it didn't take long before his breathing was laboured, his wiry arms struggling to keep up.

'Going soft, are you, Irishman?' He sent a sidelong glance towards Terence.

The man narrowed his eyes. 'It would be best if you stayed in Áth Cliath, far away from our sister. I know Ronan approves of you, but I don't.'

At that, Caragh crossed from the bow of the boat, climbing towards them until she faced both. It was clear that she'd overheard Terence's remark. To her brother, she accused, 'He took care of me, when you left. I had no one else.'

'We came back,' Terence argued.

'And he stayed, when he didn't have to.' Caragh crossed her hands upon her knees and looked into Styr's eyes. There was gratitude there, along with a tension that reflected his own uncertainty. 'After I released him, he could have gone. Instead, he helped me find food.'

Her gaze held his, and she reached out to

touch his hand. Though it was only a gesture of thanks, the coolness of her fingers sent a ripple of awareness through him. He didn't know what it was about this woman, but she affected him in a way he didn't understand. He gripped her fingers in warning, abruptly releasing them.

'I would have drowned if it weren't for Styr,' she said quietly.

He said nothing, for he should have allowed her brothers to save her. But when she'd been swept overboard, he'd plunged into an icy sea, determined to save her. He'd reacted on instinct, swimming hard to bring her to safety. She'd clung to him, so grateful for his rescue that a warmth had threaded through him. His brain had snarled at him to let her go, to ignore the way it felt to have a woman in his arms, her face pressed against his heart. Forbidden thoughts had no place between them.

Styr released her hand and took the oars again, while Terence did the same. Caragh tried to hold his gaze, but Styr wouldn't look at her. Even so, he caught the look of disappointment in her eyes as she retreated to the bow of the boat.

They would reach Áth Cliath today, and he was glad of it. He planned to search the city everywhere until he found Elena. He needed to see her again, to hold her in his arms and banish all other thoughts.

If she was here.

Within the hour, he spied the city upon the horizon while they sailed into the port of Dubh Linn. At the sight of the walled longphort with the ordered rectangular dwellings, it was like returning to Hordafylke. Familiarity pulled at him, along with a tug of regret. Perhaps Ragnar was right, and they should have settled here. At least the people had blended enough with the Irish that they had made a place for themselves.

But as they drew closer, his spirits deflated. The city was vast, far larger than he'd expected. Dozens of ships dotted the shores, some anchored on land, others further out. Immediately he began searching for a glimpse of his own ship, for it would confirm the presence of Elena and his men. But there were so many of them.

Ronan moved up to row beside him, while Terence joined his sister at the bow. 'Where do you think they are now?'

Styr shook his head. 'I don't see my ship. While they might be here, there's no certainty of it. We'll have to ask.' He glanced over at Ronan. 'Have you been to this city before?'

'No. But we should split off to find them. Terence and I can go west and east, while you and Caragh take the north. We'll meet back here by nightfall.'

'It's dangerous to take her with us,' Styr protested. And yet, he knew they could not leave her alone. He'd expected Ronan or Terence to keep Caragh with them, allowing him to search for Elena on his own.

'We have no choice, and you know it.' Ronan slowed his pace as they neared the shore. 'But I trust you to guard her.'

'Why?' he demanded. 'You hardly know me.'

'You saved her from drowning. Your actions said enough.'

Styr gave no reply, but busied himself with tying down the mainsail. The last thing he wanted was to bring another woman with him on his quest to find Elena. 'She's not coming with me.'

Ronan's expression darkened. 'Have a care, *Lochlannach*. The only reason we allowed you to come along was because of our sister.'

Words of protest stumbled inside his mouth. He didn't want Caragh anywhere near him, particularly not now. But against his better judgement, he found himself raising his shoulders in an indifferent shrug.

Ronan pressed again. 'Keep her out of harm's way and guard her well. We'll find our brother and your people.'

Styr wondered how they would accomplish this when they couldn't speak his language, but didn't say so.

They reached one of the docks near Dubh Linn, and Styr paid a copper coin to one of the men for the right to keep the boat there for the next few days.

Caragh called out to him, 'Where do you want to look first?'

He crossed to the front of the boat and lowered his voice. 'It would be better if you stayed with your brothers. Tell them you'd rather search with them.'

Caragh reached to tie back her braided hair, and her face was pale. 'Why? Because you think I'm too weak?' She moved to his side and confronted him, keeping her voice just above a whisper. 'Or was there another reason?'

He didn't trust himself around her. Though he would never act upon the unbidden visions she'd conjured, being around Caragh was weakening his resolve. He'd tasted her mouth and his traitorous mind warned that her kiss had affected him in a way Elena's never had. She was too innocent to understand, and the further away she remained, the better.

'Why?' she prompted again.

In silent answer, he cupped her cheek. He stared into her violet eyes, drawing his thumb over the curve of her lips in memory of the kiss. 'Because.'

At that, she understood. Her face flushed, and she drew his hand away. 'You've no reason to be uncomfortable in my presence. I would be like a sister to you.'

He masked any response. Never in his life could he imagine a woman like Caragh in a sisterly way. 'I want nothing from you, Caragh.'

She dropped her voice to a whisper. 'Let me make amends for what my brother did. Promise me you won't kill him.'

Her warm breath sent a ripple of uneasiness through him. 'I can't make that promise.' He didn't care that Brendan was hardly more than a young man. Elena had done nothing wrong, and if she was hurt, he would avenge every harm done to her. Without mercy.

Caragh's fingers tightened upon his shoulder, her own tension evident. 'Then I will go with you, if for no other reason than to protect him.'

'Go with your brothers,' he bade her again, and climbed out of the boat, stepping on to the docks.

Caragh hung back while Styr spoke to the Norsemen nearby, presumably asking questions about his ship. Meanwhile, she shielded her eyes against the sun and looked for a sign of Styr's ship. As her gaze drifted past several Norse boats, she realised how futile it was. Most of them looked alike, and she couldn't tell one from the next.

'Do you think Brendan is here?' Terence came up beside her, his expression grim.

'I don't know.' She shuddered, and her brother removed his cloak, handing it to her. 'We'd have seen a Norse ship along the coast, if he'd stopped somewhere else, wouldn't we?'

Terence shrugged. 'I don't trust that *Lochlannach*, Caragh. I don't care what Ronan thinks—you shouldn't be alone with him. What if he tries to force himself on you?'

'He won't harm me,' she said. 'That, I can promise you.'

There was no danger at all from Styr, because of his unyielding loyalty to his wife. She was perfectly safe with him.

Yet, she couldn't say the same for Brendan. She didn't believe he would harm Elena, but his friends might have. And regardless of what had happened, she had to accompany Styr on his search, if for no reason than to protect her foolish younger brother.

'I've seen the way he watches you,' Terence continued. 'He desires you.'

'It's nothing, Terence,' she insisted. 'I'm like a sister to him.'

Her brother cast a sidelong glance. 'You're anything but that. And I don't trust him.'

'I do. He's saved my life, more than once.'

Terence caught her hand, pulling her back before she could leave. From his belt, he withdrew a small pouch. 'Take these with you.'

She felt the weight of the coins and frowned. 'Where did you get these? And what about the animals and supplies? All that from our mother's brooch?'

Terence's face turned grim. 'We hired out our swords.' From the dull tone in his voice, she understood that whatever he'd done, had been for their family. She reached up to embrace him, but though he returned it, she sensed the trouble weighing upon him.

'You succeeded, then.'

His expression remained shielded. 'I'm not proud of what I did.'

Caragh had no time to ask further questions, for Ronan and Styr approached. Already her brother was pointing out the direction he intended to search. To Styr, he directed, 'If you'll take Caragh and go deeper into the city, we'll rejoin you here at sundown.'

She didn't miss the reluctance on Styr's face. Before he could argue again, Ronan handed a bundle of supplies to Styr. 'See to it that she eats.'

Did he believe she was a small child incapable of caring for herself? She ignored his patronising tone and started walking north, along the edge of the docks.

Within moments, Styr guided her away. 'Your brothers will search here. It's not a place for a woman.' He kept one hand upon his battleaxe, and his eyes scanned the crowd, as if searching for any possible threats. His other palm moved to the small of Caragh's back.

She knew it was only a means of telling others that she was under his protection. But even so, she grew conscious of his large hand upon her spine and the firm pressure against her skin. A strange ache resonated through her, moving from his palm, over her own skin. He'd made her feel safe on the night she'd nearly drowned, warming her with his body.

She glanced over at him, and his eyes were constantly searching, his pace swift. 'Do you know anyone in the city you could ask?'

He shook his head. 'We'll start in the marketplace.'

As they continued walking further, she was overwhelmed by the crowds, her eyes drinking in the sights. 'I've never seen so many people before.'

'Have you never left Gall Tír?'

She shook her head. 'I've lived there all my life.' And although she knew every person within the ringfort, she'd heard stories of cities so large, it was impossible to know the names of all who dwelled within its walls.

Seeing Áth Cliath, she could believe it. Though this was her own country, the Irish and the Norse were mingled together. The *Lochlannach* settlements were unusual, with long, rectangular houses set out in quadrants. Even the women were dressed differently, their long yellow hair bound up in braids. They wore long aprons over their gowns, with brooches fastened at the shoulders. And they were so tall, like exotic goddesses.

Caragh was entranced by them. Her hand reached up to her own dark locks, as if imagining them in braids.

When they reached the open market, her eyes widened at the sight of the food, the livestock, and all the merchants. Voices mingled together in different languages, lauding their wares, while others bargained for the best price.

Caragh stopped before all of it, and Styr caught her hand. 'We should go.'

'Wait.' Never in her life had she been in a place such as this, and she likely would not visit again. 'Could we look at their wares? I've not seen a place like this before.' She hid the pouch of coins Terence had given her, tying it within the folds of her gown.

He guided her away from the crowd, his gaze dark. 'I didn't want you to come with me, Caragh. And I'm not about to waste time here in the marketplace.'

Her mood diminished at his anger, and she recognised it for what it was—worry. 'We're going to find her,' she reiterated. 'But instead of searching blindly, we should ask.'

He didn't want to; that was evident enough. Impatience dominated his mood like a dark cloud.

'If she was brought here, someone might have seen her,' Caragh said. 'We'll speak with every merchant, until we learn something.'

Though he didn't disguise his reluctance, he lowered his head in a grim nod. 'So be it.'

It was the best she could hope for. She gave his hand a friendly squeeze, but he jerked his hand away, giving her a stare of warning. It bewildered her why he would feel threatened by such a gesture, but she made a silent vow to herself, not to touch him again.

The first place they visited was a spice merchant. The aroma was like nothing she'd experienced before, and she marvelled at the wares.

'What are these?' she asked the man, studying the strange coloured pieces and seeds.

His skin was dusky, his eyes shrewd as he answered in Irish, 'Cinnamon and pepper from the Far East, lady.' He held up a sample, and the exotic scent made her close her eyes. To Styr, he said, 'I will give you a good price for them.'

'No, you won't.' Styr guided her away. 'We came to ask you about a Norse woman.' He described Elena to the man, and Caragh interjected with her own questions about Brendan.

The man lifted his shoulders in a shrug. 'I

do not remember them. But if you want to buy some of my spices, they will make your food taste like it came from a king's table.'

'No.' Styr rested his hands on Caragh's shoulders, guiding her away while the merchant kept pleading with them to stay. To her he muttered, 'He knows nothing.'

As he led her forwards, the pressure of his hands distracted her. His touch was warm, and she tried not to think of it as they continued to move through the marketplace. But her wicked mind conjured up the dream of walking at his side, his hand resting upon her waist.

She closed her eyes against the forbidden vision, blurting out something to break the silence between them. 'Have you ever seen so many things in all your life? Those bracelets, and the cloth...I've never imagined anything so beautiful.'

'It's silk,' Styr told her. 'Brought over from the East.' He described the caravans from across the seas and lands where the sand stretched as far as the eye could see. Of a burning hot sun, and animals so strange, they had a single hump on their backs.

She sensed the longing in his voice and asked, 'Have you seen them for yourself?'

The exotic place sounded like a world away from anything she'd ever known.

'No. Elena never wanted to travel.' His hand dropped away from her shoulders, and she caught the tension in his voice, warning her not to ask.

Styr guided her towards another merchant who was selling meat pies, surprising her when he added, 'When I was younger, I went south with my father to the kingdom of the Visigoths. The closer you sail to the Mediterranean, the warmer the sun is. The skin of the people is darker, and their winter is very short.'

It was the most she'd ever heard him speak, and the tone of his voice spoke of a man who dreamed of travelling to distant lands.

'You love the sea, don't you?' she asked.

He nodded. 'When I was a boy, I wanted to cross the largest sea. But my mother warned that if I went too far, I would be taken by Jörmungand, the serpent of Midgard.'

'Devoured alive.' She hid a smile, asking, 'Do you still believe it?'

He shrugged, but she could see the superstition in his eyes. 'There are many things on the sea that no man can understand. I have seen fish so large, their tails are the size of my home.'

'I would like to see that. But only if I had a man like you to slay the serpent,' she admitted. A tingle of nerves caught up in her stomach when she met his gaze. The tension had returned, and she couldn't read the thoughts on his face.

She shouldn't have confessed it to him. Because truthfully, the only reason she would consider journeying across the sea was if he were with her. Her thoughts were betraying her, leading her down a path she could not travel. It embarrassed her to know that he'd seen it in her eyes.

God above, if she could simply close off her heart, she would. But every time she looked into his dark eyes, she saw the futility of her feelings. The chains of unwanted attraction had utterly bound up her common sense. With difficulty, she shored up the brittle defences around her heart.

She eyed the man selling meat pies and remarked to Styr, 'I've never seen so much food. How can this be with the drought?'

He nodded towards the ships in the distance. 'There are many who come to Dubh

Linn to trade. If a man has silver, he can buy what he needs.'

Caragh touched the pouch of coins Terence had given her, grateful for her brother's gift. Impulsively, she broke away from Styr, asking the merchant, 'How much do you think your pies are worth?'

She offered her brightest smile, desperately needing a way to distance herself from Styr. Although they had broken their fast that morn, she knew the meagre food wasn't enough for a warrior the size of Styr.

'Ten pieces of silver,' the merchant proclaimed, and Caragh laughed at him.

'What kind of a fool do you think I am?'

'A hungry one?' he returned.

'We've no time for this,' Styr said, though she caught the way his eyes lingered upon the food. He *was* hungry, whether or not he would admit it.

Caragh bade him to wait, bargaining with the pie man. 'Perhaps I would buy two pies for one piece of silver.'

The merchant shook his head. 'Not enough.'

Disappointed, she was about to ask him about Elena and Brendan, only to find herself none-too-gently escorted away by Styr.

'But what if he knows about—?' she started to say, before he gripped her hand tightly.

'Wait,' he commanded. It took no longer than a few seconds before the merchant caught up to them, holding two pies.

'Your silver?' he asked.

Styr paid the man one coin and handed Caragh both pies. She had no chance to ask any questions, before the man took the rest of his pies and disappeared among the people.

'You don't think he knew anything about your wife?'

Styr shook his head. 'He would have said anything he thought we wanted to hear.'

Caragh started to give him one of the pies, but he refused. 'You're hungry,' she insisted. 'I can see it in your eyes.'

'Not as hungry as you.'

But Caragh broke off a piece of the steaming pie, touching it to his mouth. 'I will enjoy mine more, if I know that you aren't hungry.'

He accepted the bite of food and finally took the pie. Caragh found a stack of wine barrels on the other side of the square and asked for a moment to sit down.

Her shoes were so worn, she could feel the rocky soil beneath her soles. It wouldn't take long to wear holes through the weak leather, and already she felt the swelling of blisters.

But the rest made it easier to endure. Styr leaned beside one of the wine barrels, while she finished as much as she could. When her stomach could hold no more, she gave the rest to him.

'Don't you want to save it for later?'

She shook her head. 'I know the past few days were hard on both of us. And you need your strength.' Her gaze slid over to his muscled arms, and his expression shifted, as if she'd physically touched him. Though he said nothing, his eyes passed over her. And this time, his hunger had nothing to do with food.

Her body was well aware of the direction of his thoughts, though he had spoken not a word. Against her will, a shimmer of interest echoed in her body. She imagined his hands upon her, his forbidden touch shattering every last defence.

God help them both.

'Th-thank you for letting me see the market,' she said, sliding down from the barrel. 'We should go back and find out what we can about Elena and Brendan.'

Styr inclined his head, and they returned to the marketplace, asking several other merchants about what they had seen. None had any information, but they suggested asking another man whose stall was closest to the slave market.

Strangely, Caragh didn't recognise the man's wares. She stared at the selection of ivory and polished wood, along with vials of oil.

'We're not stopping here,' Styr said, trying to move her on. But her curiosity was heightened. The man's eyes lit up when he saw the two of them. He was one of the Norsemen, shorter than Styr, but barrel-chested.

'For you, lady.' He offered her a tiny vial, contained in wood. 'Try it with your lover.'

Her cheeks went crimson, and she shook her head. 'But he's not my—'

'We're leaving,' Styr repeated, gripping her hand.

The merchant grinned at him and spoke words in his language. Styr argued back, shaking his head in refusal. Whatever it was the merchant wanted him to buy, Styr was having none of it.

'But what is he selling?' she asked. 'I don't recognise his wares.'

'Your brothers wouldn't want you here,' he said.

His declaration only heightened her interest. She ignored his wishes and moved in closer. Styr was trying to hide something, and she couldn't think of what.

'Please,' the merchant insisted. 'Take the oil. But if you wish to buy this, other women will tell you of the pleasure you will know.' He held out an ivory cylinder with a rounded, ridged top.

The moment she saw it closer, Caragh frowned. As the merchant instructed, she held it in her palm, still unclear on what it was.

'Use the oil, lady.' He began to explain more, but his Irish was broken, and he switched back into the Norse language, making it impossible to understand.

When she shook her head, the merchant took her hand and curled it over the ivory. He showed her how to move it up and down, and when she glanced at Styr, his shoulders were shaking, his mouth tight.

'What's wrong?'

He lowered his head, looking away. The man was *laughing* at her. And she had no idea why. Handing back the ivory cylinder, she saw lengths of silk in many different colours. 'And what are those for?'

'Tying up your lover,' he explained.

A snort erupted from Styr, and finally he burst out in a broad laugh. Caragh's face turned scarlet, as she suddenly understood what the man had been selling. Not only chains to tie up a lover, but the ivory cylinder was a perfect replica of a man's—

Oh dear God.

She dropped it as if it were a hot coal, hurrying away from the merchant. Styr followed, but he never stopped laughing at her. 'Are you still wondering what he was selling?'

'I cannot believe anyone would sell such things!' she said, horrified that she'd actually touched the ivory shaft. 'Why would anyone want them?'

He leaned against a wooden cart, and she glared at him while he continued to laugh. 'Should I buy you one?' he smirked, starting to walk back.

'No!' She'd never been so humiliated in all her life. 'And you can stop laughing at me.'

He did, but a dangerous smile spread over his face. 'You're too innocent, Caragh.' But his hand came around her shoulders, as he led her away from the market.

It was the gesture of a friend, of a man who was no longer threatened by her. This was the first time she'd ever seen him smile or laugh, for he'd always been so angry, so intent upon finding Elena. But for the briefest moment, she saw the anger and frustration slip away. She found herself drawn even more to this man, although his good mood was at her expense.

'I would prefer that we forget about this,' she said quietly.

His expression turned mischievous, his eyes almost sensual. 'Some women have no man to share their bed. Such things have their uses.'

'Not for me. And you didn't have to laugh.'

'The look on your face was worth a thousand silver coins, when you realised what it was.' His arm remained around her shoulders, and for a moment, her traitorous mind imagined that they were more than friends. She'd never done anything except kiss a man, but after viewing the merchant's wares, she wondered what else happened between a husband and a wife. She knew how children were made...but was there more?

Styr's hand moved away from her shoulders, once they were further away. He guided her out of the market, admitting, 'I haven't laughed that hard in a long time.'

'Not even with Elena?'

His expression shifted, his smile fading. 'No.'

She didn't know what to say, for fear of transforming his mood into sadness or anger. Instead, she let her fingers brush against his, and he took her palm, threading their fingers together.

They walked past the marketplace, and for the first time, he didn't pull away. The warmth of his hand upon hers was comforting, and for a moment, she imagined that they were friends. When he wasn't so angry, it was easy to be around Styr.

And far too easy to let down the guard around her heart.

Iona's words came back to haunt her: *You will find your happiness, when you learn to walk away from what was never meant to be.*

Was this what the old woman had meant? That she needed to leave Styr and protect her heart? The more she thought of it, the more she saw the truth in Iona's words. If she allowed herself to be friends with Styr, the dangerous attraction might transform into other feelings. Feelings of jealousy, feelings that would remind her of how Kelan hadn't wanted her.

She let go of his hand, focusing her concentration on the rising pain upon her feet and the blisters through her worn shoes.

As they continued on, Styr spoke with several more merchants, but no one seemed to have seen his wife. Caragh offered to ask among the women, but he refused to leave her side for a moment.

'It's not safe for you to be alone, without a guard.'

She acceded to him, for he knew the customs of the Norse better than herself. Then, too, more than a few of the men had eyed her, only to be deterred by Styr's presence.

'What if Elena isn't within the city?' she asked, after they had finished searching the marketplace.

He shook his head. 'I don't know. It seems likely, but without finding my ship—'

When he didn't finish the sentence, she took a breath. 'There is another place we should search.'

He knew, without asking, what she meant. They continued a little further and Styr asked a bystander where they could find the slave markets. The man pointed them in the right direction, and she saw the tension in his face. If Elena had been sold as a slave, she could be anywhere…even brought to distant lands. He might never find her.

A hollow feeling took root within Caragh, suffusing her with guilt. For if Styr never saw his wife again, his marriage was essentially over.

He could be yours, the voice of sin whispered.

She lifted her gaze to his sun-darkened hair and his brown eyes. There was no man as powerful and strong as this one. And when he'd touched her, it was as if her body craved more than he could give.

But it was wrong to even think of it. She closed her eyes, forcing back the dishonourable thoughts. A man like Styr deserved to be with the woman he loved. Not her.

The longer they walked, the more her feet began to ache. Caragh hid her discomfort, for it was not only Elena they needed to find; it was also Brendan.

She'd not seen any sign of her brother at all, and more and more, she was wondering if he'd gone elsewhere.

They walked through a maze of streets, past livestock and throngs of people. Caragh didn't know how they would ever find anyone in a place as large as this. She was accustomed to a small ringfort with only a few dozen inhabitants. Here, there were hundreds. Perhaps even a thousand.

She gritted her teeth against the swollen blisters on her soles, not wanting to reveal any weakness. When they reached the interior of the city, she saw the auction block and the chained rows of men and women. Most were Irish, but there were a few Norse men and women among them.

Although it was cold outside, the men were mostly naked, wearing only a cloth around their waist to cover themselves. She supposed it was to reveal their physical strength. The women wore a shapeless brown *léine*, their hair hanging loose. When she saw a few boys awaiting their turn to be sold, her heart twisted at the sight. What had happened to their families? And why would anyone want to sell a child?

Styr went to ask one of the Norse men about Elena, but Caragh couldn't tear her gaze from the young boy. He reminded her of Brendan, years ago, when both of them had played together as children. Though her brother had made terrible mistakes in the past few days, he was still her kin. And his life depended on what had happened to Elena.

When Styr returned, his face was grim.

'They were here, a few days ago. My men were, at least. But not Elena. They didn't see a woman.'

'Perhaps they were lying.'

'No. They had no reason to lie about her.'

His hands clenched into fists with a palpable frustration. Though he steeled his expression, she knew he feared the worst.

'She's not dead,' Caragh assured him.

'You don't know that, any more than I do.' He gripped her hand in wordless command not to speak of it before he led her away from the marketplace. Caragh cast one last look at the young boy, wishing she could save him.

But she could not delay any longer. Styr's pace had hastened, his long legs striding forwards as he moved northwest.

'Where are we going?' she asked, biting her lip against the pain of her blistering feet.

'I learned where one of my men was sold. He's still within the city, and I plan to speak with him and find out what happened to Elena.' He kept a tight grip upon her hand, guiding her through the narrow streets, across a bridge that spanned the River Liffey.

'How far away is he?' she asked, praying it could not be much further.

'Another hour. Unless we hurry,' he told her.

Caragh glanced up at the afternoon sun, which was starting to descend. 'We have to be back by nightfall. My brothers will—'

'I don't care about what your brothers want,' he snapped. 'You were the one who insisted on coming with me. And if night comes before we get back, so be it. I will find my wife, no matter how many hours it takes.'

Though he sounded impatient, she didn't miss the note of fear in his voice. 'I hope we do find them. But could we rest, for just a moment?' Her lungs were burning from exertion, and her feet were slick within her leather shoes.

He did stop walking, but appeared annoyed at the delay. Caragh moved down to the river bank and removed her shoes. She dipped them into the cool water, and the relief was immediate. He drew closer and when he saw her feet, his demeanour changed. 'When did your feet start bleeding?'

'An hour ago.' She washed away the blood, letting the cool water soothe the swollen skin. 'I'll be all right in a few minutes. Why don't we eat and then we can continue?' It had been hours since they'd broken their fast with the meat pies, and she was hungry again.

Styr ignored her suggestion and picked up

her shoes. He turned them over, revealing the holes within the leather. 'You're not walking in these.'

She shook her head at that pronouncement. 'I've no other choice.'

'I'll carry you.' He gave back the shoes and pulled one of her feet from the water. Though it was dripping wet, he dried it upon his hose and examined her blisters. When his thumb brushed against a sensitive place, she flinched.

'If we want to be back by nightfall, I'll have to walk.' She reached for her shoes, and reluctantly, he returned them. Though her feet ached, she limped along for a time.

Then, without warning, he lifted her into his arms. He strode up the river bank, moving deeper into the city.

'Styr, no. This isn't necessary.'

It was as if she hadn't spoken a single word. Doggedly, he continued, his gaze studying every street. 'It's only another mile past the river.'

'It's too far to carry me,' she said. 'Truly, you shouldn't bother.'

'Caragh, my dog weighed more than you do.' He shifted her in his arms, and his remark bruised her feelings. She didn't say anything, but it made her conscious of how much weight she'd lost. How tired she'd become over the past few months. Even when they'd caught the fish, she'd been unable to eat more than a small portion.

The famine had changed her, and not only physically. She was conscious of food in a way she'd never been before.

'I know what I look like,' she said quietly. 'I know I'm too thin.'

He slowed his pace and eased her back to her feet. Caragh faced him, holding up her arms. 'I never wanted to be like this. But don't speak as if the way I look was my choice.'

'It wasn't.' He let out a slow breath. 'But your brothers shouldn't have left you there. *They* should shoulder the blame for what you suffered.'

'They knew I couldn't make the journey to find food.' She lifted her shoulders in a shrug. 'And perhaps it…*was* my fault. I gave Brendan my share of food on occasion.' Her voice grew distant as she remembered her brother's desperate hunger.

'Then he was weak for taking what belonged to you.'

'He didn't know.' She walked gingerly, adjusting her gait to avoid stepping on her blisters. Styr remained at her side, keeping his own pace slow. 'I told him I had eaten already. Sometimes I told him it was extra food.'

The ache of hunger had dulled until she didn't feel it. And watching her brother suffer was so hard, especially when she could do something to change it.

Her mother had done the same thing, and after seeing her brother's fierce hunger, she'd understood why...even if it wasn't right to starve herself.

But now, she'd paid the consequences for her actions. She was fully conscious of her thinness, and it bothered her to be seen like this.

Styr stopped walking, and he unwrapped a bit of dried fish from their supplies. 'Eat this.'

'But you—'

'Do it,' he commanded. 'And I swear on the bones of Thor, that you won't go hungry again. Not like the past few months.'

'And how will you do that, when my brother stole your ship? You've no more coins than I.'

'There are ways,' he said enigmatically, taking food for himself. He made sure that she ate a goodly portion of fish and bread, before lifting her in his arms again.

'Styr, I don't want to be carried.'

'You slow my pace when we walk,' he countered.

And with no other choice, she let him. While he continued through the streets, she rested her cheek against his chest. In his arms, he made her feel safe, as if she could cast off her worries and rely on him.

But the lurking fear for her brother remained. What had happened to Brendan? Was he alive? And would Styr harm him? And what of Elena?

He spoke of Elena like a man who would never stop searching. But there was something else beneath his resolution. Almost a sadness, a frustration she didn't understand.

'When you find your wife, I'll stay away from both of you,' Caragh offered. 'I wouldn't want her to think that I...came between you in any way.'

His pacing slowed, and he adjusted her position for a moment. 'She knows I would never dishonour our marriage.' But again, there was a grim quality to his tone. She didn't know what to make of it.

'That's good, then.' She waited for him to continue on, pushing back her doubts. 'I imagine she will be overjoyed to see you.'

But the look on his face didn't agree with the words. Instead, he shrugged.

'Likely she'll blame me for being unable to guard her.' He continued walking, though his pace was not nearly as swift. 'She would be right.'

She reached up to touch his cheek, forcing him to look at her. 'It wasn't your fault. And I believe, when you find her, she will be so happy to see you, everything will change.'

He said nothing, a tight set to his jaw, as if he didn't believe her.

'You're a good man, Styr. You deserve the happiness she can give you.' Though he gave no reply, he tightened his arms around her. Caragh allowed herself to imagine it as an embrace instead of a duty. For she believed that, despite his outwardly rough manner, Styr was a man of worth.

As he continued to walk, she saw the shadow of guilt upon him. Why? He'd done nothing at all wrong—even the kiss had been against his will.

Was it because their marriage wasn't as strong as it seemed? Would his wife truly blame him for being captured, for being unable to save her?

From his brooding mood, it seemed possible.

As he walked, Caragh allowed herself to daydream. If she were wedded to a man like Styr, she would not fault him for the attack.

His driven need to find Elena was powerful, a force that only deepened Caragh's attraction to him. But she knew better than to reveal it. Better to bury away useless feelings that meant nothing.

Regret pierced through her heart as she thought of her past failures. She'd been so trusting, believing Kelan when he'd said he would love only her. In the end, she hadn't been the one he'd wanted.

It had stung deeply. After she'd shielded herself from any further advances, she'd turned inward, never speaking to other men or letting herself dream of a future. During the famine, there were no thoughts at all of a marriage or a family.

But now, she found herself wondering again. She'd survived, and there was no reason to abandon her own dreams. Here in the city, there were dozens of men. Black-haired men with handsome faces, golden-haired Norsemen like Styr. Strong men, young men…men who might be wanting a wife. Or children of their own.

Caragh's thoughts drifted back to the young boy at the slave auction. She had wanted children once, wanted to feel the tug of young hands upon her skirts. She'd dreamed of kissing a baby-soft cheek and cradling an infant in her arms.

It was a future she would never have at Gall Tír. But here, it wasn't so impossible.

A prickle of fear clung to her courage, along with more self-consciousness about her thin appearance. Could she even gain a man's notice? Was it worth staying in Áth Cliath for a little longer, in the hopes of meeting someone? The voice of doubt warned that few men would want a half-starved woman with nothing at all to bring to the marriage.

Styr set her down near a large rectangular dwelling. 'This is the place,' he said.

'How do you know?'

'It's as the man described it to me.' He pointed towards the door. Upon the wood, there appeared to be a monstrous face, and there were other stone carvings beside it. Elaborate runes were engraved within the limestone.

'What do you want to do?' she asked.

'If my kinsman Onund is here, he will be among the thralls. He may come outside, or he may be working within the dwelling.'

'Should we hide ourselves?' she suggested.

'We'll watch over them until we see a chance to go inside.' He took her hand and pulled her back around the edge of the stone wall. Caragh obeyed, keeping her shoulders against the fortification.

She fell silent, waiting beside him as the minutes passed. If he were alone, she suspected he would try scaling the wall to infiltrate the dwelling. As it was, she'd become a burden on him.

'You should try to go inside,' she whispered at last. 'There's a pile of peat stacked over there. I'll hide behind it.'

'No. I'm not leaving you alone.'

She thought a moment and pressed again. 'I'll be safe enough, so long as I stay hidden. And if anything happens, I'll call out for help.'

'You could be taken while I'm inside,' he argued. 'I won't leave you without my protection.'

'If there is danger there, we'll both be captured,' she reminded him. 'It's better if one of us stays behind. Give me your blade, and when you know it's safe, you'll come back for me,' she suggested. 'If you don't return within an hour, I'll get help.' With a wry smile, she added, 'I can limp back to my brothers. With any luck, I might arrive by morning.'

He didn't want to leave her; she could see the reluctance in his face. But he recognised the sense in her words. With a sigh, he gave a nod. 'Stay out of sight and don't go anywhere.'

It was evident that he didn't like the plan but could see no alternative. Caragh waited until she was certain no one was watching. She hurried across from the dwelling and moved several of the peat bricks aside to make a space for herself. It felt good to sit, and when she was well hidden, Styr approached the dwelling.

Caragh could only hope that he would find what he sought.

Chapter Eight

When the slave answered the door, Styr introduced himself and added, 'I've come to speak with your master.' He dropped his voice lower. 'Is there a thrall among you, named Onund?'

The servant's expression turned confused. 'There is, but only within the last few days.' He looked as if he wanted to ask questions, but silenced them.

'Send him to me. This concerns him, since he is one of my kin. I have come to free him.'

'Have you?' came a deep voice. 'Bold words for a Hardrata.'

Styr saw a man emerge from the shadows. He was slightly taller, with black hair and broad shoulders. His beard was trimmed close, and around his arms, he wore golden bands. Rings covered his fingers, and an earring hung from one ear. 'I knew your brother Hakon,' the stranger said. 'You've travelled far from Hordafylke.'

'How do you know my brother?'

'We were friends for many years as boys. Hakon and I sailed together for a time before I came here. I am Ivar Nikolasson.' The man invited him to sit down, but Styr hesitated. Although the man claimed to know his brother, he wasn't certain whether or not he would pose a danger to them.

'I can see from your face that you don't remember me.' Ivar motioned to a servant and ordered him to bring Onund forwards. 'Perhaps your own man can reassure you that I have not mistreated my thralls.'

He waited for several minutes while Ivar offered him a place to sit. The large interior of the longhouse was partitioned in several places to offer private sleeping quarters while a large hearth stood in the centre of the dwelling. The rich scent of roasting meat lingered in the air, and all around him, he saw evidence of Nikolasson's wealth. There were cups made of silver and a chest decorated with ivory and gold in another corner. Silks and furs lined small couches, and Ivar himself wore a tunic embroidered with silver thread.

Moments later, Onund emerged from outside. The man's expression was filled with relief at the sight of Styr. 'Thank the gods,' he breathed.

Styr stood and signalled for the man to come closer. Lowering his voice to a whisper, he asked, 'Where is Elena?'

Onund's face tightened. 'She jumped off the ship to escape her own capture. Ragnar went after her.'

A cold fist gripped him at the thought of his wife in such danger. 'Is she alive? Where did this happen?'

'We were attacked by the Danes, a few hours south of the city. They tried to swim to the shore, but I don't know if they made it.' Onund reached out and gripped his shoulder. 'I have prayed to the gods for their safety.'

Styr gave a nod, but inside, his mind was numb, as if every sense were dulled. He hardly heard Onund's words about his kinsmen.

'...the rest of us were taken as slaves,' the man finished. He waited expectantly for Styr to respond, but the image of Elena blurred with Caragh. He remembered the night she'd fallen overboard, and her struggle to swim.

Elena wasn't a strong swimmer. If she'd jumped off the ship, she must have believed she was going to die. Likely at the hands of their enemies.

He imagined her slender body falling beneath the water, her limbs lifeless, and something within him snapped.

'What about the other men?' he prompted. The cold need for vengeance threaded through him. Caragh's brother was responsible for all of it. He didn't care if the boy was only seven and ten. Because of Brendan, his men were slaves, and his wife might be dead...

A haze of fury roared through him at the thought.

'All survived,' Onund answered. 'We were brought here to be sold. I know where some of the others are.'

'How were you even taken by a handful of Irish boys?' Styr demanded. 'Were you not trained to slay your enemies?'

Onund's own anger rose up. 'Did you want them to kill Elena?' His hands clenched, his expression tight. 'We were going to attack sooner, but the boy threatened to cut Elena's throat.' He grimaced, as if regretting their actions. 'We didn't trust him not to kill her.'

The lad deserved a slow, painful death. A

blood-red rage smothered any pity he might have felt. He'd endangered Elena, and that, Styr would not forgive. As soon as he found the boy, he would sheathe his blade in Brendan's heart.

But first, he had to find him.

'Your new master,' Styr began, 'is he trustworthy?'

'I think so, yes.' A twisted expression slid over Onund's face. 'But I am a freeman, Styr. I won't live like this.'

'I'll see to it that you are released,' he promised. 'As soon as I can.'

Onund inclined his head and retreated among the other thralls. Ivar came forwards and said, 'Have you a place to stay this night? We can speak of your men, and I'll offer my hospitality.'

It was then that he remembered Caragh in hiding, and his thoughts stilled. She would do anything necessary to protect her brother. Soft-hearted and innocent, he didn't want her to know of his intentions.

'We have a ship,' he said to Ivar. 'It's enough.'

'But we have much to discuss this night, about your men and how they came to be slaves,' Ivar said smoothly. 'Dine with us and share the longhouse.'

'And what of my Irish companions?' he ventured.

'They are welcome, too.' Ivar glanced at the door. 'You are speaking of the woman who is in hiding outside, I presume?'

Styr sent him a dark look, and Ivar shrugged. 'I have men who remain on guard upon the roof of my house. I am a man of wealth, and I guard what is mine.'

Styr nodded and went outside, keeping his hand upon his blade. Caragh had remained in hiding, as he'd wanted her to, and when he helped her to stand, she limped alongside him, towards the house.

'What did you learn?' she asked.

'Some of my men are here.' But he left out the rest of what he knew, especially about Elena.

It was unlikely his wife had survived. He knew too well, how dangerous it was to swim towards the shore. The intense cold of the Irish Sea, coupled with her weak swimming abilities, would easily drown a man.

'And your wife?' Caragh prompted. 'Did they know where she is?'

Styr could only shake his head. 'I plan to

free Onund, and I hope he can show me the place where Elena…went missing.' He refused to speak of her death, as if admitting it would make it a certainty. But inwardly, his thoughts were a tangled mass of fury and doubt.

Caragh's eyes mirrored his own worry. 'I hope she is safe.'

'For your brother's sake, I hope so, too.' He didn't care how harsh he sounded. She needed to understand that he would not show mercy to anyone who threatened his family.

She blanched, her fingers clenched together. 'He's only a boy, Styr.'

'No.' He wouldn't make excuses for the young man. 'He intended to attack us, and because of it, my men were sold into slavery.' He took her by the hand and led her up into the dwelling. 'Believe me, if he earned any silver from the capture of my men, he will lose every last coin. And if my wife is dead…'

He didn't need to speak another word, nor did he bother to keep the coldness from his tone.

Caragh stared back at him, and pulled her hand away, repeating, 'He's a boy.' Lowering her gaze, she remained behind him while he led the way towards Ivar.

After Styr introduced them, the man's eyes

passed over her with appreciation. Caragh's face flushed, and Styr turned away to hide the surge of annoyance. Contrasted against her young beauty, Ivar was an older man who had likely enjoyed his share of women. And Styr didn't intend for Caragh to be one of them. He could read the thoughts upon the man's face and knew what they meant. He longed to slice the smile from the man's face.

Because you want her, his body chided. *You see her beauty and you want no one else to possess her.*

Untrue, his mind responded. *Elena has my loyalty and always will.*

He shielded the emotions, shrugging them away. Caragh was an unmarried maiden and a beautiful one. Why should he care if she smiled at a Norseman? Or if she drew his attentions? She could do as she pleased, and it mattered not to him.

Liar, his body responded.

'Is she your woman?' Ivar questioned, using the Irish language so that Caragh could understand him.

Before Styr could answer, Caragh raised her chin. 'I am my own woman. I belong to no man.'

The smile that curved over the Norseman's

face held interest and desire. 'Well said.' He gave the command for a female thrall to accompany her. 'I invite you to share a meal with us, if you are willing.'

The slight emphasis he placed upon the word *willing* made Styr's hand move towards his battleaxe. He didn't doubt that Ivar wanted Caragh to be *willing* in another manner.

His mood darkened even more at the thought.

'Would you like to refresh yourself?' Ivar offered. His gaze passed over her blue gown, and he added, 'My slaves could offer you something else to wear, while they care for your garments. That is, if you wish to try the clothing of our women.'

Caragh smiled at him gratefully. 'You are very kind.'

'Of course.' Speaking in the Norse language, he ordered his slaves to begin heating water for a bath.

When the man was out of earshot, Styr moved beside Caragh. 'He has his eye upon you. I don't like it.'

Her mouth opened slightly, and she sent him a dark glare. 'Why should it bother you?'

'I don't trust him.' His hand moved up to

cup her chin. 'Norsemen tend to take what they want.'

She pushed his hand away. 'He has thus far treated me with kindness. Unlike someone else who is threatening my brother.'

He caught her wrist before she could retreat. 'Be careful, Caragh.' Her innocence could lead her into real danger, and he didn't want any harm to come to her.

Her violet-blue eyes turned serious. 'Let me go.'

She touched his fingers, staring at him as if *he* were the threat. Didn't she understand how vulnerable she was? A man could force himself upon her, and Caragh could do nothing to stop it.

Her defiance tempted him to take her from Ivar's house this moment. It was as if she wanted to attract the Norseman, taunting Styr with the knowledge that he could not prevent it.

He gritted his teeth, but ultimately released Caragh. Her blue eyes stared at him as if she didn't recognise him any more. 'Is this the man you've become?' she whispered. 'I thought you had more honour than that.'

Without waiting for a response, she followed the women to the back of the dwelling, behind another wooden partition.

After she'd left, Ivar asked again, 'You're certain she is not yours?'

He wanted to deny it, if for no other reason than to keep this man away from her. But he didn't lie. 'I am her protector. Nothing more.'

At the gleam of interest in Ivar's eyes, Styr let his hand drift down to his battleaxe. 'You would do well to remember that I will allow no man to harm her.'

The Norseman smiled. 'She is very beautiful. Though delicate.'

'She has suffered throughout the past year, from a famine. When I found her, she had nearly starved to death.'

'Then we will be certain that she eats well this night.' Ivar's attention shifted towards the partition. From the sound of water pouring and female voices, Styr's own imagination was distracted.

Although she was thin, Caragh did possess curves. He'd noticed the softness of her breasts pressed against him, when he'd held her. She was a woman any man would desire.

Especially a man like Ivar.

Styr suppressed the snarl of anger rising up. Caragh was right; he shouldn't care. But the look in Ivar's eyes pushed him towards his breaking point, and he didn't know why. He barely heard the man's conversation, though he caught the mention of his brother's name.

'When did you leave Hordafylke?' Styr asked him.

'Six years ago. We came to trade, but I decided to stay here.' He nodded towards the house. 'I came to build my fortune, and so I have. It's time that I chose a wife and began giving her sons.' Ivar's glance moved towards the partition again, before he turned back to Styr. 'For a man with no claim upon her, you seem to have a strong interest.'

'She will make her own decisions.' He unsheathed his dagger and studied it. 'That doesn't mean I won't stop her from making the wrong ones.'

Ivar inclined his head. 'So be it.'

Styr took a sip from the goblet of wine Ivar had poured him. 'You purchased some new slaves in the past few days. They were members of the *hird*, free men who were taken captive and sold by the Danes.'

'We've had trouble with them,' Ivar admitted. 'They've been seen along the coast attacking our ships. Some believe there will be another invasion.' He refilled his own goblet and eyed Styr. 'You want your men back.'

'Yes.' But more than that, he wanted to find Elena. And he wanted vengeance against those who had taken her.

Ivar's face twisted into a smile. 'I suppose you think I should simply release your men, despite the silver I paid.'

'Or I would challenge you for their release,' Styr offered. The idea of wielding a blade against Ivar gave him a means of releasing the physical frustration within him. He wouldn't mind the fight at all.

'There are other things you possess that could be used to bargain for your men,' Ivar said.

Styr knew exactly what the man was implying. 'No.'

'Leave the woman in my care,' he said quietly. 'If she allows me to grant her my attentions, I would give her everything she desires. And your men can go free.'

'I wouldn't leave a dog in your care, Nikolasson,' Styr retorted. Before he could say anything further, Caragh emerged from behind the screen.

The women had dressed her in a vibrant red gown, with gold brooches fastening the shoulders of a white apron. Her hair was still wet, but they had braided it back with silver combs tucked within the single plait. A golden torque adorned her throat, and when the light illuminated her face, he was struck by the sight of her wearing such finery. She moved slowly, to avoid revealing her limp.

Ivar rose from his place, not bothering to hide his appreciative smile. Caragh held herself with poise, but when she sent him a quiet look, he saw the shadow of nerves.

'You are breathtaking, *kjære*,' the Norseman remarked, offering her his arm. He brought her to a low table and bade her sit upon a silken cushion. Styr didn't know what possessed him, but he took his place on Caragh's opposite side.

Ivar sent her an amused look. 'Your protector is like an older brother, isn't he?'

'He isn't my brother.' Her voice held the coolness of anger, but Styr wondered if she understood the game she was playing. Nikolasson wasn't a man who would let a woman tease his interest without responding.

Styr reached for her hand under the table, gripping her fingers in a warning. But Caragh jerked her hand free of his, sending him a look that would have frozen water.

'I like you, Caragh Ó Brannon,' Ivar admitted. 'You are very much like the women of my homeland.'

'I'm not nearly as tall as they are.' She accepted the goblet of wine he offered and took a sip.

'But you are beautiful and spirited.' He cut off a piece of roasted mutton and offered it to her. 'I am eager to learn more about you.'

Styr had no doubt of that. But he wasn't about to leave Caragh with him. 'We were discussing my men,' he said. 'Negotiating for their freedom.'

'What else can you offer in return?' Though the words were directed to Styr, Ivar's gaze drifted lower, over Caragh's body.

'She is not part of our negotiation,' he said, tightening his palm upon Caragh's hand.

Ivar gave a shrug, and offered his open palm to Caragh. 'You have captured my interest, lady. Should you desire to be…friends, you have only to say the word. And if you want me to free those men, I would do as you ask.'

'She is not interested,' Styr retorted.

But Caragh lowered her head in agreement. 'I would like you to free his men. Because it's the right thing to do—not because I ask it of you.'

The Norseman eyed her again, withdrawing his hand. 'If I did this, you would be in my debt.'

'I am not the sort of woman who offers her favours in exchange for men's lives.' She crossed her arms, revealing her dissatisfaction at the idea.

Good. Nikolasson deserved that response, and Styr was glad to see her rejecting the man's advances.

'That was not what I meant,' he corrected. 'I would merely like to make your acquaintance. Perhaps bring you gifts that would complement your beauty.'

'I am not beautiful,' she answered. Though some women might have said it in a teasing manner, Styr realised that she believed it. As if she had been told by someone. The thought irritated him.

'Then you are blind,' Ivar responded. He reached out for her palm, and Caragh hesitated before giving him her hand. She eyed him for a moment, confusion clouding her gaze. When she glanced back at Styr, he looked away.

Yes, she was beautiful. But more than that, she was strong. She'd fought to survive, and her bravery was greater than any woman he'd ever known. Beneath her fragile beauty lay a woman who had endured more than most.

Yet it was her compassion that lifted her above her kinsmen. He didn't doubt that the Irish would not have taken him prisoner. Men like Kelan would have enjoyed killing him. Styr was alive, because of her.

And yet, you want to kill her brother, his conscience reminded him.

'What has brought you to our city?' Ivar asked. 'Was it your...protector?'

Caragh shook her head. 'I came to search for my brother.' Before Ivar could ask anything else, she described Brendan, asking, 'Did you see him among the others?' Her face revealed her worry, and she added, 'He's only ten and seven.'

'A young man, then. Not a boy.'

It was exactly what Styr had been thinking, but it was clear she still thought of him as a child.

'I need to find him,' she said. 'It's why I journeyed here.'

'There is a gathering in the morning,' Ivar said. 'I could ask among my friends, if they have seen him.'

Her face lightened with relief. 'Would you?

I have no idea where to begin, and if you would be able to help…'

A slow smile curled over Ivar's face. 'I would, yes.'

'Thank you,' she breathed, smiling warmly at the man.

Didn't she understand what was happening? Irritation tensed within him, for Styr knew exactly what Ivar wanted from her. But Caragh seemed innocent of the man's interest. Or possibly she welcomed it. Tension coiled inside him at the thought. He didn't want anyone to pursue her or to—

—touch her.

He shut down the thought, feeling as if someone had driven a fist into his stomach. It shouldn't matter. Caragh was free to make her own choices, and he had no say in them.

Yet jealousy slipped under his skin, digging into his raw mood. He resented the unwanted emotion and tightened the control inside him. There was no reason to be angry with Ivar. The man had done nothing to Caragh, and if she were interested in his advances, why in the name of Thor should he care?

Leave it alone, he warned himself. *Think of Elena. Your wife.*

But as he shut out the images of Caragh

with this man, the memories of his wife that surfaced weren't the happy ones.

He'd made love to Elena, reaching to pull her warm body against his. He'd wanted her to embrace him, to lie beside him when they both fell asleep. Instead, she'd slid to the furthest side of the bed, never looking at him. Almost as if she were ashamed of what they'd done. Or worse, that she hadn't enjoyed any of it.

A dark chill centred within his heart, and he rolled away from her. 'You're unhappy, aren't you?'

Her silence was answer enough.

'I'll make an offering to Freya—' he began, only for her to cut him off.

'It would do no good at all, and you know it. We'll never have a child.'

He rolled over, staring at her huddled figure. 'Don't. We'll keep trying.'

'We already try every day,' she complained. 'I'm weary of it, Styr. I don't want to try any more.'

At last, she turned to face him. In the moonlight, he saw the streaks of tears running down her face. 'Do you know what it's like, being the only married woman without a child? Year after year, I see them, and I see their pity.'

'*Then we'll leave. If that's what you want.*'

'*I don't know what I want any more,*' she'd said.

But he'd known the truth. She didn't want *him* any more. He'd steeled himself against her rejection, hoping that distance and time would solve the rift that had formed.

Perhaps when he found her, she'd be glad to see him. It might heal their problems, giving them a new start. He wanted to believe it.

Styr glanced over at Caragh. In her eyes, he saw the reflection of the woman his wife had once been. Beautiful and alluring, with a glimpse of hope in her eyes.

He wanted to see Elena like this again. No longer living a life where she was tormented by her barrenness. He wanted to see her smile, to see happiness again, instead of failure.

It had grown late, and he needed to send word to Caragh's brothers. 'Might I use one of your thralls to send a message?' he asked Ivar. 'One familiar with this city, who can find Caragh's brothers?'

'You could accompany the thrall to locate her brothers,' Ivar suggested to Styr.

In other words, give the man time alone with Caragh.

'What sort of protector would I be, if I did that?' he demanded.

The Norseman shrugged, as if unconcerned. 'She knows I will not harm her. Don't you, *kjære*?'

'I have known you for only an hour,' she countered. 'It is too soon to tell.'

Ivar appeared amused by her response. 'So be it, then. I have yet to prove myself to you.' The look in his eyes spoke of a man eager to do so.

'Styr will remain as my guard, while you send your man to the harbour at Dubh Linn,' she said.

After Ivar summoned a thrall to send the message, she described the appearance of her brothers. 'I promised to meet them at nightfall,' she said. 'Please hurry and bid them come here.'

To Ivar, she added, 'Might we share your house this night for shelter?'

'I would welcome your presence.' With that, Ivar lifted her palm to his mouth, brushing a kiss over her skin.

Styr stood, unable to bear the sight of them a moment longer.

A warmth flooded over Caragh's face at Ivar's mouth upon her skin. The man was older, but he had a charisma about him that drew her in. His face bore a few scars, yet they seemed to add to his features instead of making him seem a threat.

Caragh glanced over at Styr, sensing that his mind was elsewhere. He eyed the doorway where the thrall had departed, as if he wanted nothing more than to leave her here. His wife was still missing, and there was no way of knowing whether or not she'd drowned.

She voiced a silent prayer that Elena was alive. Not only for the sake of her brother, but also for Styr. In his posture she saw the tension and worry, a man haunted by a fate beyond his control.

While Ivar went to speak with one of his slaves, she walked quietly towards him, for the need to ease his pain could not be denied. 'There is still hope for Elena. After we find Brendan, we'll journey along the coast. I'll do all I can to help you.'

Styr's mood was unreadable, his silence widening the invisible distance. She reached out to touch his arm, hoping to reassure him. His hand covered hers, tightening over her fingers. 'Your brother must answer for what he did.'

She didn't know what to say. His face might

as well have been cast from iron, for there was no mercy in his countenance. 'What he did was wrong, yes. But will you not forgive him for my sake?'

His masked emotions curled into a dark look. 'I'm not a man who knows how to forgive. It's not in my nature.'

A thousand pleas rose to her lips, but she doubted if he would listen. Instead, she went to stand directly before him. His hand was still covering hers, so she kept it and took his other hand in hers. Warm palms enveloped her hands, and she lifted her gaze to his, silently willing him to relent.

But instead of softening his vengeance, her touch had an entirely different effect upon him.

To her shock, Styr pulled her close. His breath warmed her ear. 'Don't trust the Norseman, Caragh. He may seem as if he's being kind, but he wants you in his bed.'

The words seemed to rush over her skin, pouring forbidden images into her mind. An unexpected vision sprang into her mind, of what it would have been like to lie with a Norseman like Styr.

He would likely take whatever he wanted, his hot skin fused upon hers. His mouth would plunder, his hands conquering her bare skin. At the very thought, an ache resonated between her legs, her breasts growing sensitive against the red garment.

He's not for you and never will be.

His gaze lingered upon her for a moment longer, as if he could read her thoughts. Caragh didn't realise she was holding her breath until he left her side to join Ivar.

The Norseman had brought out a set of dice, carved from bone. Although she'd watched men play before, there was an undercurrent between these men, one she didn't understand.

After several tosses of the dice, Styr was winning. Slowly, the pile of coins beside him grew, and Ivar's mood darkened. Caragh moved closer, and her presence seemed to intensify the game.

'Would you like to increase the odds?' Ivar asked, his gaze never moving from her face. She wasn't certain if he was speaking to her or not.

'What odds?' Styr answered.

'One roll of the dice. The winner with the highest number gets a kiss from her.' Ivar's expression turned heated, and it took an effort not to look away. He was giving her a chance to refuse, but Caragh couldn't bring herself to speak.

The truth was, she wanted to kiss Styr again, no matter how sinful it was. Her skin tightened at the thought, even though she knew he wouldn't want to. Even suggesting it was wrong.

But the temptation was too great to deny.

She offered a slight nod of acceptance, while Styr answered, 'No.'

The satisfied smile of Ivar revealed that he'd wanted a reason to kiss her, and she'd given him the means to try.

To her left, she glimpsed Styr's fury. The rage was palpable, as if she were committing an unforgivable sin.

But when Ivar won the toss, she wasn't prepared for the black look on Styr's face. Nor was she ready for the unexpected heat of Ivar's kiss that captured her lips. He didn't hesitate to reveal his desire, palming her spine and drawing her close as he kissed her. But when he tried to slip his tongue inside her mouth, she pulled back.

Her face flamed with embarrassment for what she'd done. She mumbled something about her brothers, and retreated from both of them, her mind caught up in a storm of uncertainty.

Was she trying to prove something to Styr? For what purpose?

He belonged to another woman and was devoted to her. Asking him to betray Elena was wrong. For he never would, and even if he were not wed, he certainly wouldn't claim a woman like herself.

Caragh rested her forehead against the wood, remaining in the shadows. If any of the slaves saw her, they avoided her presence. She wished she could be absorbed into the wall, for already she regretted the impulse. She'd made Ivar think she welcomed his interest, and she'd infuriated Styr.

She was beginning to question her decisions, for she was now behaving like a desperate woman. Not at all like herself.

A moment later, a strong body invaded her space, pressing her against the wall. From the moment he touched her, she knew it was not Ivar.

Styr held her motionless, his powerful body entrapping her against the wood. The heat of his skin and the feeling of helplessness both attracted and frightened her.

'Let me go,' she demanded.

'Do you have any idea what you're doing? You've just given him a reason to slip into your bed this night.' His hands clasped her wrists, as if to mimic the way she'd captured him.

Styr was behaving with jealousy, reacting with the force of a thunderstorm. She pushed back, her own anger rising up. 'And why would you care? We both know there's nothing between us.'

But he didn't let go of her. 'Don't push me, Caragh. If I weren't here to defend you, he would take you.'

His hands softened against her wrists, moving down her arms to her waist. 'He could overpower you in seconds.'

'The way you're doing now?' she challenged. Her voice was hardly more than a whisper, but she could feel the fire rising in him. Standing on the tips of her toes, she rested both hands on his face. 'You may think you're trying to protect me by proving how easy it is to claim someone as weak as I am.'

With a hard shove, she broke free. 'But all you're doing is making me think you're not as close to your wife as you say you are.'

The look of shock in his eyes turned to vehemence. 'You have no right to say that.'

'And you have no right to treat me like this,' she finished. When she'd freed herself from his grasp, she turned back. 'I hope my brothers return soon. Because it doesn't seem that I'm safe with you, either.'

Chapter Nine

A blade grazed the back of his neck.

'I find that I'm not so willing to lend you my hospitality, Hardrata.' Ivar held his knife steady. 'Especially when you're threatening one of my guests.'

Styr said nothing, but lifted his hands up, allowing Caragh to escape. He made no denial of what he'd done, though it was meant to be a warning, not a threat. An innocent like Caragh had no idea what she'd done by kissing the Norseman.

Did she genuinely want the man? Or did she have another motive?

The blade left his neck, and he turned slowly. Caragh stood between them and explained, 'He was not threatening me. Styr was warning me about putting myself in a position that could be harmful.'

Her voice remained calm, as if nothing at all had happened. As if they'd never argued.

Slowly, she took the knife from Ivar's hands. 'I know he was right. As a woman, I shouldn't have gone off alone.'

'No one in this house would harm you,' Ivar said quietly. 'Did he…bother you?' From the grim tone of the man, it sounded as if Ivar wouldn't have minded killing him.

The feeling was mutual. Seeing Caragh yield to the Norseman, softening beneath his lips, had evoked a feral sense of possession. Styr couldn't fathom why it would irritate him.

'I am fine.' She placed her hand upon Ivar's arm and sent a glance back at Styr as if warning him to stay away.

Throughout the next hour, he said nothing at all while Ivar told Caragh stories of their homeland. The man wove tales of adventure, showing her treasures of silver and gold. Her eyes were bright with interest, and a smile lingered upon her mouth.

Yet each time she glanced at Styr, he saw the unrest behind those violet eyes. She feared what he would do when they found her brother within the city. The truth was, he didn't know. Instinct forced him towards a path of revenge, but when he thought of causing her anguish, his gut tightened.

The feelings of a woman shouldn't matter. But he was acutely aware of every movement she made, every word she spoke.

And that was more dangerous than anything else.

When her brothers arrived later that night, Styr withdrew even further, until Ronan approached him.

'What did you find?' Styr asked.

'Your ship was taken by the Danes,' Ronan answered, confirming what he'd learned from Onund. 'My brother and your men were sold into slavery.' He nodded towards Ivar. 'I understand you found some of them.'

Styr told him what he'd learned, ending with, 'We are still looking for your brother.'

Ronan gave a nod, but his eyes were fixed upon Ivar and Caragh. 'What of him? You seem to be allowing him to spend time with our sister.'

'That is her choice to make.' He turned back to the man, considering whether or not to tell him the truth about Elena. Already he'd allowed the man to draw false conclusions about Caragh and him. Though he'd wanted the use of their ship, it might be wiser to break the alliance.

Before he could say another word, Onund approached them. At his side were three more of Styr's men.

'There will be a ritual in the morning,' Onund informed him. 'There have been sightings of many ships approaching, and the men here intend to summon a *volva* to predict whether or not to attack the Danes.'

'The women have begun grinding barley for the bread on the morrow,' another said. 'Ivar intends to host a feast and offer his own sacrifices.'

'Does he intend to sacrifice any of the thralls?' Though animals were most often sacrificed to the gods, there were sometimes human sacrifices, as well.

Onund glanced at his kinsmen, his face unreadable. 'He has not spoken of it.'

Which meant it was possible.

Styr knew that in times of peril, greater sacrifices were demanded. But his men should not be among them. They'd lost their freedom because he'd been unable to guard

Elena. He would not allow them to lose their lives, as well.

He rested his hand upon Onund's shoulder and squeezed it lightly. 'You will be freed in the morning. This I swear, upon the blood of Odin.' He met his kinsman's gaze steadily, though inwardly, he didn't know how he would achieve it. He needed to negotiate with Ivar for their release. To each of them, he gave one of the silver coins he'd won.

Styr bade the men a good night, and when they'd gone, Ronan confronted him. 'You've made plans, haven't you?'

'Plans to free them, yes.' He said nothing more, knowing Ronan had not understood the Norse language.

'And what about our sister? Or have you changed your mind about being her protector?'

Styr evaded the question. 'There are dozens of men, Irish even, who would make a better protector.' *Unmarried men, who can give her the kind of life she deserves*, he didn't say.

Ronan's blue eyes met his own. 'I see the way she looks at you. She hasn't looked at any man in that way, in over a year.'

He had no response to give. It would be far

better if Caragh saw him for what he was—a man bent upon vengeance and nothing else.

'You look at her in the same manner,' Ronan commented. 'And given all the invasions, I think it would be wise to ally our men. You can live at Gall Tír, and we'll join our forces together.'

'There can be no alliance between Caragh and myself.' No longer would he give the man false hopes. Ronan deserved the truth. 'I'll help you find your brother, while I search for the rest of my men,' Styr told him. 'Then we'll go.'

Ronan's gaze turned cold. 'You're planning to break her heart, then.'

'She's always known that there would never be anything between us. I was her captive. I paid my debt when I saved her life. We're even now.'

'Then you're nothing but a *Lochlannach* bastard,' Ronan countered, reaching out towards his throat.

Styr caught the man's hand and shoved him against the back wall. Already his temper was stretched taut, and he needed no man to tell him what to do.

'Don't,' Caragh protested, moving between them. When she pushed him back, there was a slight shift in her posture, almost as if she were afraid.

And perhaps she should be. He let out a slow breath of air, not regretting what he'd said to Ronan. It was better to leave her be, so she could pursue her own future.

Her dark hair was gathered over one shoulder, baring a slight glimpse of pale skin. In the firelight, he saw the gooseflesh rise upon it. Whether she was cold or uncomfortable at his presence, he didn't know. But he handed her his own cloak and returned to the back of the room. Caragh dared to glance at him, and when she did, she pulled the cloak tightly around her.

When he reached the far end of the longhouse, he made a sleeping place for himself. In his palm, he gripped his battleaxe, believing that it wasn't at all safe in this house.

Caragh sat in the darkness with her knees drawn up. She'd been unable to sleep, her mind caught up in worry. From across the room, she heard the whisper of footsteps approaching.

'My lord bids you come to him,' came the low voice of a female thrall. She spoke Irish well, but the command made Caragh's skin tighten.

'Why?'

'He knows your dreams are troubled. He wishes to speak with you and offer you a spiced wine to help you sleep.'

But Caragh held no trust towards Ivar. If he gave her a rich wine, it would only muddle her decisions more. From across the room, she spied him seated near a bronze oil lamp. Though he was shadowed, she sensed what he wanted from her.

Around her shoulders, she wore Styr's cloak, fastened with a silver brooch. Upon the heavy wool, she scented his presence, and it lent her comfort. She tightened her grip, knowing she could not obey the summons.

She stood from her pallet, the fear creeping within her veins. Darkness enveloped the longhouse, but she did not follow the servant. The woman protested in a soft whisper, but Caragh ignored her. Instead, she tiptoed across the room, past her sleeping brothers, to the one man who did make her feel safe.

Styr slept in the corner of the far end of the house. A battleaxe rested in one hand, and the moment she knelt down beside him, his eyes flew open.

Caragh touched a finger to her lips, silently willing him not to speak. Without asking permission, she lay down beside him on the cold earth. She unpinned the brooch and loosened the cloak, reaching to place it over him.

He moved towards her, his hard body against her own. 'Why are you here, Caragh?'

She turned her lips to his ear. 'You were right about Ivar. He tried to summon me to him this night.'

Styr sat up, his hand closing over the battleaxe. 'Did he harm you?' He kept his voice just above a whisper, but his tone was fierce.

'No. But I didn't believe it was safe to stay on the other side.'

'It's not safe here, either,' he reminded her. 'You should have gone to your brothers.'

He was right. Being here wasn't wise, but she couldn't say what had drawn her to him. She didn't understand the forbidden feelings he'd conjured or why she yearned to be at his side. But there had been no question in her mind that she would only find sleep if she lay beside him.

'Do you want me to go?' Her hand rested upon the cool chainmail he hadn't removed.

Styr said nothing at all, but guided her to lie back down. Her heartbeat trebled at his nearness and all the silent reasons why he hadn't sent her away. Their bodies didn't touch, but she felt the cold earth against her as she tried to sleep.

'Keep the cloak,' he said. 'You're cold.'

'So are you,' she whispered, ignoring the command.

But a moment later, he dragged her to rest beside him, her back resting against his chest. 'Little fool.' With one hand, he adjusted the cloak until it covered both of them.

But closing her eyes didn't shut out the feelings he evoked inside her. Beneath the cloak, though his skin was cool, she sensed it warming against her. She was torn between moving away from him, and craving the heat of his body.

Go to sleep, she ordered herself. She'd come to him only for sanctuary. Not to awaken any dangerous, forbidden feelings.

As she lay against him, she relived the moment of Ivar's kiss. It had been sensual, yes. But it had not taken possession of her, the way Styr's had. With this man, she'd lost sight of herself. She'd been unable to think or breathe.

Rolling over to her side, she saw that he was not sleeping, either. His dark eyes were staring at her with an expression she didn't understand. In the softest whisper, she murmured, 'This was a mistake, wasn't it?'

Styr didn't answer. Time hung between them, the seconds passing into a minute. In the end, he sat up and tucked the cloak around her before rising to his feet. He stood against the wall, watching over her like a silent sentry.

The gathering was a blend of Norse and the Irish, led by a council of men. Caragh remained at the side of her brothers, though she felt the gaze of Styr upon her.

He had kept vigil over her for the rest of the night, though her dreams had been troubled. She'd woken up once in a silent scream, imagining her brother lying dead, blood spilling from his throat. Her heart had pounded, and Styr had laid a hand over her shoulder to reassure her that it was nothing. But she refused to tell him of the vision.

Her mind was torn apart, wanting desperately to find Brendan…and fearing what had become of him.

They moved closer, but as they walked, she caught the glint of mail armour from beneath a cloak. She frowned, for why would anyone hide his armour? Styr wore his openly, his weapons hanging from his belt. But when she turned away, the man was gone, hidden among the hundreds of others.

A merchant was selling loaves of barley, and Styr paid for one with a coin, handing it to her. Whether he recognised it or not, he seemed to be continually finding ways to give her food. It was nothing but a small gesture, and yet, her foolish heart warmed to it.

Caragh broke the loaf open, steam rising from the crust, and she handed him half. They ate in silence, before Ivar approached her from the opposite side. His face held no emotion, but he greeted her, saying, 'Will you walk with me a moment, Caragh?'

She glanced over at her brothers, but they were busy speaking to a merchant, asking about Brendan. Styr said nothing at all, but his eyes followed her as she agreed.

'What is it?'

Ivar led her towards a man selling lengths of delicate cloth. 'I am a man of great wealth,' he began. 'If you wanted anything at all in this market, I could buy it for you.'

His emphasis on wealth did nothing to impress her. Though she nodded that she'd heard him, he reached out and brought her hand to touch the silken fabric.

'Nor am I a man who will allow himself to

be used,' Ivar said. 'And I can see that you're using me to try and make Styr jealous.'

'He has no interest in me,' she responded, denying his claim.

'But you want him,' he contradicted. He threaded his fingers with hers, lifting her hand up. 'I saw you sleeping beside him. You think to pit us against one another.' His hand tightened, his gaze darkening. 'I won't play that game.'

She tried to pull back from his grasp, but he held her steady. 'Hardrata's men are my slaves now. Their lives belong to me.'

He let the threat hover, while his thumb caressed her skin. 'Stay here, in Áth Cliath, and I will grant them their freedom. Let us get to know one another.'

'I think I already know the sort of man you are,' she responded, jerking her hand away.

But Styr was already at her side. From the look on his face, he'd overheard every word.

'Leave her be, Nikolasson.' His words were quiet, but the edge beneath them was undeniable. 'I will pay you for the lives of my men.'

'With what?' he countered. 'The only silver coins you have were won from me.'

Styr said nothing, but as he guided her back

to her brothers, she felt the tension in the palm of his hand.

'What will you do?' she asked.

'Find a way.'

The voices of the crowd dropped lower, and her brother Ronan interrupted them. 'I need to speak with you.'

He led her towards the front of the crowd while Styr kept close behind them. 'Brendan is here somewhere. Two of the merchants confirmed that they saw him among the slaves.'

Relief and fear rose up within her. She wanted her brother to be safe...but how would they ever help him escape slavery?

A middle-aged woman sat at the front, before the crowd. Her hair was so fair, it was nearly white, and ice-blue eyes stared straight ahead. She wore a cloak made of animal skins and in her left hand, she held a staff with a bronze bird-shaped figure upon it.

'Who is that?' she whispered to her brother.

'It is the *volva*,' Styr said, his voice resonant within her ear. 'A prophetess who will answer questions from one she chooses.'

He brought her closer, and a chill crossed over Caragh's spine. The woman was watching her, and one of the men offered her a platter of food. Her stomach churned, when she

saw the platter contained the hearts of sacrificed animals. The prophetess dined upon
them, but as she ate, she never took her eyes
from Caragh. When she had finished, another
young girl began to chant an incantation.

Though Caragh could not understand the
words, the aura surrounding the crowd took
on an otherworldly quality. Someone began
to beat a drum, and the *volva* pointed to her.

'She has chosen you,' Styr said. 'You must
go to her.'

'I don't want to,' she whispered. Everything
about the prophetess unnerved her.

'She will answer your questions,' he said.
'It is an honour.' Without allowing her to refuse, Styr gave her a slight nudge forwards,
and the crowd parted.

Caragh's heartbeat quickened, but she moved
towards the woman. She tried to keep from
limping, though her feet were still sore from
her blisters.

As she neared the prophetess, it was as if
the woman could see through her. Caragh
waited, and the woman held out her hand.

'Ask,' she said, in the Irish tongue.

Several of the men around her began voicing their own wishes, and Styr translated their

demands to know if it was an opportune time to attack the Danes.

Caragh ignored them, her eyes fixated upon the prophetess. 'Is Elena alive?' she asked quietly.

The seer's gaze moved over to Styr, and she nodded.

'Where is she now?'

The woman closed her eyes a moment and spoke. 'A green stone rises from the sea.' When Caragh turned a questioning gaze towards Styr, his face was intent upon the prophetess.

'I know the place,' he admitted. 'We passed it on our way north.'

But even more important, he seemed to believe the woman. Caragh was uncertain, but there was impatience on Styr's face, as if he couldn't wait to find his ship and return.

Her grip upon her feelings was weakening, but if Styr's wife was still alive, there was no hope. Once he found Elena, she would never see Styr again.

Perhaps that was best.

The men were closing in impatiently, and Caragh realised the necessity of voicing a question on their behalf. Most were dressed for war, wearing chainmail corselets and steel helms with more chainmail that hung down the backs of their necks. Some carried double-edged swords, sheathed within a sealskin scabbard, while others preferred the battleaxe.

'Ask her about the Danes,' an Irishman demanded. 'Our ships are prepared for a fight.'

'Are the signs favourable?' Caragh asked, as the warrior stood beside her.

The prophetess shook her head. 'They are not.' She pointed to the sky, where a flock of ravens flew above them. 'Blood will be shed this day.'

'Aye,' the Irishman agreed. 'There will be sacrifices held this day. Blood, in return for the blood of our enemies.'

At the mention of sacrifice, Caragh's skin turned cold. Though she knew the ritual of animals dying, it was not something she wanted to witness.

The *volva* was staring at her, her piercing blue eyes intent. 'You have one other question, do you not?'

'My brother Brendan,' Caragh ventured. 'Where is he now?'

The seer pointed to a large wooden cage that men were bringing forth upon a wagon. Inside, Caragh saw a group of chained slaves, crowded together. They spoke in a blend of languages, of the Irish, the Picts, and those from Alba.

But she did not see her brother.

'What is happening?' she asked Styr, as the wagon stopped before a large pile of branches and peat. Men were pouring oil upon the firewood, while inside the cage, the prisoners continued to cry out.

'They are part of the sacrifice. They will be burned to the gods, to protect us from the Danes.'

Her hands began to tremble, the fear icing through her veins. *God above, no.*

For among those about to be sacrificed was her younger brother.

Chapter Ten

'Don't move,' Styr commanded, seizing Caragh before she could run towards the cage. Already her brothers had seen Brendan and had gone to plead with the council for his life.

But Caragh refused to yield, struggling against Styr's tight grasp. 'Let me go.'

'Your brothers will bring him back,' he said. 'Let them handle this.' He refused to let her anywhere near the sacrifice, and he used his height to block her view.

'He's so young,' she whispered. 'He can't die. Not like this.' Tears flooded her eyes, as if she couldn't stop the rush of emotion. 'You have to save him.'

He remained silent, weighing the possibilities over. The *volva* had predicted that Elena was alive, and the green stone she'd described was an island outcropping south of here, near the coast. Though he wasn't certain whether or not to believe the prophetess, she'd given him a possibility.

He risked a glance at the slaves, before meeting Caragh's pleading gaze. She laid her head upon his chest, closing her eyes. 'Please. For my sake, I beg of you—save his life.' Her hands dug into his tunic, her mouth tight with fear. 'I know you still hate him for what he did. But he is my brother.'

'Elena jumped into the sea because of him.' Styr made no effort to conceal his anger and frustration. The boy had brought harm upon his loved ones. He deserved nothing at all.

'She escaped,' Caragh argued. 'We don't know what happened that day. Brendan might have tried to help her.'

She reached up, her palms on either side of his face. 'He doesn't deserve a death like this one.' Her hands were cool against his cheeks, and her blue-violet eyes were wet with tears. 'If I mean anything to you at all…if we have become friends, I ask you to save him.'

Her plea for mercy slipped past his stony resolution for vengeance. His gaze lingered upon her mouth, remembering all that never should have happened.

'For me,' she whispered.

He didn't say anything at all, his mind turning over the quandary. A woman's desires shouldn't matter. But Caragh had suffered more than most women. She'd had no one to take care of her, and she'd been strong through the worst of circumstances. After all that she'd endured, he didn't want to see her look upon him with eyes of hatred.

Her brothers were arguing with the council, but he could see they were making little progress. Every minute that passed was a minute that brought Brendan closer to death.

He took Caragh's hand in his, leading her to stand before Ivar. The man's dark eyes assessed both of them, and clearly he'd overheard their conversation. 'Do you want me to intervene on her behalf?' he asked.

'I want you to guard her while I speak with them,' Styr corrected.

Ivar gave his vow, but before Styr could leave, Caragh threw herself into his arms. 'Thank you,' she wept, gripping his waist. 'I won't forget this.'

He stared back at her, knowing that it was

not at all a gesture of mercy. And he couldn't stop himself from caressing her hair.

The blinding smile she sent him was enough to stop his heart cold.

'Will they release my brother?' Caragh asked Ivar.

The Norseman's arm moved over her shoulders in protection, as he held her hand. 'It's unlikely. They require nine slaves for the sacrifice. I would offer one of mine in their place, except—'

'Except the newer slaves are Styr's men,' Caragh finished. She understood now, that Styr was not only negotiating for her brother; he was also fighting to save the lives of his own kin.

'I want to move closer,' she said to Ivar.

'It isn't safe. You should remain here, far away from the sacrifice.'

She pressed her hands upon his chest, pleading, 'This is my brother. Don't ask me to stand back and watch him die. If Styr cannot save him...'

'We will do what we can,' Ivar said, 'but it may be too late.'

Already, the first thrall had been set on fire, his screams agonising among the throng of people who silently watched. Prayers rose to her lips, for mercy.

'They will slit the throats of the others,' Ivar said. 'That slave attempted to run away, to avoid his fate. Those who agree to die as a sacrifice will have the death of honour. It will be quick, and this night, they will dine with the gods in Valhalla for their bravery.'

Panic caught up in her throat, as she saw the terror in Brendan's eyes when he was brought to stand beside the rest of the men. He'd made many foolish mistakes, but he didn't deserve to die for them.

A tear broke free as she saw the second slave die. Styr was speaking to the men, along with her brothers. She could not hear their words, but when she saw him strip away his armour, handing it to Ronan, her pulse quickened.

He wasn't planning to take Brendan's place, was he? Bile rose in her throat at the thought of Styr falling beneath the blade, or worse, his body turning black in the flames.

She closed her eyes against the image, wanting to believe it would not happen. He had a wife to save, along with his men. He wouldn't sacrifice himself, would he?

'Take me closer,' Caragh demanded. Before Ivar could protest, she faced him squarely. 'Unless you believe yourself incapable of protecting me?'

His gaze hardened. 'Of course you will be safe.'

Caragh took his hand in hers. 'Then bring me to where I may watch what is happening.'

Ivar clasped her palm and guided her through the throng of people. In the distance, she heard the hollow beating of a round drum. Styr was stripped down to his hose and nothing else. In one hand, he gripped a battleaxe, while in the other, he held a round shield with a metal boss. Across from him stood another Norseman.

'What is he doing?'

'He has offered to fight,' Ivar answered. 'If he defeats his opponent, that man will take his place as the sacrifice.'

'And if he loses?'

Ivar met her eyes with a steady resolution. 'You know the answer to this already, Caragh.'

She squeezed his hand, her heart beating so fast, she could hardly breathe.

'What is this man to you, Caragh?' Ivar asked. 'Does he have a prior claim?'

Inwardly, her mind was crying out with fear. No, there was no claim. She should feel nothing at all for this man. Especially when he was one she would never have. He loved his wife and honoured her. Every touch between them had been of her own doing.

But she found herself nodding. 'I do care for him.'

Ivar's hand came up to cup her chin. 'He is not worthy of you, *kjære*. You should have a man who worships you.'

'There is no man who feels that way for me.' At Ivar's piercing gaze, she predicted, 'Not even you.'

He lifted his shoulders in a shrug. 'Have you thought about my offer?' He reached out for her hand, holding her fingers gently. 'You hold the power to free his men.'

'I can only think of my brother now,' she answered honestly. But Ivar's suggestion made her aware that she would owe Styr a debt which could never be repaid. He was risking his life for a boy he despised.

From across the space, his eyes met hers for the barest flicker of a second. As if to remind her that this was not his choice. Not his battle to face.

He was doing this for her, because she'd asked it of him. And in his eyes, she saw the strength and determination to win.

In that moment, her heart was impossibly lost. She could no longer deny that she was in love with a man who could never belong to her. Tears heated her eyes, but she willed them not to fall. Instead, she drank in the sight of him, trying to remember every line of his face, every feature.

She gripped her hands together, willing herself to meet his last look.

'He is a fool, *kjære*, if he does not see the woman before him.' With a dark smile, Ivar bent down and brushed his lips against hers. 'You will soon learn, that I can give you far more than Hardrata ever could. Perhaps that might one day be enough to win a smile.'

She said nothing, turning all of her attention to the fight. In the morning sun, Styr's hard body revealed his battle skills. Upon his torso were carved the deep lines of muscle. Not only in his strong arms, but also in his abdomen.

He moved like a predator, attacking his opponent with a skill she'd never imagined. His long blond hair hung over his shoulders, and upon one upper arm, she saw the gleam of a golden armband.

The enemy Norseman slashed his blade towards Styr, and he blocked it with his shield, his battleaxe arcing towards the man's head.

Ronan and Terence stood by her brother Brendan, who was still chained. His dark hair was matted with blood, his bones showing against his pale skin. Before Caragh could take another step forwards, Ivar held her back. He kept one arm around her waist, the other just above her breasts. 'No closer,' he warned.

In his arms, she watched as Styr dived to the ground, narrowly avoiding the sword. The tip of the blade caught his arm, drawing blood. At the sight of it, the people began to shout, calling out for more blood.

A cry caught in her mouth, though she pushed it back. She couldn't understand what terrible Fate had led her to love this man. But the thought of Styr dying sent a phantom pain into her own body.

The drumbeat intensified, mirroring her heart. She couldn't take her eyes off him, and when his enemy let out a roar, plunging his sword, she gripped Ivar's arm, her nails digging into his skin.

Styr raised his shield, and his enemy's blade embedded within the wood. He ripped back the shield, disarming the man, and within seconds, his enemy lay upon the ground.

Her knees went weak, and when Ivar let her go, she couldn't stop herself from running. Not to her brother, who was already unchained and guarded by Ronan.

But to Styr.

Blood ran freely down one arm, and perspiration gleamed upon his skin. But Caragh ignored all of that and embraced him hard, not bothering to hide her tears.

'Thank you for saving him,' she whispered.

His arms came around her in a tight embrace, a shocking response. She'd expected him to push her away, or to turn cold. Instead, she rested her cheek against his chest, shutting out the world for a moment in his arms. She blocked out the sounds of death and sacrifice, finding sanctuary in him.

Let go, her mind commanded. *He is not yours.*

Dimly, she was aware of him taking her away, of her brother speaking. And of Ivar's silent reproach.

'Thank you,' she breathed. 'I don't know how I can ever repay you for what you've done for us.'

'Go with them,' he commanded, guiding her towards her brothers.

'What about you?'

He cleaned and sheathed his blade, saying nothing at all. In his brown eyes, Caragh saw the promise of farewell. She guarded her heart, refusing to beg for more than he could give. For she knew already that their paths would soon part.

Her gaze met Ivar's, and she knew that there was one way to settle the debt with Styr. With one nod, she gave the promise the Norseman wanted. She would offer herself, in return for Styr's men. And the gleam in Ivar's eyes revealed his satisfaction.

She tried once more to prolong this moment with Styr. 'What about your arm?'

He simply reached for his padded tunic and ignored the minor wound, lifting his chain-mail armour over it. 'Go,' he repeated.

With one last look at him, she obeyed.

It was late afternoon by the time Styr returned to Ivar's house. Though he'd located his ship, he lacked the men to take it back again. And he still had a score to settle with the Norseman.

As he walked past the rows of longhouses, a strange sense of danger descended upon him. Though he could see nothing out of the ordinary, he kept one hand upon his battleaxe. His eyes moved over each of the people, though he tried to dispel the suspicions.

He saw a woman wearing the Norse garb of his homeland, and a trace of homesickness caught him. Already he missed the snow-capped mountains and the dark blue fjords that spanned between them. He half-wondered if he would ever go home. And whether Elena would be with him.

He tried to envision his wife's face...but instead, he kept thinking of Caragh. She had thrown herself into his arms, repeating her gratitude to him. And like a fool, he'd held her.

Gods, but he was weak. Like a man starved for affection, he'd stood there and gripped her slight body against his own. It was wrong, in the very deepest sense. And were it not for his men and her brother Brendan, he would stay far away from the house of Ivar Nikolasson. Only temptation awaited him within the walls.

He needed to find Elena and mend his broken marriage. Perhaps the distance over the past sennight would make her fly into his embrace, the way Caragh had done.

But he couldn't imagine it. Elena was cool towards him, not at all affectionate. If he found her, she would be grateful. She might even smile. But he couldn't fool himself into thinking she would want his touch.

Styr let out a breath of air, and walked towards the door of Ivar's house. He entered and saw half a dozen of his men waiting. Though he'd promised to free them earlier, when Caragh's brother had been found, he'd been unable to keep that vow.

That would change today. 'Gather any of your belongings. We leave this night,' he said to Onund. Though he wasn't certain how he would coerce Ivar into agreeing to it, there had to be something he could do.

But Onund only bowed in agreement. 'We have been granted our freedom already. Because of her.' He nodded towards a table at the far end of the room.

Several female slaves were lined up before Caragh, holding lengths of silk and golden armbands. Gifts from Ivar, no doubt.

A tightness rose up in his chest at the sight of her. She wore a gown he'd never seen before, a deep green that rivalled the hills surrounding Hordafylke. The slaves had bound back her brown hair in braids, leaving some to fall across her shoulders. Upon her fingers, she wore silver rings and they had pierced her ears to wear more jewellery.

When she lifted her eyes to his, there was nothing but sadness within them. She knew, as he did, that soon enough he'd never lay eyes on her again. By wearing Ivar's offerings, she had given her unspoken agreement to the man's courtship.

Styr knew why his men were now freed and anger prickled his scalp, at the thought of the price she must have paid. Striding across the room, he came to stand before them. To Caragh, he spoke only one word. 'Why?'

'Because it's the only way I can repay you for saving Brendan.'

'By giving yourself to this man? What did you promise him? One night in your bed for each of them?'

She paled at the accusation, but stood tall before him. Ivar crossed the room, already reaching for Styr. 'I should cut out your tongue for speaking words such as those.'

Styr caught Ivar before he could strike, holding him back. Yet, the man held fast with a strength that rivalled his own.

'Stop,' Caragh said quietly. 'Ivar, let him go.'

'She's staying with me, Hardrata. But you won't stay the night under my roof.'

'I wouldn't want to.' But he released the

man and stepped back. Caragh lifted her
hands, stepping between them. To Ivar, she
said, 'I need a moment to speak with him
alone. Please.'

Though Nikolasson looked as if he'd rather
strangle him than let him have any time with
Caragh, he relented to her plea. As if to soothe
him, she added to Ivar, 'He is leaving with
my brothers.'

Caragh walked to the furthest end of the
longhouse, and with every step, the silver jin-
gled as if she wore bells. When they were
alone, she folded her hands before her. 'You
have your men now. And my brothers will accompany you on your search. Since you saved
Brendan's life, they owe you that debt.'

'Do they know about her?'

She shook her head. 'I should have told
them. But I'll leave that to you.' There was
uncertainty in her voice, as if she held a thousand regrets.

'Your brothers won't allow you to stay here
alone,' Styr insisted. 'And neither will I.'

Her face held regret, mingled with a sad acceptance. 'I've made my decision, Styr. And
right now, I know you want to find Elena and
go back to her.'

It wasn't the truth any more. Instead, he

was fully aware of the sacrifices Caragh was making for him. He drank in the sight of her, of the brown hair the colour of polished wood. And those blue-violet eyes looking upon him, as if she wanted so much more.

He didn't move, didn't breathe at all. Inwardly, he admitted the truth to himself—that he would miss Caragh. That he welcomed the warmth of her embrace and would savour the memory of each moment in her presence.

His thoughts were on unstable ground, and he knew better than to voice the words rising up.

'I'll miss you,' she admitted. Before he could answer, she fled his presence, returning to her brothers.

His gaze followed her, and he saw Brendan seated near Ronan and Terence. Seeing the young man was enough to remind him of his purpose. He needed to question Brendan, to understand what had happened on board the ship before they were taken by the Danes. He welcomed the familiar anger, needing it to push away thoughts of Caragh he didn't want to face.

The young man owed him restitution for putting Elena in danger. By Odin's bones, he would get the truth.

He crossed the room, shadowing Caragh until he came to stand before Brendan. As soon as the young man caught sight of him, all the blood drained from his face.

Styr seized him by the throat and shoved him against the wall. Beneath his breath, he growled, 'You have much to answer for.' He pressed against the young man's windpipe, making it clear how easy it would be to kill him.

Within seconds, Ronan and Terence were dragging him back, and Caragh stood between them. 'Styr, no,' she pleaded, as if he were a wild beast, poised to strike.

With all of his strength, Styr shoved back her brothers, unsheathing the blade at his waist and pressing it to Brendan's throat. 'You owe me the truth.'

'Please,' the young man beseeched him.

He lowered his voice to a whisper only Brendan could hear. 'Was this what you did to Elena?' he demanded, drawing blood. 'Did she beg you for mercy, the way you're begging me now?'

A hand touched his shoulder, and Caragh moved before him. 'Let him go, Styr. He will tell you everything he knows.'

When he released Brendan, the young

man's hands were shaking. He sank back down on the bench, struggling to draw breath.

Out of the corner of his eye, Styr spied movement, and he spun, dodging Terence's fist before it could clip him across the jaw. Before any of them could intervene, he cut them off. 'You will do nothing to hinder my questions. I could have let your brother die today.' He stared hard into Terence's eyes. 'He may be your blood, but he is to blame for the suffering of my people.'

'You may question him,' Ronan interrupted, coming to stand by his brother, 'but you cannot touch him. He's already hurt, and—'

'You will answer all of my questions,' Styr warned Brendan, 'and if I find that you have lied to me, you will suffer for every moment my kinsmen suffered.' The fury festered within him, along with frustration at what had happened because of this young man's decisions.

'Give me your weapons,' Terence ordered, 'before you question him.'

Styr handed over the battleaxe and the blade, but his mouth tightened into a line. 'I need no weapons to kill him.' He wanted Brendan to be afraid, to understand that he had to give every truth.

The young man gave a nod, sitting down once more, as if he didn't trust himself to stand.

Before he could voice his first question, Caragh interrupted with one of her own. 'Why did you leave Gall Tír with your friends?' she demanded. 'You knew there was no food. And yet, you left me behind.' Hurt and anger blended in her voice, as she came to sit beside her brother.

'My friends thought we should capture the *Lochlannach* and take them out to the open sea,' Brendan began. 'We thought it would keep the rest of you safe, if we lured them away.'

'How did you capture them?' Styr asked. 'There were a dozen men, all trained fighters.' He'd been unconscious and whatever memories that remained were blurred.

'I don't know,' Brendan admitted, shaking his head. 'They fought hard at first, and when I took the woman back towards the ship, one of them followed. I wasn't planning to harm her.'

It must have been Ragnar, Styr guessed. His friend would have done whatever was necessary to protect Elena. 'And the others?' he prompted.

'They fought against the Irish. But the man who followed me suddenly spoke a command to them. I didn't understand it, but they dropped their weapons and came towards the boat. My friends followed, because they knew I would die at their hands.'

Brendan shook his head in confusion. 'They wanted me to give up the woman, but I knew if I did, they would kill us all.' His face paled, and Styr's hands curled into fists.

'They—they became our prisoners,' he said. 'I don't know why. They didn't struggle when we bound them.'

Styr was starting to gain an understanding. Ragnar must have ordered the rest of the men to feign surrender, until they reached the open sea. It would have been easy for the men to regain control of the vessel, especially if the Irish believed them incapable of fighting.

'We were planning to let them all go, to slip out at night and swim to shore,' Brendan admitted. 'But when we reached the southern coast, we were attacked by another ship.'

Brendan's gaze turned to Styr, his voice faltering. 'I didn't want the woman to be taken by the Danes, so I cut her free. The other man jumped overboard with her, and the rest of us were taken captive.'

'Did they make it to shore?'

Brendan stared at him, confessing, 'I don't know.'

Styr stood without a word and took back his weapons from Terence. He strode from the interior and walked outside, his mind numb with what he'd learned. Though he knew where he wanted to search, he couldn't be certain if Elena was still there. Weariness pooled within him. He didn't want to leave Caragh here, but neither did he have the right to take her with him.

He stood outside, staring at the sights and sounds of the city, unsure of what to do now. From behind him, he sensed her standing there. Without turning around, he said, 'I'm not going to kill him.'

'Thank you.' There was an audible sigh, as if she were relieved to hear it.

Styr said nothing more about it. Brendan had made poor decisions, but he'd suffered, too. And if the worst had happened…if Elena was dead…killing the young man wouldn't bring her back. A heaviness weighed upon him, not knowing what had happened to any of them.

Caragh's eyes stared straight ahead, while the sunset cast golden streaks across the sky.

'I believe you'll find her. The prophetess said she was alive.'

'I hope so.' He wanted his wife to be safe and well; there was no question of it. But with every moment he'd spent with Caragh, the differences between them only magnified. Logically, he knew it was best for them to part, to never look upon her face again.

But when her hand slipped within his, he did nothing to push her away. He simply held her warm fingers, while he wished for a moment, that another life could be his.

'Why are you staying with Ivar?' he asked. 'You don't have to.'

'I know,' she murmured. 'But I wanted to do something for you. You need your men to help you.'

'And what of your needs?' He turned, forcing her to face him. Her violet eyes were troubled, her complexion pale. 'Do you intend to share his bed?'

She lowered her gaze. 'I don't know what will happen. He seems to care for me, though he can be proud and stubborn. Like someone else I know.' Her face softened into a sad smile.

A harsh ache clenched his gut at the thought of her lying in Ivar's arms. The vision burned him like a fiery brand. 'Don't stay with him, if you don't desire him.'

Her hand moved to touch his heart. 'What choice do I have, when I can never have the man I do desire?'

He froze, disbelieving what he'd heard. Caragh's face flushed, but she turned and went back inside, leaving him to stare at the darkening streets.

She desired him. And God help him, he wanted her, too, as dishonourable as it was.

But he could not forget Elena. After all she'd endured, he could never abandon her.

The last of the fading light slipped beneath the horizon, and a strange sense of awareness caught Styr without warning. There were lights in the distance and the flare of torches. Something was wrong.

Warning shouts resounded, and within moments, an acrid scent caught his nostrils.

Smoke.

The fires began to spread, from one house to another, and he threw the door open, ordering his men to arm themselves.

'They're setting fire to the houses!' he shouted to Ivar, and the men poured forth, prepared to defend themselves. In the midst of the panic, he saw the Danes openly attacking.

'Take Caragh to your ship,' Styr ordered Ronan and Terence. 'Get her out of here.'

'One of us can take her,' Ronan argued. 'You'll need help fighting against them.'

'I'll stay and fight,' Styr said. 'You need to take her to safety. If the Danes are in the city, their boats will be empty.'

Ronan saw the truth of his words and nodded. Terence shouted to Ivar, but the man had unsheathed his own sword and was charging forwards with the others.

'Get her out!' he echoed, and Styr caught only one last look at Caragh, before she disappeared into the night.

Chapter Eleven

Bodies littered the ground, but Ivar's house remained unscathed. Styr cleaned his sword and thankfully, none of his men had died in the fight.

Ivar had a wound upon his upper arm, but it would heal. 'Take your men and go after them,' he commanded.

At Styr's questioning look, he added, 'Caragh wants you and always has.' Nodding towards Onund and the others, he said, 'Your men helped defend my house. They may take their freedom, so long as you guard her.'

Ivar's mouth curved in a bitter smile. 'The only reason she offered to stay was for you. And unless you're an utter fool, you should claim the woman who loves you. Before the Danes do.'

'She doesn't—'

'Open your damned eyes, Hardrata. Because if you don't go after her, I will.'

Styr eyed the man, not certain what he was agreeing to. Even so, he didn't want Caragh here any more. It wasn't safe.

'You and I know the Danes,' Ivar continued. 'They will build their fires upon the bodies of their enemies. And her brothers aren't enough to guard her. Go,' he ordered.

Sheathing his sword, Styr ordered his kinsmen to follow him. They moved through the streets, cutting down any man who dared to attack.

As they moved along the edge of the River Liffey, Styr kept his battleaxe in hand, his eyes searching for a glimpse of Caragh. The deeper he moved into the city, the more he realised Ivar was right. The Danes had slaughtered the Norse and Irish alike, and the fighting hadn't stopped.

He moved with a purpose, needing to ensure that she was safe.

The sounds of Death surrounded them, mingled with fire and smoke.

Caragh kept her head down while her brothers pushed her through the crowd. She saw women cut down in the streets, the Danes slaughtering anyone who stood in their way.

Terence shoved her through a narrow passageway between houses, ordering, 'Don't look. Don't think. Just run.'

And she did. Her lungs burned, her sides aching as she followed them towards the harbour. But just when she spied the gleaming dark water, a hand snaked around her waist, dragging her back.

A cry escaped her, and Ronan swung hard at the man, his blade biting into a wooden shield. Terence tried to aid him, but within moments, they were surrounded by invaders. The dark-haired *Gallaibh* were fierce fighters, bearded men whose ruthless eyes revealed the desire to conquer.

Fear pulsed within her, while her brothers fought, back to back, against the insurmountable odds. She struggled against her captor, but although she had regained some of her strength, it wasn't nearly enough.

His foreign words made no sense to her, but when he shoved her against a wall and reached for her skirts, his intent became clear.

No. She refused to stand here without fighting. When he tried to pin her, she let her body go limp, and she hit the ground hard. Her fist seized a handful of dirt, and when he jerked her up, she threw it into his eyes.

He roared in fury, reaching for her. She ducked to avoid the strike of his fists, but a moment later, the man seized her, gripping his forearm across her throat.

'I should break your neck,' he said in Irish, and his breath smelled of ale. She tried to push against him, but he only tightened his grip, cutting off her air.

The world swam with blurred images, her hands fighting hard against the man who slowly strangled her. She couldn't see her brothers or anyone else, the fading consciousness sliding away.

She glimpsed the face of Death, as her lungs burned from lack of air. A part of her mourned the fact that she hadn't had the chance to talk with Styr to admit the feelings she'd held inside her.

And now she was going to die.

Styr embedded his battleaxe in the Dane's spine, catching Caragh before she could fall.

Thor's blood, she'd nearly died. Her skin was waxen, but thank the gods, she gasped for air. He lifted her in his arms, while his men aided Ronan and Terence in fighting the enemy.

All around them were the bodies of the fallen, but Styr kept his battleaxe in one hand, holding Caragh with the other arm. Her head slumped against his shoulder, but he continued towards the waiting boat. One man dared to attack, and he slashed his battleaxe, cutting the man down.

No one will harm her. The need to protect Caragh, to keep her safe, went deeper than his bones.

When he reached the boat, he brought her inside, awaiting her brothers and his men. Not once did he let her out of his arms, and at long last, her eyelids fluttered.

'Caragh,' he murmured. 'Are you all right?'

She coughed, and he held her, rubbing her back as she regained awareness.

'Where am I?'

'On board your brothers' ship,' he responded. 'We're waiting for them to join us.' Her arms came up around his neck, and when she embraced him, he gripped her hard.

'You came for me,' she whispered. 'I thought I was going to die.' She drew back, her dark blue eyes meeting his. 'And all I could think was that I never told you.' Her voice was soft, as if holding secrets.

'Never told me what?' But he knew before she said a word. Her heart lay in those eyes, and in her, he saw the offering.

A faltering smile crossed her face. 'I'm such a fool, Styr. You made me so angry at Ivar's house. He could have given me anything. And yet, I let myself fall in love with a man I can't have.' She touched his cheek, the sadness filling up her countenance. 'I'm sorry. But I needed you to know.'

He didn't know what to say. Her words should have provoked a sense of guilt. Instead, he saw her love for what it was—a gift.

'I know you will return to your wife,' she said. 'I know you love her and not me. But when I was about to die, I wished I had said it sooner.'

He lifted her hand to his mouth in a silent kiss. There were no words to tell her that he did care, far more than he should. When he'd watched the Dane trying to kill her, the raw fear had struck him down. He couldn't let it happen.

'You honour me,' was all he could say.

He kept her in his arms, not revealing his own troubled spirits. Her affection was a kindness he'd never expected, and for a moment, he let himself dream of what his life would have been, had he wed a woman like Caragh.

'Will you allow me a boon?' she said, when she caught sight of her brothers approaching.

He nodded his assent, not asking what it was. But when her hands moved to either side of his face, he guessed what she wanted. Violet eyes watched him with a longing that stole his breath away. And when she brought his face down to hers, he didn't stop himself from kissing her back.

She was a beautiful woman, loving and warm-hearted. Yet, he knew this was a kiss goodbye.

He wasn't prepared for the rush of heat that filled up the empty crevices of his heart. Her tongue touched his, and the kiss shifted from a farewell into a carnal response that staggered him.

Elena's kisses had been good, but none of them had made him feel such a visceral need. He didn't understand why Caragh's touch affected him in such a way, but he didn't stop it from happening. For it felt right to kiss her, to be with her.

'I'm sorry,' she whispered against his mouth, when she pulled away. 'But after what happened this day, I needed you. Just for a moment.'

He saw the looks on the faces of her brothers. They'd seen him kissing Caragh, and Terence's expression tightened with dissatisfaction. The rest of his men arrived on board the boat, and they, too, eyed him with suspicion.

Ronan gave the orders to pull up the anchor and untie the boat from its moorings. The men took their places at the oars and began to row, while in the distance, the fires burned through the city.

Styr continued rowing alongside the men, and Terence came to sit by him. 'We're taking you to your ship, *Lochlannach*. You'll take your men and go.'

And leave our sister alone, were the unspoken words.

Styr said nothing but only continued to row. Caragh borrowed a cloak from her brothers and was sitting at the side of the boat.

It wasn't long before he saw the outline of his vessel. The bronze weathervane marked it as his, and only a few of the Danes remained on board. Styr gave the order for his men to release arrows, and within moments, the ship was theirs again.

It had grown so dark, they needed torches to see clearly, but his men took their positions at the oars. Styr took the rudder and the Irishmen removed their ropes, releasing his ship.

'Thank you for looking after our sister,' Ronan said. 'But we'll take her home now.'

'Safe journey to you,' Styr bade them. He searched for a glimpse of Caragh, but in the darkness, he could no longer see the far side of the boat where she'd been sitting. It seemed she had already voiced her farewell, and he'd not see her again.

It was likely for the best. At the moment, he needed to get his ship out to the open sea where they could open the sails and gain speed. The night was clear, and the full moon was bright. It would take many hours to reach the place of the green island. If the moonlight illuminated the shore, it was possible that they could make camp at the site where Elena and Ragnar had disappeared.

Gods, but he was grateful to be back on board his own ship. His men began to row, using their strength to move the boat across the waves.

When Styr took his place at the side rudder, he spied a lone figure, huddled within a cloak.

And he knew.

Tearing off the cloak, he saw Caragh's dark hair. 'What do you think you're doing?' His mind spun with the realisation that her brothers would think he'd stolen her. He needed to take her back, and—

'Coming with you.' She stood aboard the ship and reached for one of the torches. Holding it, she stood across from her brothers' boat, lifting her hand to them. 'And now they know that this was my choice.'

'They'll come after you.'

She shook her head. 'No. I spoke with Brendan. He knew what I planned to do.'

'Why?' he demanded, taking the torch from her and returning it to the iron sconce. 'You have no place with us.'

'Don't I?' She regarded him steadily, taking a seat near the rudder. 'All my life, I've done what others told me to do. I obeyed my parents and my brothers. I stayed at home and did what I could to take care of Brendan. I've never done anything that *I* wanted to do. Not until now.'

She lowered her voice so that only he could hear her. 'You kissed me back.'

'Yes.' He offered no excuses for it, but there were none to give.

'I just wanted to stay with you, until the end,' she whispered.

And then, he understood. She needed to know if Elena was alive, to know whether or not he would return to his wife. But more, she wanted to know whether he felt any love for her at all.

His chest tightened, holding back the words of dishonour. Caragh's bright spirit and her fascination with new experiences and places made it easy to enjoy her presence. Around her, he could be himself. He didn't have to think about the way she wanted him to act or whether or not the moon was in the correct phase to have a child.

He could simply *be*.

'Stay,' he said. He refused to think of the implications, or worry about what the morning would bring if he found Elena. But the thought of finding his wife no longer brought a sense of relief or joy. It was an obligation he had to fulfil.

The thought of living with her, sensing her disappointment in his inability to give her a child...made him wary. He knew the truth of his marriage. It had reached the breaking point, and he didn't know what he wanted any more. Elena hadn't been happy in years.

But if he ended their union, she had another choice. She could find another man to marry, and perhaps have the baby she wanted. He didn't have to imprison her in a marriage filled with resentment and lost hopes.

He could set both of them free. All he had to do was speak the words of divorce in the presence of witnesses.

And Thor's blood, it tempted him. He closed his eyes for a moment, breathing in her scent. Wishing it was Caragh who belonged to him.

She took his hand, gazing up at the stars. 'It's beautiful, isn't it?'

He leaned in, his hand catching the hair at her nape. Without taking his eyes from her, he admitted, 'Yes.'

He didn't know how long they sat beside one another, but he held her hand in his, grateful for her presence.

The winds eased their travel, bringing them near to the green stone within a few hours. The fragment of rock rose up from the sea, coated in moss and grasses. The sight of it, reflected against the moonlit sea, tightened the nerves inside of Caragh. From the moment Styr saw it, he'd grown more distant, as if plagued by thoughts he wouldn't voice. The men drew the ship in as close as they dared, and Styr carried her to the shore, never minding that his clothes grew soaked in the sea.

They made camp, building a fire and eating the food his men had brought along with them. Though she knew she ought to be tired, a restlessness heightened within Caragh. And when they made camp, Styr set up her tent far away from the others.

Away from him.

She lay inside the shelter, darkness enveloping her. When she'd dared to come with Styr, she'd not imagined what it would do to her heart. It was a physical ache to be apart from him. Right now, she wanted to lie beside him, to feel the powerful warmth of his body against hers. She needed him in a way she didn't understand.

And when she crossed the camp of sleeping Norsemen, she entered Styr's tent, not knowing whether or not he would let her stay.

He jerked awake at the slight sound when she moved through the opening, and she said, 'It's me,' before he could draw a weapon.

Styr let out a sigh and she heard the sound of a blade slipping back within its sheath. 'Is something wrong?'

'I didn't want to be alone this night,' she admitted. 'I just wanted to sleep beside you. If you will allow it. I needed—'

You, she wanted to say. But she didn't finish the words, afraid he would turn her away.

For a time, she could hear only the sound of his breathing. She sensed an invisible tension, as if he were making a decision.

'I'll go, if that's what you want,' she whispered, frustrated with herself for even daring to ask.

But his hand caught hers, and he dragged her down upon him, seizing her mouth in a kiss. He wasn't wearing armour, and the touch of his hard, bare chest was dizzying. His skin was so warm, she found herself unable to stop from moving her hands over him, exploring his flesh. Every ridged muscle, the fine texture of his hair.

He stole her breath, and she felt as if she could touch him for ever.

'You shouldn't be here, Caragh,' he said.

'I know.' He was right. Even to be in his presence like this was so terribly wrong. 'I didn't come here for this,' she admitted. 'I just wanted to lie beside you for one last night.'

He drew her against him, her back nestled against his chest, his arms around her. But instead of lending comfort, her heart beat faster. Every part of her body craved more. And she couldn't understand it.

Against her hips, she felt the rise of his arousal and knew that he was not unaffected, either. It was a grim torture, for she wanted him in a way she shouldn't.

'I wed Elena when I was Brendan's age,' Styr began. 'Our parents arranged it.'

It was the first time she'd heard him openly speak of his marriage, and she reached for his hand, saying nothing.

'Elena was beautiful, and I knew the arrangement would bring together our tribes.' He released her hand, bringing both of his arms around her. 'She was a quiet woman but strong in her own way.'

'What do you mean?'

'She planned every moment of her day, from the time she rose to the time she fell asleep at night. She worked in our garden every morning, wove cloth or sewed in the afternoon, and cleaned our house every evening. Each day, exactly the same. There was never any change, but she didn't want it to be different. It was her own sort of control, her own power.'

His hand moved to hers. 'We were happy

for a time, but she wanted a child. I couldn't give that to her.'

Beneath his voice, she sensed his frustration.

'We tried for years,' he admitted. 'And never once did her belly grow round with my child. Elena believed the gods were punishing us for something we did. Or didn't do.'

Caragh turned to face him. 'It's not your fault,' she whispered. 'Some men and women are not blessed with children.'

'The first two years, we kept trying,' he said. 'During the full moon or during the crescent. At night and during the morning, until we couldn't bear the sight of each other.' His hand came to touch the side of her face. 'It was impossible to please her.'

'Why did you stay?' she ventured, not knowing how he would respond. A fragile hope burrowed within her heart, that perhaps there might be a chance for the two of them.

'Because I didn't want to give up. A warrior never surrenders in any battle. It's not my way.'

'And now?' Caragh asked, resting her hand upon his heart. His legs were tangled with hers, and although his body remained aroused, it didn't threaten her.

'I thought of sailing away, of giving her distance.' He covered her hand with his, before bringing it to rest at her waist. 'When I offered to leave, she said she would come with me.'

He expelled a breath. 'This, from the woman who never altered her day by a single moment.'

'She didn't want to give up on your marriage, either,' Caragh said, her throat closing up. She could understand that. If she were wedded to a man like Styr, she would follow him across the seas.

But hearing the truth from him only warned that there would be no happiness for them. Not if he and Elena wanted to stay together.

He said nothing, but only held her tighter against him. 'Every day I've spent with you is a betrayal of her.' The words were a blade twisted inside her, wounding her heart. Then he added, 'I won't forget a single moment of it, Caragh. Or you.'

His embrace only deepened the heartbreak. But leaving him now would only heighten the loneliness. Her eyes blurred, and she admitted, 'I shouldn't have come here.'

'Why?'

'Because it only makes me desire you

more.' She started to sit up, and he caught her wrist.

'I can't give you an answer,' he admitted. 'Not until I see her.'

'You're her husband. I understand that.' Though she tried to keep the pain from her words, they caught in her throat. 'You must go to her.'

'I have to see that she is provided for.' He kept his hold upon her wrist, drawing her back against him. His hands moved down her side in a caress. 'And if she wants to return to Hordafylke, I will arrange it.'

'Without you?' she ventured.

He turned her upon her back, his body above hers. 'What do you think?'

She couldn't breathe from the intensity of heat that rushed over her. Against the juncture of her thighs, she felt the hardened length of his shaft, and she couldn't stop herself from opening to him. Between her legs, she ached, and even her breasts were sensitive to the weight of him.

'She deserves to be happy,' he said. 'And perhaps it shouldn't be with me.'

Caragh shielded her heart from the wild hope that beat within her. Though she wanted desperately to believe that he might divorce his wife and stay with her, he'd made no promises.

'You deserve to be happy, too,' she whispered, reaching her arms around his torso.

He shook his head. 'The gods have cursed me. For I have no sons or daughters to carry on my blood.' He moved to his side, drawing his hand over her hip.

She recognised the warning. He was telling her that even if they did come together, there might never be a child. But she didn't want to believe it.

'You might…with me,' she whispered. She couldn't believe she had dared to speak of such a thing. Not when they had been so careful to avoid touching.

'Do you want to know what it would be like?' His whisper was a half-growl, and she wasn't sure what he meant by that.

'Yes,' she breathed, 'but it would be wrong.'

'I won't lay a hand upon you,' he said, his voice resonant within the darkness.

'But I don't—'

'You're going to touch yourself.'

Chapter Twelve

Never in his life had he wanted a woman this badly. Caragh's hands around him had awakened an arousal he couldn't deny, instead of lending comfort. He wanted to lay her back and taste her bare skin. Learning what pleased her body.

But then, she was a virgin. Asking her to be intimate in this way would likely embarrass her instead of bringing her pleasure.

'Or you could return to your tent.' He offered the escape, uncertain of whether she would seize it.

When he heard no movement from her, the air within the tent seemed to grow warmer. He went rigid at the thought of what was about to happen between them.

At first, he'd believed that she would run away. Instead, she'd met his challenge, leaving him with no choice but to continue.

'I want all the time that remains between us,' she murmured. 'Even if it's stolen.'

He moved to her, not touching her, but so close he could feel her breath against his cheek. 'If you stay, you obey my commands. Without question.'

She took his hand and laid it beneath her gown upon her heart. Beneath his fingers, he could feel the harsh beating of her fears and inhibitions. But he lifted his hand away.

'Remove all of your clothing,' he ordered. 'Lie down upon it.'

In the darkness of the tent, he could not see her. But he imagined the delicate skin, the soft curves of her breasts. Her nipples a pale pink, her slender waist flaring to hips he wanted to hold while he drove himself within her.

'I'm ready,' she whispered.

He heard the nerves in her voice, the uncertainty. But he would have traded every last piece of silver for this night. He would give rein to his desires, the forbidden dreams of her.

And, if the gods were willing, he would

free himself from Elena and one day make love to Caragh the way he wanted to.

He stripped away his own clothing, lying across from her. 'Do you feel the cool air upon your skin?'

'Yes.'

'I'm going to tell you where I would touch you now, if I could. You're going to touch yourself where I command it.'

Caragh said nothing, but her breathing remained unsteady.

'Place your hands upon your breasts,' he said. 'Stroke your nipples until they harden.' He moved beside her, gritting his teeth against the taut erection. It was torment, telling her all the places where he wanted to touch her.

Yet, he would not dishonour Elena by lying with another woman, much as he wanted to. His conscience warned that this act between them was nearly the same.

But his wife no longer wanted him. And Caragh did.

'It aches,' she confessed. 'I feel it all the way between my legs.'

'Don't stop,' he ordered. 'Use your fingers to roll the tips and imagine that I am the one touching you now.'

He heard her emit a shuddering gasp, her body arching against the pile of clothing.

'Lick your fingers and then touch your nipples,' he commanded. 'As if it's my mouth on top of them. Suckling each one, and imagine my tongue against the sweet tips.'

A moan broke forth from her, and he couldn't stop himself from curling his fist around his erection, squeezing the shaft and imagining that she was impaling herself upon him.

'Now move one hand downwards,' he ordered. 'Over your ribs and your belly. Down between your legs.'

'I—I'm wet,' she said, as if not understanding what was happening to her.

'It's your body preparing itself for lovemaking,' he said. 'Take one finger and slide it inside.'

She let out a low hiss, and he added, 'Keep touching one of your breasts while you slide it in and out.'

'Styr,' she pleaded. 'I can't. I need you.'

'No.' His voice came out in a low growl. 'You will not argue with me. Tonight, you are my prisoner. And you won't leave this tent until I hear you cry out in release.'

His words were nearly as erotic as the touch

of her own hands. Caragh had never imagined her body could be awakened like this. And though it was wicked, she wanted to know what it was to take a lover. He was guiding her, teaching her mysteries she'd never known.

She obeyed because she trusted him implicitly.

'Two fingers now,' he ordered. 'Stretch yourself and move your fingers in and out while you caress the other breast.'

She did, and the added pressure of touching her breast echoed the rhythm below. It should have shamed her to be openly touching herself, but she imagined that it was his hands upon her body. That it was his thick manhood invading her flesh, sinking against the wetness and withdrawing.

She was trembling now, her breathing quickened into short gasps. Something was happening to her, and she couldn't know what it was.

'Remove your fingers,' he ordered.

'I don't want to,' she murmured, revelling in the sensation that was so close, the trembling feelings rising up within.

'Obey me.' He reached for her wrist and removed it, guiding it until the heel of her hand rested upon her mons. With his fingers, he commanded hers, bringing her to a small fold of flesh above her entrance. 'Circle your finger over this,' he said. 'Keep stroking yourself until you start to tremble. And imagine that it's my tongue upon you.'

The words shattered her inhibitions, and she found herself experimenting with the pressure, learning how to touch and how to bring forth the deep arousal she'd conjured earlier.

'Do men do that?' she whispered, arching when her body responded with more warmth. 'Use their tongues upon a woman's—'

'Sometimes,' he said.

'And do women taste a man's flesh?' she enquired.

He was so quiet, she didn't know if she'd offended him. 'My wife never did,' he admitted at last.

'She never touched you?' The very idea seemed impossible. Even now, she wanted to explore his body with her hands, kissing him and finding out what brought him pleasure.

'I don't want to talk about Elena,' he countered. And he commanded her again to touch herself, to draw out the aching pleasure until she was starting to shake. The pressure was building inside, and she couldn't stop her hitched breath, nor the keening cries as she came closer and closer.

'Styr,' she begged, not knowing what it was she needed.

'Don't stop,' he commanded. 'Keep going.'

The needs were so strong, she instinctively quickened the pace, crying out as her body tightened with a wave of heat so intense, she was hovering on the brink of collapse.

But when Styr's warm mouth closed over one nipple, she lost control. The sensation of his tongue suckling her while her fingers moved upon her wetness was too much. She bucked her hips, gripping his head as a frenzied storm of shaking hot pleasure boiled through her body, making her so wet, she couldn't stop herself from plunging two fingers inside. The rhythm of release shattered her apart, and she reached for him, closing her hand over his silken erection. He was hot and moist as her thumb brushed the tip of him. It took only a few strokes of her hand before he let out a harsh breath and spilled his own seed.

He murmured words in his own language, words that sounded like a blend of an apology and a curse.

'Put on your gown and leave this tent. Now,' he commanded.

'Are you certain—?'

'If you don't go right now, I'm going to break every vow I ever made.'

With shaking hands, she pulled the gown over her nude body, her breasts sensitised against the fabric. Between her legs, she still longed for him, but she'd pushed him too far. For he'd nearly done what she'd wanted.

She left his tent, tiptoeing outside into the night. The coals of the fire glowed red, while flames licked the banked pile of wood.

His revelation, that Elena hadn't liked to touch him, had revealed a side to their marriage she didn't understand.

But more, he'd offered her a hope she'd never dared to imagine. He would see to it that Elena was safe. But afterwards…it might change.

He hadn't turned her away tonight, and he'd given her a pleasure she'd never dreamed of. The only way it could have been better would be if he'd been inside her.

The unexpected kiss upon her breast, the feeling of his tongue swirling over the nipple, had been such a shock, she could only imagine what it would be like to share his bed.

As she curled up within her own sleeping space, her body was so warm, she hardly needed a coverlet.

But fear and worry slid over her sense of honour. Styr had made her no promises. Everything depended upon Elena and what she would say.

Though Caragh wanted to believe that Styr would abandon the marriage and stay with her, she didn't know what would happen. He'd never spoken of his own feelings. If he held any at all.

Tears filled up her eyes, as she forced them to close. Tomorrow, their fates would be drawn together. Or irrevocably severed.

Styr awoke at dawn, surprised that he'd slept as late as he had. It was as if all the exhaustion of the past few weeks had caught up with him. Last night, he'd dreamed nothing at all, finding a peace.

But in the morning, he sensed the phantom fragrance of Caragh, as if she were still here.

He never should have bent his head to her breast, but he'd been unable to stop himself. She'd been so close, almost agonised in her need. And when his touch had brought her such a violent release, he'd revelled in it. If he could have spent the rest of the night watching her come apart, he would have savoured every moment.

Just the memory of last night brought him a physical ache, and he adjusted his erection within his hose, donning a padded tunic and chainmail to hide what he could. He crossed the sleeping camp, staring at the hills and wondering if he would find Elena this day.

When he reached Caragh's tent, he opened the flap and ducked inside. She was still asleep, her hand half-open as if waiting for him to hold it. Instead, he reached into his pouch and withdrew the ivory comb. He laid it in Caragh's palm, and the moment he did, she awakened.

Her face flushed, as if in memory of last night. When her hand curled over the comb, she asked, 'What is this?'

'A gift for you.'

She turned it over, examining the ivory. 'It has a woman's face upon it.'

'The goddess Freya,' he explained.

Her violet eyes met his, a sadness descending over her mood. 'This was meant for *her*, wasn't it?'

He made no denial. 'I want you to have it.'

She sat up, and her gown slipped, baring one shoulder to him. At the sight of her skin, desire welled up once again. But the look on her face spoke of a woman who held regrets.

'I don't want a gift to remember you by,' she admitted. 'I'd rather have you.' With her knees drawn beneath her, she looked like an innocent girl. 'You're going to find her today, I know it.'

He nodded. 'I need to talk with her.'

'I want to believe that we can be together,' she said. 'That I can love you.'

Her words held an emotion he'd never guessed, and he moved closer, needing to touch her. But she shied away, turning her face. 'I'm afraid, Styr. You've been with her for so long. When you see her again—'

He cut her off, embracing her. 'Don't.' At this moment, he couldn't say what would happen. But he let his actions speak for him, drawing her against him. 'Wait for me here while we search. And when I return to you, we'll go back to Gall Tír. We'll start over.' He took the comb from her and drew it through her long brown hair. The ivory contrasted against the dark strands, and when he glimpsed the carving of Freya, he believed there was a reason why he'd never conceived a child with Elena. It was never destined to be.

Caragh took the comb from his hand and

returned it to him. 'Give her the comb, the way you intended to. And don't return to me until you are free.'

The solemnity on her face proclaimed her resolve. 'My men will guard you.'

But Caragh shook her head. 'No. My brothers are waiting for me. I'll return home with them.'

Styr frowned, for he'd not bothered to look out from the shore. He left her tent, shielding his eyes against the sun. Just as she'd predicted, a small fishing boat lay anchored a short distance away.

'I knew they wouldn't let me go,' she admitted from behind him. 'My brothers are too protective. And I suppose they were right to come. It's probably best that I don't meet your wife.' She drew a *brat* over her head and shoulders, wrapping the wool around her against the chill.

He hadn't thought of it, but likely it would be terrible if Elena and Caragh shared the same vessel for travelling. Better if he gave command of his ship to Ragnar and let him take Elena and his men home again. Or anywhere else they wanted to travel. Then he could return with Caragh and her brothers.

'I'm going to begin searching for them,' he said. 'Stay here, and don't leave until I return.'

She nodded, and at the sight of her worry, he bent and kissed her cheek. 'It will be all right. I promise you.'

But as he took his leave of her, a sense of dread filled him at the thought of what he must say to Elena.

'Let go of me,' Caragh demanded.

Onund had gripped her by the arm, holding her fast. 'You are commanded to stay here until he returns. You may not follow them.' His expression was like granite, his bearded face shielding any trace of sympathy.

His imperious attitude darkened her mood, and she tried to pry his hand away. 'I won't interfere. They won't even know I'm there.' She craned her neck to meet his eyes, hoping he would understand. 'I just want to see them together.'

If she could see the look in Styr's eyes when he saw his wife for the first time, she would have the answer she needed. She would know.

Onund loosened his grip upon her. He stared at her as if trying to discern her purpose. 'I saw him watching you. And I saw him go to your tent this morn.'

She shielded her feelings from him. 'He did nothing to dishonour his marriage.' Though she wondered if that were true. In the end, he'd hungered for her, and she'd writhed at the touch of his mouth upon her bare breast. Even now, the memory sent a ripple of desire through her.

'Their marriage is a shadow,' Onund admitted. His expression narrowed upon her, as if trying to read her thoughts. 'It was duty that kept him at Elena's side. He should have put her aside long ago, choosing another woman to give him sons.'

His answer startled Caragh, for she'd not known that the others were aware of their marital difficulties. Nor had she realised the emphasis the *Lochlannach* placed upon bearing children.

'Whatever choice he makes, I want him to be happy,' she told Onund.

The man folded his arms across his chest, and Caragh doubted if he would allow her to take a single step inland. 'Styr needs sons,' he repeated. Taking her hand, he led her through the sand towards the hills.

As they approached the top, he added, 'You will remain hidden.' Onund reminded her, 'You cannot reveal yourself. No matter what you see.'

'I won't,' she swore. Grateful for his assistance, she walked alongside him. Styr had gone with a handful of men earlier, tracking the path of Ragnar and Elena. There was no way of knowing how far they'd gone or whether they would find them.

But with every footstep closer, her dread heightened. Within her bones, she sensed that Styr would never leave Elena behind.

Onund led her through the meadows, towards a river that wound through the land. Traces of smoke from a fire revealed the presence of a campsite.

'Stay back,' Onund warned. There was a small copse of trees, hardly more than a dozen, nearby. He guided her there, and when they reached the edge, he warned, 'Not a word. You don't reveal us, or Styr will have my head for it.'

She nodded, crouching low. Her stomach burned when she saw Styr speaking to another man who she supposed was Ragnar. Their features were similar, though Ragnar's hair was a darker gold blended with brown, and he was shorter.

There was a tension between them, though

she didn't know what they had said to one another. Styr was eyeing his kinsman with suspicion, his arms crossed in front of his chest.

Then, a moment later, the woman emerged from within a crude shelter. Her face softened with relief at the sight of Styr, and she looked as if she wanted to embrace him.

The ugly claws of jealousy sank into Caragh, though she knew Styr was bound to Elena and had shared her bed. The image of the two of them together made her lungs constrict, and she gripped her skirts at the thought.

'Do you want to go?' Onund whispered, seeming to read her thoughts.

Caragh didn't move. She was waiting to see if Styr would deny Elena, if he would tell her the truth of what had happened between them. Instead, she saw the woman offer a tentative smile, her hands moving to rest upon her womb.

Then the shock of disbelief upon his face.

And she *knew*. Without a single word from either of them, she knew that after so many years of trying for a child, it had come to pass. Styr would never leave his wife and unborn child. Not for a woman he'd known in so short a space of time.

The pain was a physical blow, drowning her. Caragh took a breath and nodded to Onund. She didn't want to hear any words or excuses. Right now, she wanted her brothers to bring her home. Somewhere she wouldn't have to see Styr or his wife again.

She'd been a fool to let herself be caught up in the dreams of a life with him. Last night, she had gone to him, and he'd warned her to leave.

She should have gone.

Caragh hurried through the field, not caring if anyone saw her or not. Onund kept up with her pace, and when she reached the shore, her lungs were burning, every part of her grieving.

'Will you help me go to my brothers?' she pleaded. 'Their ship isn't far.'

'My orders were to keep you here.' But the man's face held sympathy, for he knew the humiliation inside her.

'Don't make me stay.' The tears burned against her cheeks, and she picked up her skirts, prepared to swim if she had to. 'I already know the choice he's made. And it isn't me.'

'It's possible you could be his concubine,'

Onund countered. 'If you conceive a son, he might put her aside.'

Caragh wiped the tears from her face. 'That isn't the life I want.'

Footsteps drew closer, and she saw Styr standing at the rise of the hill. His eyes locked with hers, and she saw the regret in them.

Caragh hurried to the furthest edge of the shore, raising her hand to wave at her brothers. Surely one of them might see her and they would bring the boat in closer. The desperate need to leave superseded all else.

But Styr was already overtaking her.

'Caragh,' he began. She didn't turn around, trying not to reveal the desolation on her face.

'She's carrying your child, isn't she?'

'Yes.' There was no joy in his voice, only a grim resignation. 'It happened before we left for Éire. I knew nothing of it.'

'It doesn't matter when it happened. You have to stay with her now.'

His silence was the answer she feared. When he came forwards, his hands rested upon her shoulders. 'I am a cursed man. I should be overjoyed at this blessing. And yet, it is another set of chains.'

She turned around, and he didn't hesitate

to pull her into an embrace. 'I can't turn my back on them.'

'I know.' It should have consoled her to know that he, too, was unhappy about it. But there was no means of changing it. Their child had been conceived before they'd set sail. She had no right to ask him to leave Elena, and she would not do it.

Her brothers' boat was drawing closer, and Styr cupped her cheek, wiping a tear away. 'I can't say the words I want to say.'

'Go back to her,' she bade him. 'Not once did you dishonour her.'

'I dishonoured her a thousand times in my mind,' he said. 'And the gods have punished me for it.'

He held her again, so tightly, she felt as though he wanted to absorb her into him. 'May your child be born well and whole,' she whispered. 'A fighter, like his father.'

She stepped out of his embrace, walking towards the boat that drifted closer. And she refused to look back.

Chapter Thirteen

That night, Elena held his hand as they walked along the shore. 'I've seen the woman before,' she said quietly. Though her tone remained even, he knew she'd seen them embracing.

'Caragh Ó Brannon,' he admitted. 'Brendan was her younger brother.'

'She took you as her captive, didn't she?'

He nodded, hardly caring what Elena suspected. Right now, he was haunted by the look in Caragh's eyes when she'd learned of the baby. It infuriated him that he had come to resent this child. It wasn't right and it wasn't fair.

'Do you…have feelings for her?' His wife's voice was heavy, filled with accusation. And what could he say? That he'd fallen beneath Caragh's spell until he could think of no woman but her? That he didn't want to remain here any longer, and it was killing him not to go after her?

'Why would you ask me something like that?' He avoided Elena's question, adding, 'I only knew her for a week.'

'I have eyes, Styr. I saw you with her.'

'She left with her brothers. I told her farewell.' He shrugged it off as if it were nothing. As if the gnawing hole inside him didn't exist.

'You were embracing her.'

He spun, confronting Elena. 'Nothing happened between us.' *Liar*, his conscience retorted. He'd betrayed her in countless ways, worst of all last night.

His temper threatened to flare up, but he suppressed it. Hadn't he stayed? Countless other men would have taken Caragh as a concubine, but he'd remained loyal to his wife.

'Then why are you so angry?' she shot back. Her eyes pierced through him, discerning the truth. 'If she were nothing to you, you wouldn't be acting this way.'

The familiar coolness slid over her expression as she collected herself. Styr had no response, for anything he said would reveal his frustration. Instead, he redirected the conversation. 'I heard from Onund that you jumped from the ship to escape.'

She inclined her head. 'We were attacked by the Danes and there was only one chance to escape. Ragnar helped me reach the shore.'

'Both of you could have died,' he said.

'I wasn't about to let myself be sold into slavery.' Her green eyes welled up, and she admitted, 'This might be the only baby I'll ever have.'

He sobered, letting out a slow breath. For a long time, he didn't speak but stared out at Caragh's boat disappearing in the mist. Guilt filled him up, and he deserved the aching loss of her. Finally, he spoke. 'Do you know how long I searched for you? I thought you had died.'

Elena stood behind him so he could not see her face. 'I didn't think they would let you live, either.' She moved closer, standing by his side. 'But I'm glad you returned.'

The awkwardness stretched between them, and he didn't know what to say. He turned to walk back to the beach, letting her follow.

'How long have you been here?'

'Several days. The Danes wounded Ragnar, but he kept me safe.' A flush came over her cheeks at the mention of the man. 'We found food and built this shelter.'

A memory flashed through Styr, of Caragh's struggle to survive. She'd nearly starved without her brothers to help her, and he wondered if there were enough supplies to see them through to the harvest. He hadn't forgotten her unbridled joy when he'd helped her find fish. Or the way she'd embraced him in her happiness.

It occurred to Styr that he hadn't greeted his wife properly. Not once had he welcomed her with an embrace, when he owed her that. He turned, intending to take her in his arms, but when he reached towards Elena, she instinctively backed away.

'What are you—?' Then she seemed to realise his intent and apologised. 'You caught me unawares.' She leaned in, offering a slight hug. Then she stood on tiptoe and kissed his cheek. But the gesture rang false, as if she'd felt obligated.

To change the subject, he asked, 'How are you feeling?'

'The same,' she admitted. 'I wouldn't have known about the baby, if it weren't for the fact that I haven't bled in two moons.' She reached down to touch her slim stomach. 'It seems so strange to think of a child growing inside me.'

As she continued to talk about her pregnancy, his thoughts grew distant, his mood sombre. He wouldn't abandon Elena now, not while she needed him. Perhaps when the child was born, it might mend their broken marriage, making it easier to care for her again.

But as he walked back with Elena, he couldn't help but wish it was Caragh who was pregnant with his child.

Three weeks later

Elena wasn't a fool. She knew her husband had feelings for the Irishwoman. Oh, he'd been polite and respectful, seeing to her needs and comforts. But he might as well be gone. At night, he lay beside her, but he never tried to touch her. He kept a slight distance between them, and the longer it went on, the lonelier it was.

At least she had the baby to console her. A third month had passed with no bleeding, and she was positive that there must be a child. But it bothered her that her body remained slender, her breasts the same size. Shouldn't she be changing more than this? Instead, she felt nothing at all.

They had settled just south of Dubh Linn, near some friends of her mother's, but the threat of the Danes lingered. Elena had never felt quite safe here, and she was grateful for Ragnar's presence when Styr was away. At least he listened to her and didn't utter one-word responses.

This morning, Styr had gone to the marketplace, leaving her behind. She had cleaned every inch of their house, sweeping it four times. The table and chair were tidy, and she had begun digging a garden, ensuring that each row was perfectly straight, one hand-width apart.

But despite her efforts to maintain order, she could do nothing to change her husband's mood. She had no doubt at all that he'd fallen in love with the Ó Brannon woman, from the way he was pining for her. And though he swore he'd never touched her, that her accusations were unfounded, Elena might as well have been married to a stone.

She'd prepared Styr's favourite foods, arranged for his armour to be cleaned, and had done everything to make his life comfortable. But he hardly noticed any of it.

Ragnar was busy working upon his own house, and she hoped to speak with him. She knew very little about what men wanted from a wife. Perhaps he could help.

But the longer she stood near him, the more he continued wielding a hammer, pounding the beams into place.

'May I join you?' she asked, coming to sit near him.

He said nothing, but from the way he continued hammering, she could tell that his mood was even worse than Styr's. She came forwards to offer him a drink of water, but he tossed the hammer to the ground, pushing the drink away.

'Stay away from me, Elena.'

She was so taken aback by his anger, she didn't know what to say. Before she could leave, he wiped his brow upon his sleeve and apologised. 'I'm in no mood to see anyone just now.'

'I came to ask for your help. But if it's not a good time, I'll go.' She didn't understand what was bothering him, but she knew better than to press him. He rested his palms upon the wall for a moment, taking time to calm his temper. When he faced her, she grew nervous, seeing the dark look in his eyes. Perhaps it wasn't wise to ask advice from him.

Ragnar let out a breath and walked to stand before her. 'What is it?'

'It's Styr,' she admitted. 'Ever since he came back, I don't know what I can do to please him.'

A tightness invaded Ragnar's expression. 'We are *not* having this conversation.'

She flushed. 'No, I didn't mean…that. We haven't—not since the baby.' By the goddess, why was she even talking about it? But the words spilled forth as if they were waves, crashing forth against her will.

'He won't even talk to me. He's so distant, I don't know what to do.'

'Why do you stay married to him?' Ragnar demanded. 'If you have no feelings for one another and you don't talk, what reason is there?'

'He's been good to me,' she said. 'And there's the baby.'

'You're not pregnant, Elena.'

Her hands moved to her womb, and she stood up. 'Yes, I am. It's been months now. I must be.'

'I've had sisters who have had children. If you were truly with child, you would be much bigger by now.' He stood and returned to his hammer. 'Go and speak with the midwife. She'll tell you.'

A bleakness spread over her at the thought. Her eyes filled up with tears, and she hugged her waist. 'If there's no baby—'

'Then you have no reason to remain wed to him. Let him go, Elena. You'll be happier for it.'

She got up to leave, feeling as if someone had cut her in half. Her eyes burned as she made her way to the door, before a hand pulled her back.

'Come here,' Ragnar commanded, drawing her into an embrace. His arms came around her, pulling her face against his. The kindness broke her apart, and she let the tears fall. Throughout the worst nightmare of her life, he'd been there, never faltering in his friendship.

'I've already lost him, haven't I?' she wept.

'You haven't lost me.' His hand smoothed her shoulders, and she clung to him.

Elena was grateful for his presence, but the idea of divorcing Styr seemed wrong. She wasn't ready to give up on their marriage. Not so soon.

When he returned to his house that night, Styr found Elena huddled in their bed. He couldn't tell if she was asleep or whether she wasn't feeling well, but it was early yet.

But when he moved closer to see her, her eyes were rimmed with red, and she'd been weeping for some time now.

'What is it?' he asked.

She shook her head, drawing back the coverlet. 'The baby.'

Fear shot through him, that she'd miscarried the child. But when she moved to sit up, her posture slumped over. 'I was wrong,' she said dully. 'There never was a baby. I began bleeding today.' A sob broke from her, and she continued, 'The midwife said…sometimes a woman doesn't have her moon time, if she faces peril or times of fear.'

There were no words to console her, but Styr drew her into an embrace. To his surprise, the loss of the child hurt more than he'd thought it would. Elena wept against him, clinging hard as she admitted, 'I wanted this so much.'

'I know.'

'And I haven't been a good wife to you. Not the way I should have.' She drew back, gesturing towards the house. 'I tried to keep everything orderly. But it wasn't enough.'

'I never cared about the house.' He kept her

in his arms, understanding that her tears were about more than the baby.

'You wanted to travel across the seas,' she said at last, leaning her head against his heart. 'And I never let you go.'

'I knew you didn't want to travel with me. And if I was away, you couldn't conceive a child.' He shrugged it off, for it didn't matter.

'That was your dream, not mine,' she admitted. 'I should have given you my blessing, but I was too afraid to be alone.' She reached up to touch his cheek, and offered, 'I still love you, Styr.'

Her words hollowed out another piece of him. After all these years, she deserved the words in return. But before he could say them, she covered his lips with her hand.

'Don't say it. I've known you too long, and that isn't what you feel for me. Not any more.' Another tear broke free and rolled down her cheek. She smiled through her tears, adding, 'We had some good years together.'

'We did.' He smoothed back her hair, a harshness rising in his throat. 'And we'll have more.' It was a hollow promise, but the best he could do. It was strange to be grieving the loss of a child who had never been conceived.

But perhaps he was grieving the loss of what there had once been between them.

Elena captured his hand and stood up from the bed. In her eyes, he saw the heartbreak. And amid the pain, there was a glimpse of the woman he'd cared about.

'Will you walk with me?' she asked. There was hesitancy in her voice, as if she were suddenly nervous. He nodded, still holding her hand.

The gown she'd worn was fitted to her slender form, and a dark blue apron hung over it, pinned at the shoulders. Her reddish-blonde hair was braided, with several strands hanging loose around her face.

He opened the door for her, and though it was past evening, it was not dark. She kept her hand in his, leading him towards Ragnar's house.

'He'll finish it in another few days,' Styr predicted. His friend had built the house and several of their kinsmen lived with him. It surprised him that Elena would lead him here, to a house filled with men. Her despondent mood made it more likely that she would want to be alone to weep.

When they entered, the men were seated at a long table, a feast of meat and ale spread before them. Styr greeted Onund, Ragnar, and the others, but Elena caught their attention, raising her hands.

'There is something I would ask of you,' she began. The men turned to listen, and Styr had no idea what her intention was.

'I ask you to bear as witnesses.' Her sea-green eyes locked on to his, and she faced him. 'I have been wedded to Styr for five years now. In that time, I have been barren, and it is unfair of me to bind him in this marriage.'

She let go of his hand, and shock roared through him when she pronounced, 'I divorce you, Styr Hardrata. In the presence of these witnesses.' Three times she repeated the declaration, leaving him stunned.

He wasn't the only one. The other men were as startled as he, and none of them knew how to react. She'd not told him anything of her intentions, giving him no means of arguing.

Without another word, she left the longhouse, returning to the house they had once shared.

Styr followed her, hurrying until he'd caught up. 'You think to divorce me? Just like that, with no word of explanation?' He was furious with her and embarrassed that she'd done it before so many witnesses, leaving no doubt of her intentions. 'Why? I thought you wanted to try again!'

She held the door open and waited for him to enter. He slammed it behind him, and she sat calmly upon a footstool.

'We don't belong together, Styr. We never did, and the gods refused to give us children.'

'Did I make you that miserable?' he shot back.

'Yes!' She stood up again, facing him down. 'And don't tell me I didn't do the same to you.' Her hands were trembling, but her green eyes were furious. 'You tried. Both of us tried, but you were never happy. It doesn't have to be this way.'

She turned away, admitting, 'I saw the way you looked at her, Styr. I saw the way she held you. She loves you. And you love her, the way you never loved me.'

He couldn't bring himself to deny it. But the anguish in Elena's face was echoed by regret in his own heart. Without a word, he touched her shoulders, embracing her from behind.

'I want you to go to her,' she continued. 'Marry her if she's the one you want. And perhaps you'll have the sons I could never give you.'

He couldn't imagine what courage it took

to give her blessing, after what she'd endured. 'What about you?'

Elena moved in his arms to face him. 'I'll stay here, for now. I don't know where I'll go after that.' She shook her head, and he dried her tears.

Leading her towards the bed, he bade her sit down. Instead, she chose the floor, leaning back against the raised straw pallet. He came and sat beside her.

'I'm sorry I wasn't the husband you needed,' he admitted at last.

'It wasn't terrible,' she said. 'There were some good moments.'

'Is this truly what you want?' he questioned. 'A divorce?'

'I've already done it, Styr.' She managed a smile through her tears. 'I don't need your permission to declare it before witnesses.' Leaning her head against his shoulders, they sat for a few moments, and he understood how difficult it was for her to let go of their years together.

Then he remembered the gift he'd brought for her. He stood and retrieved the ivory comb from his belongings. 'I bought this for you, before we left Hordafylke.'

She studied it, noting the image of Freya.

'It's beautiful.' She ran it through the strands of her hair, trying it out. Then she held it in her hands, sharing the memory of the day they were wed and of how afraid she'd been.

During the next few hours, they reminisced over the years of their marriage, laying each one to rest. They talked long into the night, until her voice grew hoarse, and his eyelids grew heavy.

And when he awoke in the morning, Elena was gone.

Chapter Fourteen

Caragh walked through the neat rows of barley, pulling a few stray weeds. Her brothers had gone out fishing, and she'd busied herself with inspecting the harvest. It would not ripen for another few months, but at least they had the promise of more grain to sustain them. The tribe had planted more, after the seeds Terence and Ronan had brought back from their travels. She hoped that the sun and rain would be kind to them this season, allowing them to restore their losses.

Despite the countless hours she'd spent working, it did nothing to diminish the heartache. She'd let herself love Styr, and it burned to know that once again, the man she'd cared about had chosen someone else.

She strode through the fields, hastening her pace. It wouldn't do to dwell on it any more. She'd known from the beginning that he was not free to be with her. As she crossed through the open meadow, she shielded her eyes to the morning sun. There was her brothers' boat, moving out to sea. And to the east…another ship.

She frowned, not recognising it at first. Was it the fishermen returning to Gall Tír?

But when she saw the striped sail, her stomach plummeted. The *Lochlannach* had returned. For what purpose? Were they invaders or was it Styr's ship? Neither was particularly welcome.

She hurried down to the shore, grasping her skirts. Some of the elderly Ó Brannons were busy scraping hides while others prepared meat for drying. Caragh went out as far as she dared, peering hard at the water. And when she saw the bronze weathervane of Styr's ship, her tension didn't diminish.

Why had he come? Was he wanting to settle here with his wife and later, their children? The thought of seeing him each day with Elena filled her with a crushing pain. A part of her wanted to flee, to hide where he wouldn't find her. But then, she wasn't a coward. She might not know why he had returned, but she would stand here and face him.

She sat upon a large stone on the water's edge, waiting. His ship drew closer, until at last, she saw him tying up the sail, steering closer to land.

He was still as handsome as she remembered, his dark gold hair tied back. The weather had grown warmer, and he wore no armour this time.

And then he saw her waiting. His stare locked with hers, as if remembering the night they'd shared together.

Caragh studied the boat but saw that he had come with only two men. Elena was not with them.

If she could have shielded her heart with stone, she would have. Styr had left her behind, choosing the woman he'd married and their unborn child. There was nothing that would change that.

He strode through the water, moving towards her. The waves sloshed around his thighs, but he ignored the frigid water. 'We need to talk,' he said.

'I have nothing to say to you. Or to your wife.' She stood from the stone, ignoring him.

'Elena is not my wife any more,' he called

out to her back. Her face flooded with colour, but she continued walking away. Whether it was true or a lie, a storm of confusion muddled her thoughts. When she reached the grassy hillside, she stopped walking but didn't look back at him.

Was he expecting her to fall into his arms, to somehow rejoice that she was his second choice? Had something happened to Elena or their unborn child?

Anger and sorrow choked her, but Caragh got no further before he caught up with her, catching her in his arms. 'As I said, we need to talk.'

'Put me down,' she demanded, trying to push her way out of his arms. When he only tightened his grip, she relented. 'All right, I'll talk with you. But not here.'

Not where others could see her being carried off by a *Lochlannach*. Styr didn't appear to trust her promise, for he didn't let her down at all. 'It's been too many weeks, *søtnos*.' He embraced her, as if he wanted to meld her skin into his.

In passing, he nodded to his men who had begun unloading their ship, carrying her past the ringfort and towards the open meadow.

'Styr, please,' she said. 'I can walk.'

'I don't want you to run away,' was his response. 'You've a right to be angry, but we'll talk in private.'

'What about your child?' she asked. 'If you're no longer married to Elena—' Her words broke off as she realised what had likely happened. Even to mention it was cruel.

'There never was a child,' he admitted. 'She believed there was, but it was a mistake.'

In his voice, she heard a trace of regret, almost as if he wished the child had come to be. 'Please, let me down,' Caragh repeated.

He did, but he didn't release her wrists. His grip was firm enough to remind her that he wasn't going to let go.

'What do you want from me?' she asked quietly. 'Why did you come back?'

He took her face between his hands and kissed her hard. His hands tangled in her long hair, pulling her to him as he coaxed her mouth. The familiar rush poured through her with awakening desire. And though she accepted his kiss, she didn't return it.

'You're angry,' he murmured against her mouth.

'You can't believe that I'll let you come from another woman's bed into mine.' She turned her face from him, hiding the hurt within.

'I never lay with her. Nor did I touch her.'

Caragh shook her head. 'It's too soon, Styr.' To her embarrassment, the weeks of hurt welled up within her, and she blurted out, 'You had no choice, I know. But I don't want my heart to bleed like that a second time.'

'It won't,' he swore. 'I don't intend to leave you again.'

His intense gaze reached inside her, pushing back against the barriers around her heart.

'I don't know what's right any more,' she admitted. 'Perhaps we should be friends for a time,' she offered. 'We could get to know one another without…'

'Without Elena between us,' he finished.

She nodded.

A dark expression came over his face, as if he didn't like the idea of waiting. His hands moved down to the base of her spine, and he remarked, 'I won't be bringing you flowers or trying to win your heart, Caragh.' He reached below her hips, picking her up until her body was flush against his.

'I'm a *Lochlannach*. And I take what I want.' To emphasise his words, he kissed her, invading her mouth with his tongue. He ravaged her mouth like the warrior he was, claiming and consuming her until she was breathless. Against her body, she felt the length of his arousal, and it sent a rush of need between her legs.

His mouth travelled down her jaw, to the soft part of her throat. 'Perhaps you'll be my prisoner, this time.'

Her mind spun with images of being chained and at his mercy. A sigh escaped her when he lowered her again, sliding her against him.

But she raised her chin and said, 'No.' Before he could carry her off again, she pointed a finger to his chest. 'I hardly know you. And you know very little about me.'

'You like food,' he offered. 'And you're not fond of sailing.'

'I'm not fond of drowning,' she corrected. She'd learned to overcome her dislike of the water, especially after she'd continued to fish alongside her brothers. Never again would she let her fear prevent them from getting food.

'You like the colour blue, and you have a sense of adventure. You like to try new things.' He took her hand in his, and added, 'You cheat when we play games.'

'I do not!'

'I saw you move a few pieces when you thought I was distracted.'

He'd seen that? She frowned, but before she could say anything, he finished with, 'And you like kissing me.'

'Sometimes,' she admitted.

Styr took her hand in his, leading her up to the open meadow where new sheep grazed upon the tall grasses. 'I brought you gifts from Dubh Linn,' he told her.

Caragh tried to keep the interest from her face. She couldn't let herself be swayed by offerings, but he said, 'Come to the boat and I'll give them to you.'

A sense of warning flared up. 'If I go with you now, you'll steal me away.'

He cocked his head. 'Would it be so bad to spend a night with me on the boat, watching the stars?'

It did tempt her, and he offered, 'I'd take you south to the lands of the sun. Where the warmth would change the colour of your skin darker.' He traced a single finger down her throat, and the touch burned through her.

'You would taste foods you've never had before. Spices and wine that linger upon your tongue.'

'Would I see my brothers again?' she ventured, going along with the dream.

He nodded. 'Whenever you wanted to go back, I would take you there.'

His hand moved around her waist, but she stopped walking. 'What happened with your wife? Tell me.'

'I already did. She learned there was no child, and she divorced me.'

Elena had divorced him? At her shocked expression, he continued, 'She saw us together before you left with your brothers.'

Her face darkened with shame. 'I didn't mean to come between you, Styr. And I shouldn't have gone to you that night. It was wrong of me.'

His fingers moved up her ribs in a light caress. 'I haven't stopped thinking of it, Caragh. Only the next time, I want my hands upon you.'

A flare of desire shuddered through her at the thought. But she couldn't simply drop the shields around her battered heart. 'I want a man who will protect and love me.' She raised her eyes to his, the apprehension rising within her. 'But I need time.'

Another barrier hung between them, and she questioned whether or not to voice it. His first marriage had ended because there had been no children. Though she didn't want to hurt him, neither did she want to ignore the truth. If she chose him for a husband, there was a very real possibility that he could not give her children.

'There is time now,' he acceded. 'I've come to stay, Caragh.' His hand moved to touch the small of her back, and the gesture made her next words all the more difficult.

'I won't deny that I've missed you,' she began, trying to choose the right words that needed to be spoken. 'And my feelings haven't changed.' She took a breath and met his eyes. 'But you only left her because she could not bear you a child. What if the same thing happens to us?'

Her words were a sharp blade between them, for he didn't know if he could grant her a child. Though it was possible that it was Elena who was barren, Styr had known men who had married again and again, never to bear sons of their own. If he couldn't give Caragh children, were they condemned to the same fate as his first marriage? Would she grow to hate him, pushing him away and not wanting to share his bed?

It was a truth he hadn't wanted to face.

The reality of her words made any other conversation impossible. He guided her back to the ringfort and found that Onund had brought their supplies to shore, anchoring the ship off the coast.

She made excuses about having to begin preparing a meal, but he caught her hand. 'This isn't finished, Caragh.'

She shook her head. 'No. But I don't know what to say to you or what to feel right now.'

He let her go, and once she'd disappeared into her own house, her brothers approached. Neither appeared pleased to see him. While Ronan kept a short distance away, eyeing Styr's ship and the few men he'd brought with him, Terence made no effort to disguise his rage. He strode towards Styr, and when he reached him, he swung his fists.

Styr caught the man's hand before it could strike his jaw, holding it in place. 'I didn't come to fight.'

'That's good, *Lochlannach*. It means I can kill you quicker.' Terence followed up with his other fist, clipping Styr across the opposite jaw.

Pain radiated through him, but he smiled at the man, no longer caring that this was

Caragh's brother. 'You won't succeed.' If the man wanted a fight, he welcomed the chance to release his frustration and anger.

'You made her cry,' her brother accused. 'And now you dare to show your face again?'

'I'm going to wed her. You'd best get used to my face.' He circled the man, knowing that Terence wouldn't fight fair. Not when it came to guarding his sister.

'And what does your wife have to say about that?' he taunted. Before Styr could respond, he added, 'Brendan told us. Were you ever going to tell Caragh?'

'She knew, from the beginning. And Elena is my wife no longer.'

Terence threw another punch that struck Styr in the ribs. He grunted against the pain and blocked another blow.

'You're nothing but a bastard who doesn't deserve to breathe the same air as Caragh,' he taunted. 'She should have left you chained to rot.'

Without warning, the man unsheathed a blade, darting towards Styr. He saw a piece of driftwood lying nearby, and when Terence lunged, he dodged the strike and reached for the wood, using it to block the man.

In one swift motion, he swung the wood

towards Terence's head, intending to knock the man unconscious. But at the last second, he heard Caragh cry out, and he halted the motion.

She came running from her home, and the distraction rewarded him with a slice against his arm.

'Terence, don't!' Caragh exclaimed, rushing forwards. Though his arm bled freely, Styr didn't think the wound was too deep. He was amused when Caragh drew her hand into a fist and punched her brother in the shoulder before she came to his side. 'That's enough. Leave him alone.'

Terence sent them both a dark look, but relented.

'Why were you fighting?' she demanded, urging Styr to sit so she could tend the wound.

It occurred to him that he could take advantage of the minor cut, especially if it meant she would tend him. 'He was angry at me for hurting you. And he thought I'd lied to you about Elena.'

Caragh found a cloth and dipped it in water, washing the blood away. She held it in place, informing Terence, 'You will not harm him. Whatever comes is between the two of us. Not you.'

The desire for murder burned in Terence's eyes. To Styr, he ordered, 'You don't hurt her again. If she cries one tear because of you, I'll—'

'Go and eat,' Caragh interrupted. 'Both of you. I'll join you soon.'

'He's not eating with us,' Terence insisted. 'Let him dine on seaweed and whatever he can find crawling on the bottom of the sea.'

Styr said nothing, knowing that he'd have done the same for his own sisters.

'Go,' she repeated.

Her older brother Ronan started to guide Terence away, and he added, 'We'll expect you to join us soon.' The unspoken words were: *Or we'll come and fetch you.*

'I'll come when I want to. Not before.' She crossed her arms, glaring at them.

'You deserve better than a man like him,' Terence said.

'I deserve the right to choose.' Waving them on, Caragh stood firm on her decision. She waited until they'd gone, before turning back to Styr. 'Will you be all right?'

He didn't answer at first. 'It might grow poisoned from the blade.'

She rolled her eyes. 'It's a scratch.'

'And what if it gets worse?' he prompted.

'What if I get a fever and you have to stay all night at my bedside?'

'I could cut it off and save myself the trouble,' she remarked drily. 'See, it's stopped bleeding already.'

This wasn't at all working the way he wanted to. 'I'd like it if you stayed all night at my side. The way you did a few weeks ago.'

Her face flushed. 'Styr, I can't.'

'Then you'll return to your brothers, feed them, tuck them into their beds at night, and never marry. Is that it?'

'There's no harm in taking care of my family.'

'They're grown men. They should marry and have their own families,' he said. Though she'd cared for them over the course of the past year, he wanted her to break free of them.

'Are you hungry?' he asked.

'I have a meal prepared,' she answered. 'It's enough.'

'Bring some of the food in a basket,' he said. 'I'll take you out on the water, and we'll sail and eat.'

She cast a reluctant glance towards the hut. 'How do I know you'll bring me back?'

'My men are here,' he pointed out. 'I'm not about to abandon them.' When she didn't answer, he added, 'And you'll see the gifts I brought for you.'

In her eyes, he saw the slight interest, and he took her hand, leading her along the shore. 'Will you come?'

Caragh wasn't certain why she'd decided to sail away with Styr, but the idea of leaving everything behind and feeling the wind in her face was suddenly appealing. She closed her eyes, breathing in the salty air while the sun warmed her face. When she opened them, she saw Styr's taut muscles flexing as he fought the power of the wind.

He caught her watching him, and his gaze turned heated. As if there was no one else in the world but the two of them.

He'd never openly pursued her, and it took a strong effort to guard her heart. For so long, Elena had been between them. And now, he had ended that path, choosing Caragh instead.

What if he found her wanting? The lack of a child had torn apart his first marriage, and she feared that it might happen again. She'd been honest with him; she did want a baby. She wanted to feel the warmth of an infant against her breast, touching the small feet and curled fists. It might not happen if she wed him. And if it did not, would it come between them?

'Keep looking at me like that, *søtnos*, and I'll never take you back again.'

She braved a smile, and he tied off the ropes, coming to sit before her. 'Do you want to see the gifts I've brought?'

'You didn't need to bring me anything,' she began, though it was difficult to push back her curiosity.

Styr reached into the bag and showed her a length of crimson silk. She touched it, and marvelled at the softness of the cloth. 'I've never felt anything like this before.'

'You'll sew a gown from it. And wear it on the day we wed.'

She brought it to her cheek, a rise of nerves gathering in her stomach at the thought. Though she wanted to wed him, a thousand doubts and fears made her nervous.

'We should sell it,' she suggested. 'The harvest might fail, and—'

'It won't.' He folded up the cloth and set it aside. 'Caragh, there's nothing wrong with accepting gifts of value.'

'We have so little,' she confessed. 'I can't forget what it was like when we nearly starved. I don't ever want to face that again.'

'You will become accustomed to wearing finery, as a *jarl*'s wife.'

'But my brother Ronan is chief,' she protested.

'My men will not follow an Irish leader.' He stared out at the horizon, and pointed to the stretch of green lands further inland. 'We will settle there, near the river. And you will be their lady.'

She'd never dreamed of such a life, or of such responsibilities. But she could see that it meant a great deal to Styr.

'My brothers own those lands,' she reminded him.

He inclined his head as if he'd expected this. 'I will negotiate for the territory, in return for grain, livestock, and more silver. Your people will not know hunger again.' He proved his words by withdrawing a small leather pouch. Inside, Caragh found a great deal of silver and gold.

'When I returned to Áth Cliath, I relieved the Norsemen of their wealth,' he admitted. 'They should have known better than to wager against me.'

She closed the pouch and handed it back. 'I thought you wanted to sail across the seas to distant lands.'

He turned back to look at her, as if he were startled that she'd remembered. 'Some day, perhaps.' He withdrew a folded piece of leather and passed it to her. 'These came from the southern lands.'

Inside, Caragh found oval-shaped nuts that were sticky to the touch.

'Those are almonds, dipped in honey,' he told her. 'The traders brought them to the city.'

She savoured the honeyed almonds, holding them in her mouth until at last she tasted the crunch of the nuts. When she offered one to Styr, he raised her fingers to his mouth, kissing the tips as he took the almond. Then, he rested his arm at her waist, sitting beside her while the boat took them along the coast. The wind had slowed, but she enjoyed the way the vessel skimmed the water.

'Where are we going?' she asked.

'Does it matter?' His hand moved up her spine, his gaze upon her.

No, it didn't. Being with him, knowing that he'd sailed hundreds of miles to return to her, was a strong temptation. Her head argued that she needed to be careful, to guard her heart.

He didn't choose you, her head warned. *He chose Elena first*.

She closed her eyes, silencing the words

she didn't want to face. Caragh stared out at the sea, admitting, 'I am glad you returned.' His hand moved up her back in a soft caress, weakening her resolve. Somehow, she forced herself to continue. 'But I'm also afraid.'

'Of what?'

'What if I cannot bear you a child, either?' Though she didn't want to push him away, she felt the need to confront the barrier that had driven Styr and Elena apart. She loved him, but his first marriage had broken apart without a child.

He cut her off, touching his hand to her lips. 'We can speak of it later, Caragh. For now, I want this time with you.'

Her protests fell silent at that. He was right. They had been apart for nearly another month, and she had missed him desperately.

She moved her hand to his chest, unable to resist slipping her hand beneath his tunic. His skin was warm and firm, his muscles taut beneath her fingertips. He inhaled when she touched him, and he moved her hand away for a moment while he removed his tunic. His body was bared to her, and she saw the years of strength and pain scarring his chest.

'I did miss you,' Caragh said again. She couldn't resist running her hands over him.

Her fingertips grazed his nipples, and they hardened, his body responding to her. When she bent and touched her lips to his skin, needing to taste him, he let out a groan, his hands catching in her hair.

'Show me how much,' Styr demanded. He laid her back on the bottom of the vessel, lying beside her. His mouth was on hers, hungrily kissing her until she wrapped both arms around him.

So very much, she wanted to whisper. Her body was aching as his tongue slid against hers, his hands loosening the ties of her gown.

When she touched him, rubbing her hands over his scalp, caressing a path down his neck, he froze.

'You don't have to touch me,' he said. 'I'd rather take care of you.' To show her what he meant, he touched her ankle, his hand stroking a path up to her knee.

The words struck her cold, and she frowned. 'But why? Is there something wrong?'

He eyed her, his face masked as if he didn't understand why she desired him.

'Styr,' she said quietly, 'I'm not Elena. And I want to touch you. I need to.'

His skin revealed gooseflesh as the wind moved over him. Caragh placed her hands upon his shoulders, exploring his skin with her hands. He stiffened at the touch, but she massaged the skin, caressing him as she learned the planes of his body.

She replaced her hands with her mouth, kissing him the way she'd wanted to. It seemed so forbidden, to draw her mouth and tongue over the firm shoulders, her hands reaching forwards to touch his chest. He let out a hiss of air when her hands moved lower.

She held her hands upon his stomach, too nervous to dare any more.

'My turn,' he growled. His eyes were heated, and she hesitated to allow it.

'Perhaps we shouldn't start this now,' she hedged.

'You think I'll give you a choice, *søtnos*?' He moved to sit behind her, drawing her hips between his legs. She felt the undeniable heat of his erection against her spine.

Styr began with her hair, touching her scalp the way she'd touched him. His hands moved down to her neck, where he found the tension and gently worked out the knots. She leaned her head down, her hair falling over one shoulder. It was so relaxing, having him touch her in this way. But when she felt him loosening her gown more, she froze.

'Don't be afraid of me,' he urged, and he lowered the gown to her waist. The wind blew over her bare breasts, making her nipples grow erect. His palms moved over her back, massaging warmth into her skin, drawing her beneath his spell.

And when he moved his hands over her breasts, she gave a cry, pushing back against his hips when he cupped her. His thumbs moved over her nipples, drawing out the tips and sending a rush of desire between her legs. She was wet, aching for him to fill her. With every caress of her breasts, she felt the answering throb between her legs. Her hands gripped his thighs, her body shaking as he palmed her, arousing her with only his hands.

She remembered the shocking heat of his mouth upon her nipple and how it had sent her past the brink. She wanted him desperately, but she hardly trusted herself around him. With Styr, the world dissolved, sending her spinning into sensations she'd only dreamed of. Caragh gripped his hands, pulling them away to free herself from the prison of desire.

He spoke to her in his native language, capturing her waist and turning her to face him. She tried to cover herself, but he captured her wrists.

'Don't hide your beauty from me.'

'I'm not beautiful,' she whispered. 'I'm too thin.'

'You were hungry,' he corrected. 'And that's starting to change.' His hand moved from her cheek, down lower, to the curve of her breast. 'I'm not leaving you again, Caragh. If I have to steal you away from Éire, I will.'

She trembled as the wind caught up, cooling her skin. Styr drew her to him, until her bare breasts touched his chest. Both of them were cold, but the contact of his flesh only quickened her breathing.

'You're mine,' he said, holding her to him with her head tucked beneath his chin.

I want to be. But the fears and uncertainties pushed to the surface of her courage. It would be so easy to simply open her arms to Styr, rejoicing in his return. Yet, she couldn't forget the countless nights when she'd cried herself to sleep, mourning the loss of him. She'd become a hollow shell of a woman, hating the person she'd become.

She extricated herself from his embrace, pulling her gown back up. Taking a deep breath, she voiced the words that needed to be said. 'But we still need to talk about what will happen to us if I cannot have children.'

'We won't know until we try.'

She took a breath, steadying herself. 'Would you end our marriage?'

He stared at her, as if uncertain of what to say. His hesitation multiplied the fears inside her, but at last, he admitted, 'Yes.'

The hurt balled up inside her, her throat closing up. She could not wed a man who wanted a child more than he wanted her.

'It would be the right thing to do,' he said quietly. 'If I cannot give you a child, then I'll let you go.'

His words were knives, slicing away at the tremulous fear within her. Did he truly believe that children were more important than all else? That she would want another man, all for the sake of a babe in her arms?

She tried to shield herself against the pain, voicing the other truth that plagued her. 'If Elena were still carrying your child, you never would have left.'

His eyes grew harsh at the accusation. 'What would you have me say?' he demanded. 'Never would I turn my back on my son.'

She had no answer for that. But she wanted so much more from Styr. She wanted him to love her, to be with her, even if there were never any children.

Was it worth risking her heart, knowing that he might break it a second time by leaving?

The heavy weight of silence spread between them, and she waited for him to speak, to say anything at all. She needed reassurance from him.

'I love you,' she said at last. 'And I won't lie to you. I do want a child. A son with your eyes, or a daughter with your smile.'

She reached out to touch his hand, and his arms stilled upon the oars. 'But I won't live from one month to the next, wondering if this will be the day when you leave me. I'd rather be alone than endure that heartache again.'

Chapter Fifteen

Styr spent the rest of the evening brooding among his men. He'd brought Caragh back to her home with all the gifts he'd given her, but his foul mood lingered.

Thor's teeth, but women were impossible to understand. He'd come back to her, hadn't he? Yet somehow what was supposed to be an afternoon spent in her arms had become an argument that twisted him into knots. He'd given her the truth, even if she hadn't wanted to hear it.

If she wanted a babe and he could not give her a child, he'd rather release her from their marriage than have her look upon him with hatred. He cared about her too much, wanting only her happiness.

He wished he could find the right words—to talk to her, to tell her all the reasons why he wanted to be with her. Damned words were of no use to him. He didn't know what to say or what she wanted to hear.

Styr rubbed the scar on the back of his head, unsure of what to do. But he wasn't going to abandon this. Not yet.

They made camp and Onund went out to hunt. Styr had spitted a trout he'd caught and was waiting for the fish to cook.

'May I join you?' came the voice of a wizened old woman. He'd seen her before, but didn't know her name.

Styr gestured for her to sit across from him, and she smiled, saying, 'No, I can't, my boy. If these old knees bend, they won't get up again.'

'Are you hungry?' he asked, though he suspected that wasn't the reason for her conversation.

'No,' she said. 'I came to lend you my advice, since you're failing in your quest.'

He lifted a peat brick and tossed it on the fire. 'And what quest is that?'

'Why, to win our Caragh's heart. She wept over you, you know. She tried not to let us see it, but you hurt her. You'll have to atone for it.'

Styr said nothing, for he wasn't about to

beg. He wanted Caragh, but what more did she want?

'Give her time,' the woman suggested. 'Build her a house and show her that you're not leaving.'

He studied the old woman and saw that her face was sombre. 'I have no intention of giving her up.' But neither did he want to wait for weeks, giving Caragh the chance to say no.

'I think you already know what to do, *Lochlannach*.' The old woman smiled. Leaning on her walking stick, she hobbled back to her husband.

An idea took root in his mind, one that suited his intent perfectly.

Over the next few days, Caragh hardly saw Styr at all. He'd negotiated a truce with her brothers, and she half-wondered if it was in return for keeping his distance.

But on the night Ronan and Terence took Brendan to visit a neighbouring clan, she found Styr awaiting her inside her home. He was seated on a stool, both hands enclosed in manacles, while a longer chain looped around the post where she'd once held him captive. His hands were in front of him this time, with each bound separately, to give him more freedom to move.

And he wore nothing but his hose.

At the very sight of his muscled chest, words failed her. He was magnificent, his sun-darkened skin gleaming against the fire. His shoulders were corded, lean and strong, while his stomach was flat and ridged.

Caragh couldn't imagine what had happened to him, but the heated look in his eyes drew her closer.

'Wh-what are you doing here?' she asked, pushing back the storm of unexpected feelings. 'Who's done this to you?' Had Ronan or Terence ordered him chained? She wouldn't put it past her brothers. But if that were the case, they wouldn't have confined him here.

'Close the door,' Styr answered. 'This was my decision, with the help of Onund.'

'Why?' she blurted out, not understanding what would possess him to do such a thing. It reminded her of the first nights they'd spent together, when she'd held him captive.

'Because I'm not good with words.'

Caragh bit her lip to keep her mouth from falling open. *He* had chained himself here? For what purpose?

She studied him, taking another step closer.

He was bared to her, his body chained so that he could not leave.

And she understood what he was trying to say.

'Promise me,' she whispered. 'No matter what happens between us.' Her hand came up to cover his heart. 'Our marriage will not rest upon the condition of having children.'

He leaned in, resting his cheek against hers. 'I want to give you children.' His hands moved to rest upon her waist. 'I want to watch you grow round with my child, your breasts heavy with milk.'

His words held a power that entrapped her, as if she were the one wearing manacles. Against her body, she felt the rise of his arousal.

'Your brothers are gone this night,' he reminded her, nipping her cheek with a light kiss. 'We're alone.'

Her body responded to his sensual promise, aching for him. Against her gown, her breasts tightened.

'What do you want from me?' she whispered.

'Everything.' His voice was resonant, pushing past her defences. 'Did you think I was going to let you walk away?'

She had no idea what to say, but eyed the chains. 'This wasn't quite what I had in mind.'

'It's more interesting.'

Her eyes widened, her skin warming at his suggestion. But she could not resist the urge to run her hands over his shoulders, feeling the strength of his bare skin.

It felt wicked, having a man chained for her pleasure. Deliciously so.

'This isn't fair to you,' she whispered.

A slow smile curved over his mouth. '*Søt-nos*, there isn't a man alive who doesn't dream of this.'

She realised, then, that this was his way of atonement. When he'd left her before, she'd nearly crumbled under the weight of her grief. He had chosen to stay with his wife out of honour and duty to their unborn child. She'd understood that, though it had devastated her.

'If you wed me, I don't want you to leave,' she said. 'I want a child, yes, but more than that, I want you.' To emphasise her words, she ran her palm over his cheek, down his throat, to rest upon his heart. 'With or without a child. It's you I need.'

Styr held himself motionless at her words. When Caragh moved beneath his chained arms to kiss him, he claimed her lips, as if disbelieving what she'd said. Pulling back from him, she ordered, 'Look at me.'

He did, and she framed his face with her hands, seeing the yearning that mirrored her own. 'I don't love you for the child you may or may not give me. I love the man before me.' She pressed another kiss against his heart, and he drew his chained hands against her hair, holding her as best he could.

'I don't want you to hate me, years from now,' he admitted.

She looped her arms around his neck, pressing her cheek against his skin. 'I'll only hate you, if you walk away.'

In his eyes, she saw the uncertainty, the belief of a man who saw himself as unworthy. And she realised that he was as broken as she had once been.

'When you left, it was as if a part of me was gone,' she continued. Emotion welled up in her eyes as she reached down to touch the lengths of chain. 'I never should have taken you prisoner in the beginning. I understand now, what you suffered, not knowing if Elena was alive or dead. It was wrong of me.'

His hands came around her waist, pulling the chains taut until her body was pressed against his. She could feel his desire, and she warmed to it. 'I love you, Styr. And though I may not ever be what Elena was—'

He cut her off at that. 'She cannot compare to you. Not in any way.' He took her mouth again, kissing her and shaping her lips to his. When she opened to him, she accepted his tongue within her mouth, matching his invasion with her own.

His deep voice was a breath of heat upon her skin. 'From the moment I saw you, Caragh, you captured me.'

The desire to touch him, to feel his bare skin against hers, was an ache that could not be denied. At his words, she reached back for the ties of her gown, loosening it until the linen slid over her shoulders, over her bared breasts, and falling to her feet.

When Styr saw her body, he ached to touch her. Her slim lines had filled out, her breasts a generous handful that he wanted to caress. No longer could he see her bones, but a softer flesh covered the body he adored.

'I am yours to command,' he said, and by the gods, he prayed she would take advantage. Against his hose, he was rigid, almost afraid he would lose control the moment she touched him.

She drew near to him, her unbound hair

falling across her shoulders in a dark pool. He lifted his chained hands, and she stepped beneath them, her expression shy. The length of the fetters grazed her nipple, and she gasped at the sensation.

'It's cold.'

'Is it?' He covered one nipple with his palm, gently teasing the other with the chain. She gasped, and he distracted her with his mouth, tasting the sweet flesh while his hands moved over her hips, lifting one of her legs until he could loop the chain between them.

She was so caught up in the attention he gave to her breasts, that she hardly noticed the length of chain until it slid between her thighs, moving upwards until it rested upon her womanhood.

A cry escaped her when he rubbed it gently upon her. 'What are you—?' A shudder broke forth as he drew it over her flesh.

His hands caressed her rib cage, his mouth still suckling her breasts while he tormented her below.

'Remove my clothing,' he ordered. But she was so caught up, her eyes closed at the sensation, she hardly heard him.

'Caragh,' he demanded, 'look at me.'

Her blue eyes were hazed with pleasure, her

hands gripping his shoulders. He repeated his request, and she fumbled with the ties of his hose, drawing them over his hips.

Her fingers brushed against his erect shaft, and it was as if she'd touched a torch to his skin. He nearly lost his seed at that moment, and he froze, trying to gather up the threads of his shredded control.

'I'm sorry,' she said, pulling her hand back. 'I didn't mean to hurt you.'

It was the sweetest pleasure he'd ever felt in his life, but this was not meant to be a moment for his own release. To distract her, he moved the chain between her legs. Although he saw the flush of arousal deepening, her breathing growing faster, she never stopped her own torment. Her fingers curled around him, stroking him from the base of his shaft to the blunt tip.

He was losing command of himself, a prisoner to her touch in truth.

'I love touching you,' she admitted, exploring his rigid flesh with her hands. 'You're like warm stone.'

'If you do that for much longer, I won't be able to pleasure you,' he gritted out. He lowered the chain and dropped to his knees. Her sex was wet, her legs spread apart for him.

With no warning at all, he placed his mouth upon her intimately, and her knees buckled.

'Hold on to the post,' he ordered. With his hands upon her bottom, he used his tongue upon her flesh, revelling in the salty taste of her arousal.

Caragh was lost in sensation, drowning in him. Her hands moved to touch his hair, trying to guide him back up. She couldn't stand the fierce pleasure that rocked her core, and when he entered her with his tongue, she couldn't stop the tremors from sweeping over her.

'Come for me,' he demanded. 'I won't stop until you let go.'

Oh God above, she couldn't take this. Her body was on fire, her mind enslaved to him. She remembered the night he had forced her to touch herself, and the memory of that pleasure was returning.

He seemed to recall it, too, for a moment later, he rose from between her thighs and guided her hand to the wetness between her legs. With his hand upon hers, he took her back to the searing rhythm, and that was all it took for her to crumple, a cry of ecstasy tearing forth. He leaned against the post, lifting her up with his chained hands beneath her bottom. His hips rocked against her, and she opened to him, trembling when the hard ridge of his manhood slid against her wet seam.

Slowly, he settled her until she felt him entering. His arms tightened, but he did not fully penetrate. The sensation of his manhood filling her was so welcome, she cared nothing for the slight discomfort of losing her virginity. And when she was fully seated upon him, she wrapped her legs around him, feeling that it was right to have him inside her.

Styr licked the underside of her breast, his warm breath sending chills of desire rippling through her skin. He remained sheathed within her, not moving at all, but using his mouth to draw out the heat and need.

'What is your command?' he asked her, his eyes burning with wickedness.

She could hardly speak, much less give him orders. The cool length of the chain was against her bottom, his hands holding her steady.

'I want you to find the same release I did,' she said. 'I want to please you.'

Leaning in, she kissed his mouth. He responded with aggression, his tongue plundering her, while below, he lifted her gently. Every touch of his mouth and hands had aroused her to the point of desperate need.

Her body no longer belonged to her; it was his conquest.

'This pleases me more than all else,' he answered.

Caragh began to move against him, rising and sheathing herself while staring into his eyes. He helped her, his body thrusting inside hers as she rode him.

Each time he filled her up, her body clenched. He was insatiable, his mouth moving over every part of her skin as he lifted her. With one arm, he held her bottom balanced, while he reached around, stretching the chain around her waist. He moved his fingers between them, finding the nodule that had brought her such pleasure before.

'I wanted to do this from the first moment I saw you,' he confessed. 'You fascinated me. And the longer I was with you, the more I wanted you.' He stopped thrusting, using his hand upon her instead. 'You were forbidden to me, and I never thought we would have this.'

She was fighting against the touch of his fingers, but could not stop the keening cries that escaped her. Styr kept up the pace, demanding, 'I'm going to take you there again, Caragh. I'll watch you come apart with me inside you.'

He leaned her back slightly, and the angled pressure caused a delicious friction. She couldn't stop herself from panting to the rhythm of his fingers.

'I love you,' she told him, locking his gaze with hers. 'Stay with me. No matter what happens.'

'I love you,' he answered. When the words were spoken, it seemed to transform the intimacy between them. And with his hands, he pleasured her until she trembled violently against him, his body still buried inside her.

'Please,' she begged. 'I can't bear it any more.' She was moving in counterpoint to him, her body crying out for release.

Styr kept the same pace but impaled her deeply, his hard shaft embedded to the hilt. In and out he moved, every penetration swift and deep.

Caragh couldn't speak, she was trembling so hard. 'I need your hands on me,' she begged. And when she guided his fingers between them, he found the place she wanted. It took only a few strokes before the shattering sensations flooded through her, making her cry out with release. She clenched against his erection, and he went rigid, his expression fighting to maintain control.

When the languid feelings spread over her, she wanted him to lose himself, to forget all about her and sate his own desires. 'Let me touch you.' Reaching down, she cupped his sac and he tensed at her actions.

He let out a stream of words in his native language, and perspiration beaded across his brow.

'Or should I take you in my mouth, the way you tasted me?'

The very promise made him groan. Styr resumed his thrusts, his body so tense, she wondered when he would let go of his control. To urge him, she wrapped her legs around his waist, and he rewarded her by increasing the rhythm.

It was primal and hard, their bodies so caught up, they were one. And when she felt herself trembling a third time on the brink, she pulled his mouth down to her bare breast, and he rewarded her with a deep pull against her nipple.

It took only a few more penetrations before his breathing shifted and he groaned, collapsing against her. Caragh's heart pounded so fast, she couldn't catch her breath. But she felt alive in a way she never had before. Being with Styr, sharing this act with him, was everything.

And she loved his skin upon hers.

Her brothers made him pay dearly for the rights to the land. Over the next few weeks, Styr journeyed back to Dubh Linn to bring over sheep and horses, as well as enough grain for every person in their clan. And when they'd at last agreed to the price, Styr spent his time building longhouses similar to those in the city.

Caragh had come to see him each day and sometimes brought him water. Her presence only increased his desire to finish their home sooner. Her brothers had refused to give their permission for the marriage to take place until the dwelling was completed. Although Styr knew he could have taken her to wife at any moment, with his men as witnesses, he knew Caragh wanted her brother's blessing.

Being apart from her was slowly killing him. He hadn't touched her in nearly a month, save for a few stolen embraces.

He was working atop the roof one afternoon, laying thatch, when she approached with her brother Brendan standing behind.

Shielding her eyes against the sun, she called out to him, 'Will it be finished tonight?'

'If I keep working until sundown.' Styr climbed down the ladder, noting the soft smile on her face that belonged to him alone. His body stirred, and he didn't resist the urge to pull her close.

'My brother wanted to speak with you,' she admitted, and Brendan stepped forwards.

'I've come to ask that there be peace between us,' he began. 'For Caragh's sake.'

The young man's face was sombre, and though Brendan appeared nervous, he continued his apology. 'I thought I was protecting my people when we took your men and your wife captive. She—she's safe now, isn't she?'

Styr gave a nod, still not revealing his thoughts. He knew Caragh wanted him to forgive her brother, but Brendan's actions had threatened all of them.

'I know this won't matter to you, but my blade is yours, if ever you have need of it. I owe you a debt that I can never repay.'

Styr glanced at Caragh, and saw the plea in her eyes. 'My men will need help building their homes,' he said at last. 'Give them the labour of your hands until our work is done. That can serve to repay your debt.'

He flushed, his head bobbing with thanks. Caragh's blinding smile made Styr glad he'd compromised.

'There—there's one more thing I can do for you,' Brendan offered, his face turning crimson. 'I—I could keep my brothers away for the rest of the afternoon. So that you and my sister can be alone.'

Caragh looked at her younger brother, aghast that he'd said such a thing. But his offer caused Styr to break into a laugh. He took her hand and called back, 'I accept your offer, Brendan, and gladly.'

'I can't believe what my brother just said,' Caragh murmured. She was holding a cup of cold water from the stream, and Styr accepted the cup, drinking deeply.

'He's more intelligent than I realised.'

A bead of sweat rolled down his cheek, and she reached out to touch it, drawing a line down his throat, to his chest. Heat flared through him, and Styr dropped the cup, dragging her inside.

He took her mouth, kissing her hard against the wall. Gods, but he would never get enough of the taste of her. Caragh's arms came around him, and she pressed close. 'If you finish the house today, we could wed this night.' Her mouth was swollen, her eyes bright. 'I've made a gown from the silk you brought me. I hope it pleases you.'

'You could wear nothing at all, and it would please me,' he gritted out. His hand moved up to the underside of her breast. 'Though I would kill any man who looked upon your beauty,' he murmured against her throat, caressing the hard nub of her nipple.

'You're not playing fair.' She shuddered at the touch of his hands, gasping when he cupped her fully.

'Not for something I want this badly.' He kissed her hard, offering every promise of what was to come. She melted against him, opening while his tongue invaded her mouth. When she kissed him back, pulling him tightly against her, his arousal made her breathing quicken.

'I don't want to wait until tonight,' she whispered. Her arms tightened around his waist, her face pressed against his heart. Styr gripped her hard, breathing in the scent of her hair.

When she raised her head, she stared hard at him. 'A madness possesses me when I'm with you. I don't understand it.' She steadied herself, then ventured, 'Was it like this with her?'

'What happened with Elena is in the past,' he said, not wanting to darken this day. But when he saw the look of worry pass over her, he realised she needed to know that he no longer held any feelings for his first wife.

'No,' he said. 'It was never like this. Not in five years.' Kissing her to force her not to speak, he murmured against her lips, 'Elena is a good woman, and I wish her every happiness. But protecting her and being her husband was my duty.

'We were friends,' he admitted. 'Lovers, even. But I never felt for her the way I feel for you now.' He slid his hands beneath her skirts, touching her bare leg. 'I love you.'

Caragh was watching him, her eyes gleaming with emotion. She reached up to touch his face, and he rested his forehead against hers. He brought his hands over her heart, down to her breast. 'If any man took you from me, I'd destroy him.'

She gripped him hard, and he answered the embrace, his hands moving over her body. She was whispering words of endearment in her language, and a moment later, she touched his hose, reaching for his arousal. 'I want you, Styr. This very moment.'

She started to raise her skirts, and he turned her to face the wall, bracing her hands on either side. He freed himself and palmed her bare legs, lifting her skirt to her waist. Stepping between her legs, he slid his arousal against her. She was already wet, and before he could say a word, she reached down and guided him inside her.

Scalding heat enveloped him as she pushed back, and he filled her, primal in his need. Their coupling was fierce, and she bent over, meeting him with every thrust. He took her hard, but she seemed to welcome the swiftness of their lovemaking as her breathing quickened.

And when she arched against him, trembling hard with the force of her release, he let go of his control, revelling in the way her body accepted him, squeezing hard against his length. He spasmed against her, holding tightly to her waist while he rested his head against her shoulder.

'I can't get enough of you, *søtnos*.' Withdrawing from her, he lowered her skirts and turned her to face him. With a wry smile, he admitted, 'You may not sleep tonight.'

She kissed him, resting her cheek against his. 'There will be time enough for sleep later.'

He brought her over to a low bench to sit, pulling her on to his lap. Her cheeks were flushed, her arms around him. Then she drew his hand down to her womb. 'Even if we never have children, Styr, having you at my side will be enough.'

'You say that now, but—'

'No. I know you've dreamed of going to those lands across the sea. We could go together,' she offered.

'Some of those places aren't safe for women.'

She moved her hand over his shoulder. 'You would protect me, wouldn't you?'

'I'd take a sword in the heart for you.'

Caragh moved her hand upon his chest. 'I want to sit beside you and let the sails take us where they will.' His dreams, of journeying to foreign places, mirrored her own. As long as he was with her.

'What of your family?'

'We will see them every summer,' she said, 'and spend our winters in the warmer lands, just as you said.'

He touched her cheek, guiding her into a

kiss. 'I always thought the gods had cursed me. I made sacrifices and raged against them.'

She saw in his eyes that he believed it. 'You were never cursed.'

'No. And neither was my first marriage a mistake. It led me here, to you. The greatest treasure I could ever have.'

They wed upon the sands, speaking their vows before friends and family. Caragh wore the crimson silk he had given her, the soft material clinging to her body. When they were married, Caragh took his hands in hers. 'There is no woman on this earth who loves you as much as I do.'

He kissed her hard, and she welcomed the familiar warmth of his body pressed against her. 'I am your prisoner, now and always.'

'As I am yours,' she whispered.

With a smile, he took her hand, walking with her towards the feast that awaited them.

As the last of the sun gleamed against the dark waters, she saw the outline of his ship… and knew their journey had only begun.

* * * * *

A sneaky peek at next month…

HISTORICAL

IGNITE YOUR IMAGINATION, STEP INTO THE PAST…

My wish list for next month's titles…

In stores from 6th September 2013:

- ❏ Mistress at Midnight — Sophia James
- ❏ The Runaway Countess — Amanda McCabe
- ❏ In the Commodore's Hands — Mary Nichols
- ❏ Promised to the Crusader — Anne Herries
- ❏ Beauty and the Baron — Deborah Hale
- ❏ The Ballad of Emma O' Toole — Elizabeth Lane

Available at WHSmith, Tesco, Asda, Eason, Amazon and Apple

Just can't wait?

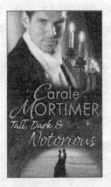

Join the Mills & Boon Book Club

Want to read more **Historical** books?
We're offering you **2 more** absolutely **FREE!**

We'll also treat you to these fabulous extras:

- 🌹 **Exclusive offers and much more!**
- 🌹 **FREE home delivery**
- 🌹 **FREE books and gifts with our special rewards scheme**

Get your free books now!

visit www.millsandboon.co.uk/bookclub
or call Customer Relations on 020 8288 2888